Women:
Wise, Wicked, Worn

C.A. MacKenzie

Women: Wise, Wicked, Worn
Copyright ©2018 Catherine A. MacKenzie

MacKenzie Publishing
Halifax, Nova Scotia
April 2018

ISBN-13: 978-1927529539
ISBN-10: 1927529530

Cover image courtesy of Chelle at Morguefile

80CB
𝔐𝔞𝔠𝔎𝔢𝔫𝔷𝔦𝔢 𝔓𝔲𝔟𝔩𝔦𝔰𝔥𝔦𝔫𝔤

Author's Note

These stories fit into a common theme—thus the title. No explanation is necessary!

Several stories have been previously published in my books *BETWEEN THESE PAGES, PAPER PATCHES,* and *BLOOD DREAMS.* Some have been published in anthologies. Others appear here for the first time.

All these stories have been edited and proofread by individuals other than myself. Despite that, no doubt errors still exist. The "rules" state a writer may have one typo/error every 10,000 words. Given that this collection is over 80,000 words, I'm "authorized" (haha) to have eight errors. One error is one too many, and I hope you don't find any.

I hope you enjoy this collection.

Please, if you have a second, leave a review (good or bad).

Cathy

Contents

Blood Dreams

No, don't let them take me." Corinne twisted and squirmed. Her eyes darted from her daughter, Anne, to the nurses, and back to Anne.

"Mom, it's okay. They're just taking you down for your treatments."

"No. They do more than that. They do things to me. Horrible, horrible things."

"Mom, stop it. You're acting crazy again. You know what happens when you act like that."

Corinne raised her arms. "Look. See the holes? You can't help but see them. They poke and jab at me. They never give up."

"Mother! Stop it right now."

Corinne glared at her daughter. It was hopeless to convince her; it always was. Anne believed what Anne wanted to believe, whether a truth or a lie.

The male nurses clasped straps over Corinne's wrists, and she gave up her fight. She stared at the conglomerate of dulled paint and plaster dangling from the ceiling.

The clusters reminded her of bats that had hung from the rafters of the barn on the old homestead. Even though she and her younger brother, Calum, had known the bats roosted there, they still played in the dilapidated building. They climbed the wood-splintered ladder to the loft area where they saw up close the upside-down apparitions before screeching and scrambling down the ladder as fast as they could. The bats, awoken from their sound sleep, zoomed about the rafters like leaves hurled about by a tornado. Once Corinne and Calum were safely outside, their stomachs constricted with laughter. Corinne's often hurt so horribly that she cried.

"I think Daddy's got me on his bench vise," Corinne once said to her brother. "My belly's killing me."

No matter how frightened they were of the creatures, they played their bat game a couple of days a week. The adrenaline rush exhilarated them, yet Corinne suffered recurring nightmares as a result.

The rattle of the gurney jolted Corinne to the present. While the nurses rolled the bed down the hall, Corinne's eyes silently pleaded with anyone who looked her way, but when she saw only pity and disgust, she knew she was doomed.

She squinted at the calendar pinned to the wall. The month of October and the numbers were easily decipherable, but she couldn't make out whether the thirteen was positioned under Thursday or Friday. With her luck, it would be Friday the thirteenth. She had glanced at the red numbers on the bedside clock radio as they wheeled her out of the room: eight o'clock.

It was always early in the mornings when the hospital staff attacked her. They didn't always draw blood. Anne had been in her room, but why? She usually visited only once a week. Had another week passed?

Corinne moaned, resigned to her fate. No one ever helped or protected her from these monsters. And monsters they were, poking and jabbing, stealing her blood. Afterward, she was dizzy and faint, barely able to open her mouth. Not that she had anything to say. What was the use?

Plasma would be replaced within twenty-four hours, provided one drank enough water. She figured that's why they put her on intravenous after taking her blood; she was elderly, and it took much longer for her blood to return to normal than it did for a younger person. She also knew if she didn't have enough iron in her diet, she would become anemic, which accounted for the iron supplements they daily stuffed into her. She would still be tired, however—needing to sleep for the rest of her life to recover from the bi-monthly blood purloining. Even in her ailing condition, she was aware blood donors were not permitted to give blood more than every couple of months.

Why were they stealing her blood so often? She answered her own question: because they could. No one was the wiser. No one believed her. Those monsters knew that. Oh yes, smart ones they were. Smart and heartless and cruel.

She suspected, as well, that she received the odd blood transfusion when her health took a turn for the worse. Through slits in her eyes while feigning sleep, she had seen blood bags hanging by her bed and felt the searing liquid coursing through her veins. She suffered nightmares that the bag was one of those horrid bats from her youth come back to haunt her and infuse her with its blistering blood. When she awoke, some mornings she'd notice discarded bags on the table beside her bed, and she'd wonder if she had digested the contents or whether furtive vampires had leeched them dry. The transfusions didn't help; she was still exhausted, still had no energy.

"Ow!" The jab of the needle into her arm caused the sight of bats to disappear. "Ow," she repeated with more force. Although her voice was barely audible, it echoed through the cold, sterile room. White apparitions loomed like the ghosts of bats swirling around.

"Roll her over," one of the nameless voices said.

Hands slithered underneath her body and heaved her to her side. She waited for them to force her head-first into the plastic-covered pillow but seconds later realized they wouldn't chance suffocating her. No, she wasn't worth anything dead. Or was she?

Cold hands rudely parted the back of her johnny shirt and probed her butt cheeks. Grateful for the cushiony fat, she sensed more than felt the needle. But what were they doing with her buttocks?

"Another." The voice seemed far away.

"Almost done." Another distant voice.

The reassuring words weren't said for her benefit. A needle jammed in deeper than the previous one. She felt it linger inside her longer than it should have. What the hell were they doing to her? She opened her mouth to speak, but her throat was thick with phlegm.

When she thought she couldn't stand the pain any longer, the frigid hands let go and pushed her to her back. She fought against nausea. Her mouth filled with bile. She smelled her feces before she felt her anus loosen.

The nurses didn't seem to notice—yet. What would happen to her when they caught a whiff?

"Okay, missy." One of the male nurses returned.

Oblivious to the smell, he grasped her arm. It didn't take him long to insert a needle into the top of her hand, not with purplish veins snaking over pale skin that resembled a travel map of scattered highways without a purpose except to race off the edge of creased paper.

She winced when the needle entered, but she couldn't experience any more pain than she already had. The bag by her side slowly filled with her blood. She watched it for a time, feeling the life draining from her and again imagined bats feeding on her flesh. She supposed it was natural and fair, the bats doing that. She had disturbed their rest. She and Calum should have let them be.

Calum. What happened to him? He had disappeared when in his twenties. Took off one day and never returned. She pictured him in some wild place and hoped he was enjoying his life. *He can't be having a worse time than me. Unless he's dead, of course. Then again, I'd rather be dead than endure these god-awful indignities.*

She sighed and glanced again at the nearly full bag. They'd have to transfuse her again. Why did they withdraw her blood then transfuse her? Was her blood that valuable that they had to take it and replace it with someone else's? She hardly thought so, but why? She couldn't figure things out. Maybe she'd ask Anne the next time she visited. After reflection, she changed her mind. Anne didn't believe her, no matter what Corinne told her. Anne wouldn't believe her mother was slowly being drained of life.

Corinne knew she was delusional again. The withdrawing of her blood always did that to her—caused her thoughts to jumble and flow in a madhouse of nonsense and nightmares. She closed her eyes to the white-cloaked bats leering over her and willed herself to sleep, hoping she wouldn't snore. The snoring annoyed the nurses, and they'd shake her awake and tell her to quit. If she didn't, they would force her to stop, and she knew what that meant. While nurses pinned her to the bed, others would cover her mouth with their firm, abrasive hands until she couldn't breathe. Her eyes would bulge, her arms would flinch, and her fingers would spread.

Why did they bother? Why did they try to quash an eighty-nine-year-old who simply wanted to rest in peace?

Eventually, she slept and snored, and when they shook her shoulders and slapped her face, she was too weak to fight back. She feigned sleep as best she could and let them have their way with her.

***

Dozens of grey bats swirled above Corinne's head, and the rough breeze washed over her while the bats hissed and hummed. One dropped on her hand and sucked at her discoloured flesh. Later, she felt the pinch of sharp teeth jabbing on her buttocks. She tried to scream, but as usual, the sounds were restrained as though someone held a meaty hand across her mouth. Her tongue, looking for escape, roamed inside its cavern and caressed cushiony, toothless gums. She wondered when her teeth had been removed and why she hadn't remembered someone taking them out. Without teeth, she was defenseless against the attacks. In another lifetime, she had watched the Hitchcock movie, *The Birds*, and wondered how she would survive an onslaught of flying creatures huger and more horrifying than those in the movie.

She tried to raise a hand, the one the bat had glued itself to, but was unable to. Her hand was immobile. Heavy. She tried her other hand but discovered a band around her wrist bound it to the bed rail.

Corinne kept her eyes closed, too frightened to open them, too scared to see her surroundings. Her legs were heavy, as well, and she could barely wiggle her big toe.

"Open your eyes."

The faint words startled her. Why had the voice materialized the exact instant she had decided to keep them closed?

"It's okay. Open them."

The same voice. But louder.

"No." Had she spoken?

Bats still zoomed around her face. She smelt their odour, the same stench that had permeated the run-down barn. She yearned to cover her nose and attempted to move her left hand, but the dratted bat still fed off it, its heavy body weighing down her arm. The longer the blood drainer, the weaker and disoriented she would be.

"It's me. Calum."

Corinne heard the voice again, louder that time.

"Calum?" She wasn't certain she had spoken.

"Yes. And thank you."

"Thank you?"

"Thank you for the blood. I need it, you know. I need it to live. Your days are over."

"My blood?" Corinne opened her eyes, but she couldn't see. She needed to swat at the bat wings that covered her eyes, but she couldn't move.

"Yes, your blood."

A man giggled. No, more like a foxy, evil snicker than a giggle.

"Wha—"

"Oh, you're a funny woman, Corinne. You know what's going on. Why do you fight it? Just give it up. Relax. Let your body float away."

"Calum?"

Corinne tried again, desperately wanting to open her eyes, unable to determine whether she was asleep—in the throes of a nightmare—or whether she was awake and hearing imaginary voices.

She pictured Calum the last time she had seen him—a tall, thin boy-man, for he hadn't yet matured even though he was twenty-two. His unruly hair had always looked as if he had just climbed out of bed. He hated brushes and combs, much preferring to use his fingers.

"I'm going away for a while," he had told her before he slammed the door on their lives. Calum had a farfetched goal of hitting it rich in Hollywood. "I want to be a famous actor," he had said numerous times.

"Please don't go." Corinne had pleaded with him, to no avail.

"Oh, let him be," their father had said. "He's a man now. Time for him to strike out on his own. He'll come home soon, dragging his tail between his spindly legs. You'll see."

Corinne's mother had sat in the corner and wailed. "My son, my son." She had always been drawn to tears; everything had upset her.

Corinne knew that was the last time she'd see her brother.

Except—he was back. *Or was he?*

"Corinne. Corinne." The voice changed into a sing-song lilt, the volume intensifying. "Come with me."

An imaginary force still possessed her limbs. The bat still fed on her. She couldn't view the brutes, but she heard them droning overhead, circling around her bed, readying to pounce. A light bore through her eyelids, and she wanted to squint, but she couldn't summon that wee bit of strength.

The feeding continued, the blood draining from her body, the poking and jabbing intensifying. She heard Calum's voice in the distance. Her parents stood at the barn door, watching her climb the rickety ladder, one foot following the other, one hand and then the other grasping the rod above her, over and over until she reached the dampness of the loft. Hundreds of grey-brown bats swayed from the rafters, their high-pitched sounds reverberating throughout the barn. Corinne plugged her ears before protecting her eyes from the sun's radiance.

***

"She went quickly. There was no pain," the male nurse told Anne.

"But she was fine before you took her away. What happened?"

"Her heart gave out. You knew she had a weak heart."

"Yes, I know. But it was so sudden." Anne brushed the tear from her face. As much as her mother irritated her, especially over the past several weeks, Corinne was still her mother.

"Sometimes that happens," he said. "The doctor will be here in a few."

The nurse left the room, leaving Anne alone with her mother.

While Anne stared down at the lifeless body, the tears returned. She touched her mother's arm, stunned to see pinpricks lacing across her skin. Her mother's whining about stabbings and piercings flashed through her mind. She also remembered her mother jabbering about a bat invasion. Anne had laughed at her.

She peered closer to examine her mother's arm. She jumped when the door creaked.

"I'm Doctor Simmons," he said, holding out his hand.

Anne hesitantly placed her hand in his, her soft skin sensing the roughness of his.

"Sorry we're meeting under these circumstances."

She nodded. "I noticed the bruises and scabs on my mother's skin. I guess they're from drawing blood?"

"Yes. The nurses tell me it was a continuous process to find veins."

Anne scanned her mother's arms, noting the numerous puffy blue veins. "I see." She didn't know what else to say.

"I must ask that you leave now. I'm sorry," the doctor said.

"Yes, okay." Anne stole another glance at her mother's still face before leaving the room.

***

Though the morning was dark and dreary, with a light drizzle, an eerie calmness settled over the burial.

The tarp of fake grass hid the abysmal pit as if the few mourners were too fragile to know what lay beneath. The burnished coffin sat at one side of the tarp.

Anne glanced around at the dismal group. Her mother hadn't had many friends. At that age, most people didn't. She was grateful for three of her friends who had the decency to pay their last respects to a woman they barely knew.

After the final prayer, four funeral home employees, dressed in usual funeral finery, adjusted the ropes around the coffin in preparation for the move to its final home. The tarp was removed, and the men lowered her mother into the pit.

She glanced to the sky and back to the ground. Where would her mother reside: Heaven or Hell? Or did those places even exist? Anne was not religious. Her mother had attended church every Sunday until she moved into the nursing home, where she had been bedridden the final months of her life.

Ah, Mom. Anne sighed, remembering her mother's crazy rants the last few days. Although her mother had become more delirious, Anne had not expected death so soon.

The coffin hit the bottom with a thud. Mourners usually departed then. Why was that? Why couldn't she watch the dirt bestowed upon the deceased?

She turned. Sure enough, everyone was leaving.

She lingered, needing a few moments. She yearned to drop a flower or a shovel-full of dirt into the hole as actors did on television and in the movies. Did anyone do that in real life?

The funeral director appeared beside her. "The women's group is providing sweets in the hall. It's best we go now."

"Why can't we watch the rest?"

"Nothing to see. Machinery moves the dirt. Grant will do that later today. The stone should be delivered tomorrow or the day after. Come back in a couple of days."

Anne hesitated but followed the funeral director. After a couple of steps, she stopped and glanced back.

An immense black cloud slowly descended and hovered over her mother's final resting place, which brought to mind the disgusting bat game her mother and her uncle had played in the barn, the story her mother loved to tell. Anne wished she had met Uncle Calum, but he died in his mid-twenties, beaten and left for dead in an alley of a cheap hotel. She was sad for her mother, who had never gotten over her only sibling's death and often said she looked forward to reuniting with him in Heaven.

She shivered at the memory of her mother's prickled arms—the well-defined holes surrounded by blue-tinged bruising.

She shook her head. They were simply pinpricks made by the nurses delving for elusive veins.

"Mom was delirious," she mumbled.

"Pardon?" The funeral director turned.

"Oh, nothing," Anne said. "Just talking to myself."

She turned around one last time. The storm cloud broke apart, releasing dozens of bats. They circled her mother's open grave, reminding Anne of a game of follow the leader, and disappeared into the hole.

The Ending

I gripped the black umbrella and pulled it closer to my head lest the wind gust underneath the floppy panels and thrust it from my hands. Rain and hurricane force winds had been in the news, and I was stuck in the middle of it.

I pictured the umbrella with wings as it soared through the air like a wayward balloon, perhaps one blown up at a funeral since it was black, similar to white doves or butterflies set free at weddings. But it took every bit of strength to hold firm to the shaft, with not much left over for imagining circumstances that might or might not be.

When the figure appeared before me, I glimpsed a muddled blur— dark ski cap and dark trench coat—and my preoccupation with weather and saving my $6.99 umbrella faded. The nameless individual loomed in front of me for several seconds before he snatched my bag and raced away.

The day was Friday, about four o'clock. I had just left the bank.

David, my common-law spouse, had come home from work for a few minutes before his scheduled appointment. "You have time to run to the bank, pick up a bottle of wine, and get back home before the rain starts. Stay on Spring Garden Road and you'll be fine," he had said.

I had glanced out the window. "But look at the sky. It's pitch black. Why don't you stop?"

"I don't have time, and traffic will be awful. Besides, the bank'll be closed before I'm done."

"Let's do it next week then."

"No, I want it done now. Take the umbrella. It's only a couple of blocks."

"It's five blocks! And the wind is picking up. Look at the trees across the street." I didn't mind the walk, but he was being obstinate and I needed to retaliate.

When it came time for him to leave for his meeting, the rain had started, so David changed his mind and dropped me at the front door of the bank. "I'll be home in an hour or so," he said. "You can get home before it gets really bad."

We had moved into a condo a few months previously. I enjoyed living in downtown Halifax. Walking was the best perk; not having to pay for parking or deal with horrendous traffic, rush hour or otherwise, were two more. Everything was close by—movie theatres, restaurants, shops. I rarely drove the car.

So that day, amid a hurricane forecast, gusty wind, and torrents of rain, I finished the business at the bank and hastened down Spring Garden Road. Halfway home, I realized I had forgotten the wine.

"Call a cab if need be." David's words resonated. But he knew I wouldn't call a cab, as I knew I wouldn't. It was only five blocks. What fool would call a cab for five blocks? Despite inclement weather, I enjoyed walking, and what did it matter how dishevelled I'd be when I arrived home? There'd be no one to open the door to greet me. I could straighten up easy enough. It was only water, after all, and a little bit of water hurt no one.

More of his words rankled me. "Empty the safety deposit box," he had said. "We don't need it."

David didn't believe in banks, not with low interest rates and high taxes. According to him, until we decided what to do with the money from the sale of the house, we'd be better off with the cash hidden under our mattress, so to speak. The teller had looked at the cheque, askance that anyone would request cash, and we had to wait several days until the bank acquired the funds. When the money came in, David had stashed it in a safety deposit box at the bank.

The wall safe had been the main reason David wanted to rent that particular unit in the condo. "Look at this," he had said. "A brand new safe. Secure. And no one knows it's here since it was installed after the last renters moved out." With our own personal safe, David figured the money should be there instead of in the safety deposit bank.

I had balked at renting the condo. "The rent's so high. Can we afford it?"

"Of course we can," he had said. "As soon as the housing market falls flat again, we'll buy another place. If we like living here, maybe a house downtown."

Dumbfounded, I stood in the rain, my umbrella discarded to the sidewalk, my bag gone. Stolen. Everyone but me had taken cover from the barrage. Unknown to anyone, I suffered more than a mere downpour. My space had been invaded, my privacy violated.

I felt I'd been raped, and an old memory washed over me, an occurrence years before David entered my life when someone broke into my car and stole money I'd stashed in the glove compartment. At the time, it had seemed brilliant to put cash in envelopes designated for specific bills so I'd not be so liable to spend it on other things. In the end, though, that asinine plan was akin to David's.

Why was I walking the streets with half a million dollars? Why hadn't the money been invested?

Tears dribbled down my face, melding into the pelting rain. The nondescript building behind me drew me like a magnet, and I leaned against it, grateful something strong held me up. Hammers pounded against my skull. I was being attacked again. My breaths alternated between gulps and sobs.

Vaguely, I remembered a police station several blocks away. I headed back the way I had come. I passed the bank. Should I go in, tell the cashier or another individual I'd been robbed of almost every penny David and I possessed? No, what would they do? It wasn't their money. No one would care. They'd simply notify the authorities, which I was about to do.

When I reached the station, I'm sure I resembled a dog emerging from an ocean, an animal unable to shake itself dry or become warm. Helplessness morphed into fear and rage—fear at David's reaction, rage at my accoster.

The heavy wood door closed behind me. I collapsed against it and slipped to the floor. A stranger ran to me, helped me up, asked if I was okay. Someone else propelled me into a chair.

"What happened?" Eyes raked over my body. Fully dressed, I couldn't have been raped.

"I've been robbed," I mumbled before I burst into tears.

A woman officer put her around me, wiped my face. "Are you hurt?"

"No...he...he...just took...took...my...bag. All...my...money." I shook as I spoke.

"Calm down. We need to ask you some questions."

"Anyone we can call?" someone asked.

I managed to give them David's information and was in the middle of my statement when he barged in. We hugged. He was wet, too.

"Still raining?" I asked. Such a mundane question after losing what amounted to our life's savings.

"She's in shock," a female said.

"What happened?" David's frantic, high-pitched voice hurt my ears.

"Calm down, sir."

"Darlene, the money?"

I sobbed again. Or maybe I had never stopped. My vision blurred.

"Darlene, you okay?" His voice lowered.

"David, the money. I—"

"The money's not important. As long as you're okay."

"Of course it is," I said. "That's our future."

"It's only money. We—I can make more."

"Can you catch the guy?" I asked the officer.

"We'll do our best, ma'am. We have a car out now."

Faces blurred, as did more questions and my answers. I wasn't sure what I was saying half the time.

One of the officers volunteered to drive us home. The three of us left the station, the rain still pummelling the pavement and the wind whipping across our faces. Traffic was almost nonexistent.

The officer escorted us to the fifth floor of our building. Were we supposed to invite him in? I wanted to be alone. To get warm.

"Thank you for the ride, officer," David said. "Let me know when you have news."

David had been strangely subdued at the station—once he simmered down after the initial shock. His manner changed when we were alone, which had been my fear.

"What were you thinking!" he screeched. "How could you let someone run off with my money?"

I glared at him. "Your money? I thought it was ours. And what do you mean, let someone run off with it? It was your stupid idea in the first place. What kind of fool keeps that kind of money lying around?"

Even the police had been dumbfounded at his reasoning.

David lowered his voice. "Sorry, honey, you're right. I thought it was the right thing to do."

"I hate that it's always your money! What about us? Yes, I know it was your house before I came along, but I thought we were in this life together. Partners. What's yours and mine is ours, you always say."

I hadn't contributed financially to the relationship, but what did he expect? I had been a clerk at Mill's Department Store, not a highfalutin architect like him. He knew my situation when we moved in together. We had discussed it. "What's mine is yours," he had said.

Suddenly, though, it appeared we had nothing—or very little. David had worked hard to pay off his mortgage, and except for his RRSPs, he didn't have much else in savings. Thanks to me, he—we—didn't even have that.

***

Weeks passed. The police had no leads. Feeling responsible, I telephoned the station every day, more or less to assuage my guilt. The police wanted me to disappear.

David kept assuring me all was fine, that he harboured no ill will toward me. And he didn't seem to, which amazed me. I often thought back to the day of the robbery; every day, in fact. I couldn't get away from that afternoon—the episode flitted into my mind when I woke and shadowed my mind before I dozed. Some nights I lay awake replaying the scene. What could I have done differently? The answer was always the same: I shouldn't have been transporting that amount of cash. David shouldn't have allowed it, but it was his idea. His stupid idea.

Months disappeared without news—good or otherwise—from the police. Though no one told me, I knew the file had been relegated to the bowels of the department, into a cold case box.

David rarely mentioned the stolen money. He worked harder and longer: gone earlier in the mornings, home later at nights, even working the occasional weekend.

I hadn't worked since I moved in with him but took a part-time job at a grocery store—due to boredom, to take my mind off the robbery, to help with finances. To assuage my guilt? Finally, I was paying my own way in our relationship, not asking David for money for incidentals. David's salary paid the bills, groceries, entertainment. "I'm slowly getting our savings up," he said.

We continued to rent the condo with the useless safe in the wall.

***

About six months after the robbery, I suspected David of having an affair. He had turned slightly indifferent toward me. It was nothing I could definitively explain, just women's intuition.

When I confronted him, he denied it but fessed up the following day. He had the nerve to blame it on stress due to the stolen money. An hour later, he said, "I've grown out of love with you. I was waiting for the right opportunity to tell you." I'd never forgotten those words and the cold manner in which he delivered them.

Right opportunity? He mentioned the money again and how that had been the start of his waning love.

Fell out of love with me because I had been robbed?

"Get out!" I screeched.

"Me get out? This is my apartment if you'll remember. I pay the bills on it. I'm the one who goes to work before it's even daylight and comes home in the dark! What do you do except work four hours a day in a grocery store and waste time on your so-called great Canadian novel?" He sneered at his last words before adding, "And I don't know what you do. You could be fucking someone all day. How do I know?"

"How do you know? Well, you don't, do you? But I'm not like you, off cheating every day like you've admitted. You want out, fine. I'm gone."

I raced to the bedroom and fell to the bed. What was I to do? Run home like a wounded stray puppy to Mommy and Daddy? My parents lived a four-hour drive away. I had no vehicle. After we moved into the condo, David had suggested I sell mine. "We don't need two vehicles living in town." He was right—then, at that moment. But the situation had changed. I needed transportation. And I had none.

Without a word, the condo door slammed. Running to his whore, I guessed, while giving me space to pack up and disappear from his life as if we had never existed. What a sham of a relationship. I was glad we hadn't married. "We will someday," he had said. The small diamond radiating from my left hand supposedly proved it, but the promise never materialized.

***

Even before I met David, I'd been writing a book, sort of a creative nonfiction about my life. I led a dull, ordinary life, so I took great liberties with my words and embellished ninety percent. I didn't know how the story would end. I had no idea how my own life would end, so I hadn't yet figured out how to end my character's life. As does every first-time novelist, I dreamt of penning a bestseller, having my books alongside the likes of Joyce Carol Oates or Alice Munro or Margaret Atwood.

I had read enough how-to books on general writing, including settings and plots and characters, to realize my dream was just that— an impossible dream, a fantasy. One famous author advises wanna-be novelists to write the first book, stash the manuscript in a drawer, and write a second. And repeat with a third. Very rarely does an unknown get her first book looked at by an agent, let alone published. Ditto for the second and third books. But an "unknown" has to get known some time, doesn't she?

Heeding the author's advice, I wrote that first novel to get it out of my system, a book so emotionally charged with me and my feelings, portrayed through my characters, of course. For I was writing fiction— though creative nonfiction—but with enough creativity, a friend or relative would never identify the real characters—or me. But my story had no ending.

David knew a book publishing deal was farfetched. He, more so than me, knew my dream would never come to fruition. Despite his claims otherwise—despite the faith a partner should have in the other—David had less belief in me than I had, which should have been my first clue. I can usually spot liars—can detect them two miles away, behind cloudy eyes and fake grins—but I was either too wrapped up in my writing or too in love. To sport a cliché: love *is* blind.

***

After the door slammed signalling David's departure, I composed myself. I wiped my tears, tossed a few clothes into a suitcase, and gathered some personal items. Surely after I found a place, he'd let me return to get the rest of my things.

When I was about ready to leave, I glanced around the living room. My eyes stopped on the ship painting as if it was the focal point of the room. The gilded mirror over the propane fireplace normally drew one's eyes, for one saw the opposite wall in the mirror, giving the illusion of a larger room.

Always illusions.

I'd never been a snoopy person. I've gone through life being too trusting, burned by a prior boyfriend and a couple of girlfriends. I thought David was different. I never loved anyone as I had him, never trusted as much, yet ironically, he was the one who piled the most wood around me, threw in the match, and giggled as it fired up.

I removed the heavy painting from the wall. The artwork, a ship sailing the high seas, was valuable, one that had been passed down through David's family. I wasn't sure if the value was more sentiment or money. Knowing David, it was the latter. Careful to not damage it, I laid it face down on the carpet.

The safe stared at me; I stared back: a battle of wills. The grey mocked me with its locked door and barricade of thick steel. I wanted in, but it wouldn't let me. I hadn't thought of opening it until that second.

The handle wouldn't budge. Locked! Of course. Even I knew it was locked. What purpose to have a safe if it weren't locked? But there would be nothing in it. David had another safe at work; he had let that slip one day.

The key. Where would it be? Any normal person would carry it on him to be sure of its safety. I would if I had a safe. The key would be in a secret pocket in my purse. Though I was never without my purse, after the robbery it was obvious carrying everything on my person wasn't a smart idea. But my purse hadn't been stolen, just the extra-large shoulder bag containing the cash.

The day of the robbery, my purse, fashioned of imitation leather, was so light I barely felt it as compared to the larger bag. The bag holding the money hung on my right shoulder. Coincidence the robber had taken the most valuable bag? Yes, I reasoned. In his hurry, he snatched the first one he saw: the more obvious one, the bigger one.

Where was the key? I raced to the bedroom, where I searched the logical places—David's sock drawer, his small jewellery box, his roll-top desk. Not wanting to give up entirely, I tugged again on the safe's handle. I pondered the fact it was a keyed safe. Newer models were combination safes, which would have been harder to crack, but I suppose the result was the same: search for a key or a combination. The safe wasn't new despite David's claims.

When I knelt to pick up the painting, I noticed a strip of tape on the lower back. I assumed it covered a rip since it was important to protect paintings from dust and insects. I rubbed the tape and felt a ridge. The key? I slit through the paper with my fingernail, but the ridge was simply a wide staple on the wood frame. Despite that, I tore the tape from the paper to reveal more of the inside.

The key, taped against the side of the wood frame, almost winked at me. I stopped breathing, not trusting what I saw.

No doubt it was a duplicate. The tape I had removed from the backing hadn't been disturbed and David had been into the safe often. He wouldn't delve into the painting each time, so he probably carried a duplicate on his keychain.

I gulped. My fingers shook. I nearly dropped the key in my haste. Who knew when David would return.

When the metal grey door swung open, I ogled the sight. What was that?

I withdrew an envelope—an empty one. My stomach lurched. My heart beat like crazy.

The envelope looked familiar, like the ones containing the money I had taken from the safety deposit box.

The money that had been stolen from me!

The fucking bugger!

I slumped to the floor. If he wanted to be rid of me, why didn't he tell me? I snickered. He had. Minutes previously.

Common-law spouses are entitled to half, whether married or not. He hadn't wanted to pay me off, so he concocted a grandiose scheme. He had no inkling I'd break into the safe. No way would he have thought I'd find the key. He could have covered his tracks by not leaving traces in the safe, but he figured he was safe.

I snickered. He should have been a writer. I couldn't have come up with this hair-brained plot. Thing is, it worked—except I found out and wasn't supposed to.

I tossed the key on the floor. I eyed the painting, hesitating only a second. I stomped on his precious painting, relishing the sound of the canvas tearing, watching that ship sink beneath my feet.

I grabbed additional clothing and a few more items I couldn't live without before calling a cab to take me to a nearby motel. I'd decide the rest of my life later.

One can't always predict an ending. One can't always get the ending one desires, either. Often the ending isn't even what you assume it is.

In the end, I was glad we hadn't married, but thanks to him, I walked away with the ending to my novel. I was confident I'd find a publisher despite it being my first novel. *The Ending* might not be a bestseller, but I was positive it would sell. Who can make up this stuff?

Truth *is* stranger than fiction, to quote another cliché.

Women Must Stick Together

Before moving to the rental property in the country, Mona had looked forward to relaxing at night with the windows wide open, listening to limber branches sway or crusty leaves rustle. Crickets' chatter and water lapping at rocks in the nearby water garden would soothe her to sleep. The buzz of silence would prevail at other times, and she was positive she would hear the quiet, as crazy as that sounded.

Since moving, however, the only time she experienced peace in the evenings was inside the house, with the windows closed tight. Night noise rang in her ears then, a faint but discernible hum as if sounds floated like dust particles, which was better than the alternative when the windows were open.

Though savouring peace and solitude, she had enjoyed the rumblings from the trains that had lumbered down the tracks near her previous home in the city. Choruses of *clickety-clacks* and forlorn *woo-woos* had been oddly relaxing after a hard day's work, easing the stress of waiting tables and fending off obnoxious, horny men.

She lay coverless and naked on the bed. Temps must have surpassed thirty-five degrees Celsius, which had forced her to open the window. Perspiration covered her. The white curtains were as flimsy as the breeze, providing little relief from the heat even when unexpected whispers of air caused the gauzy material to billow.

For some odd reason, the occasional flapping resembled angel wings, probably because her mood had been the farthest side of angelic since relocating. The Miles' house and its occupants were within sight and sound, respectively, constantly ruining the nights. Nothing should mar the peacefulness of the countryside; nothing should intrude upon her little bit of heaven except nature's laughter.

Even in the city, living in a large apartment complex with neighbours above, under, and either side of her, she hadn't had to endure such nonsense. She would never have moved to the country had she thought a neighbour's commotion would constantly hinder her sleep. To drown out the Miles' screeching, she sometimes imagined trains in the distance. She was only fifty-eight kilometres away from the railroad tracks that ran by her previous home; surely she could hear them. And she did—if she pretended and strained hard enough. But that was only an auditory illusion.

Mona groaned. Though the heat had drained her strength, she brandished her arms and clenched her fists as if preparing to punch someone in the face. Maybe she would. Those dratted neighbours would pay for their sins, maybe sooner than later. If she had to put up with their wretched bitching much longer, she'd lose her cool, and who knew what would happen then. When her temper was incited, anyone within twenty feet of her best seek cover.

She'd never actually seen the couple—Mr. and Mrs. Miles—and only knew their surname from the real estate agent when she viewed the property she ended up leasing, which was located next to them. But she'd heard them spew cuss words enough to envision two frightful faces and bizarre bodies, a canvas that remained wet no matter how often the wind blew or how long it was left to dry in the sun.

She pictured Mr. Miles stomping through the house, a hairless head atop a blubbery body, with perspiring palms and feisty fists smashing everything in his way. Tiny and tired Mrs. Miles would be no match for her bruiser husband who, obviously, felt compelled to conquer women. Mona envisioned them in bed, too, the ancient bedsprings creaking under the brute's oppressive weight and the hapless woman beneath him, barely able to breathe. But all that was more depiction than Mona wanted to fathom. She didn't want to visualize repulsive couples copulating. And ugly they were; she was certain of that.

In Mr. Miles' defence, she figured Mrs. Miles had a bit of a mouth, compelling him to lay his hands on her. Mona heard Mrs. Miles' loud and piercing voice at nights when the couple was hard at it and couldn't fault the man for losing his cool, even though abuse against women wasn't right in any circumstances. She was a woman, after all; females must stick together against domineering males of the world, and she reprimanded herself for putting any blame on small and defenseless Mrs. Miles. But Mona herself had lost control in the past and had experienced the difficulty of maintaining one's good nature when the world didn't particularly follow the path one desired.

"Enough already!" she screamed, throwing meandering thoughts aside and bounding out of bed. "I've had it. Truly had it!" She had it up to her eyeballs and beyond, farther even than her height of five foot four, at the nonsense she was forced to listen to night after night. And that night the racket was worse than usual—if that was possible.

She stumbled around in the dark, finally switching on the light and slipping into a pair of jeans—underwear be damned—and a T-shirt. She paused at the sudden velocity of the male voice and hoped she'd arrive in time to save the poor woman.

Mona didn't have a plan in mind, no inkling what she might do when she reached their house or how she'd subdue hefty Mr. Miles. But she had to do something. The pitiful, downtrodden woman needed help, and the nearest house was kilometres away, which left only Mona.

After a final glance about the bedroom, she went to the kitchen. The dozen or so knives, all different shapes, sizes, and severity, all recently honed to razor-blade thinness, leered at her from the under-counter fluorescent light. *Eeny meeny, miney, moe*, she thought. "Eeny, meeny, you're the one."

When she finished her singsong, she selected the largest of the knives, luckily the one her finger had landed on because that's the one she would have picked anyway. The thickest didn't necessarily make it the sharpest knife on the wall, but she'd need the largest against Mr. Miles—whether she did or didn't arrive in time.

Despite Mona's sticky clothing and the sweating she'd suffered earlier, the warmth of the night comforted her while she ambled across the field, flashlight in one hand, knife in the other. Once upon a time, the Miles' house had been the main house and hers the servants' quarters.

She had moved to the country because she didn't want to live in a cookie-cutter house or have houses flanking hers. She wouldn't have settled on 2329 Willow Wood Road had she known the sole neighbours were insufferable and unpleasant. With a narrow field and a fence separating the properties, she had thought a safe distance existed, enabling her to use discretion as to whether she'd consider the unknown couple true neighbours or not—as in, can-I-borrow-a-cup-of-sugar folk. She had never expected to hear their vile voices every evening, which afforded her zero chance of ever wanting to be friendly.

Though heavy, the knife seemed like a feather in her hand, whereas the small LED flashlight was dead weight. The shouting increased as she neared the house. A light shone from a front room, which Mona assumed was the living room.

She stepped on the wide front porch and peered in the large window. The room was awash with light, but no one was there. She still heard the man screeching, his voice thundering to the outdoors. She shivered. Rivulets of sweat dribbled from between her breasts as if insects slithered to her waist. She fanned her arms to allow circulation under her armpits.

Carefully, she opened the door, hoping the ancient hinges wouldn't give her away. She entered the hall and gently closed the door behind her. She peered to her left, which was, as she had suspected, the living room. To her right was another room, probably the parlour from what she could glean in the dim light.

The ruckus, still going strong, was happening on the second floor. The dark staircase was slightly illuminated by a shadowy light at the top of the stairs. From one of the bedrooms, she figured, for that's where they'd be. In the bedroom. In bed. Mr. Miles on top, crushing his wee wife beneath him. Mrs. Miles would be panting, trying to catch a breath, waiting for him to enter and finish the deed.

Mona reconsidered. No! They were squealing—or Mr. Miles was. They wouldn't be in the throes of passion nor would he be raping. The noise wasn't like that.

She crept up the worn, wide steps, hoping again that ancient creaks wouldn't announce her presence. But the couple was too rambunctious to hear a subtle noise from an intruder. The male voice, raspier and more spiked in person, was louder than any sound a female would make.

Mona reached the top of the stairs. Her armpits smelt worse than previously. She paused while more moisture gathered between her breasts. Her T-shirt was plastered to her back as if she'd been whipped, the blood gluing fabric to skin. Even her crotch felt moist, gooey even. If she found the couple in the middle of sex, she prayed she wouldn't be turned on by the repulsive sight. What would that say about her? She shuddered at the thought of enjoying such a gross spectacle.

The lit room was at the far end of the hall. She clutched the railing that continued from the staircase and wrapped to her left. She glanced down between the railing and the stairs and saw a light from the living room. Taking baby steps, she slipped across the hardwood. She ignored three dark bedrooms, assuming two closed doors were a closet and a bathroom.

A sudden shriek by Mr. Miles caused her to jump and almost scream. Despite her anxiety, she clearly discerned snippets: "You bitch...take that...and this..." and heard slaps that could only be against Mrs. Miles' sallow face or her bony butt. Mona pictured red splotches, perhaps a tad of blood—maybe a lot of blood. Maybe the woman's nose had been broken. Maybe her lip cut or a tooth knocked to the floor.

How had Mrs. Miles put up with thrashings and horrid words lambasted at her? Mona had been told by the realtor that the couple had owned the property next door for at least thirty years, and since Mona had heard commotion the first evening after moving in, she figured the episodes had been occurring for a long time. Why hadn't the woman left? Mona knew that was easy for an onlooker to say. Life was hard, and only individuals living in those situations knew the severity. Women left when they were ready, not before. If they left before they were ready, they'd return to their abuser. Mona knew. And understood. No, she wouldn't judge the other woman. She probably shouldn't be helping her either. A stranger shouldn't intrude where she wasn't wanted, shouldn't intervene without being invited.

But mayhem every night! She had to do something. If not for Mrs. Miles, for herself—for Mona—so she could enjoy the peace she was entitled to.

She stood outside the last bedroom, from where light splayed into the hall, and wished she could block her ears from the piercing voice. She heard the woman's quiet voice acquiescing, "Yes, dear; sorry, dear," and the unmistakable sound of sobs. Tears would be rolling down the woman's cheeks, mixing into the blood and diluting it; and thick drops would be seeping into her dull grey hair or plopping to the compressed pillow.

Mona had heard enough. No female deserved that. To top it off, it sounded as though Mrs. Miles was compliant, as if used to the rampage, which ensured she would suffer again in the future. That wasn't right. Women must stand tall for all women even if a woman wasn't aware she was being damaged. Mrs. Miles was one of those unwitting individuals.

Mr. Miles' voice rose. "You damned well be certain you do. Say you're sorry again. I want to hear you grovel." He laughed then, a laugh from deep within a rotten soul.

Mona gripped the doorframe before peering into the room. The glare blinded her at first, and several seconds elapsed before she could see clearly. Not believing her eyes, she blinked. *What?*

She blinked again. And again.

She backed away from the door. The episode couldn't be playing out as she'd seen. She had been mistaken. The light played tricks.

She gulped and slowly exhaled to cleanse her lungs, to give her strength to view the scene another time.

After a few seconds, she peeked into the room again, proving her eyesight was excellent.

She turned and stared at the knife, the blade sharper than she had originally thought, grateful she had grabbed the biggest one; she would need it. Though the scene had presented itself for mere seconds, she couldn't mistake the actors and their roles. The people she'd just witnessed didn't match the ones she'd envisaged. Mrs. Miles, the central person etched firmly in her mind, was huge, more monstrous and macabre than Mona imagined any man could be. And Mr. Miles—well, she couldn't believe she'd been so wrong about him.

As if a zealous soldier on the first day at war, she charged into the room, the knife outstretched. The larger individual still ranted and the smaller one murmured meek okays, but Mona was oblivious to the words. Her mission had been to save a defenseless woman.

But was the woman defenseless?

Mr. and Mrs. Miles hadn't yet realized someone had entered the room. The heftier figure, with layers of fat folding upon each other, was bending over the figure on the floor. Their naked bodies glistened from the overhead light bulb and the humidity and heat.

Mona gaped at the burly woman's boobs, immense breasts that swayed and brushed the hairless chest of the man below. The elongated masses ending with dark, large nipples reminded Mona of two upside-down chocolate-dipped ice cream cones.

Mr. Miles suddenly glimpsed Mona and managed to cover his genitals but not before she saw the tiny upright critter posed as if thumbing a ride. Mrs. Miles, noticing his eyes darting away from hers, turned. Her eyes flared when she saw Mona.

Mrs. Miles stood, ready to pounce like the rabid feline she was. Mona clenched the knife, moved toward the obese woman, and lashed at one mammoth breast. Mrs. Miles eyed the spurting blood and reached down to cover the gash.

Mr. Miles, still on the floor, remained motionless, his hands still cupping his privates. His forlorn eyes gazed at his wife. His lips slowly parted. Bubbles appeared before drool leaked from the corners of his mouth.

Mona leapt at the corpulent woman once more, who was obviously stunned, perhaps in shock. Mona slashed the left breast, causing the woman to release her right breast to comfort the other. Blood spurted uncontrollably. Her blubbery belly, with its rolls of fat, hung toward her knees. Mona couldn't see her pubic hair. Was she shaved? A decisive "no" went through her mind. A woman looking like that would never shave. How would she even find herself?

Mona revved back to life. Mrs. Miles was still alive and could smother Mona with one fleshy bat-winged arm. Without another thought, she plunged the knife into the grotesque gut again and again until the woman collapsed to the floor. The deafening noise, a tree-dropping-in-the-forest kind of sound, jarred Mr. Miles to attention. Forgetting his nudity, he stood, probably the fastest move he had made in years.

"Sweetie," he moaned. "Oh, my sweetie." He fell to his wife, his skeletal body barely covering one of her lumpy legs.

Despite her injuries, Mrs. Miles opened her mouth. "I'm here, I'm still here. Get that woman, you bitch! Get her!"

"What? Who? Me?" He scrunched his face and flailed his arms.

Mrs. Miles pushed her husband away, turned over, and heaved to all fours. Skin from her shredded, scarlet breasts swayed to the floor, blood pouring from her chest.

Without thinking, Mona dug the knife into the woman's butt, and Mrs. Miles screeched, one of those evil screams Mona had endured at night.

"Take that, *you* bitch," Mona yelled.

Mrs. Miles plunked to the floor, face first.

Mr. Miles sprang into action. He swatted at Mona and tried to wrestle the knife from her hand, but the thin, tiny man was no match for her. Mona plunged the knife into the side of his cheek, surprised to see the blade emerge out the other end. His eye sockets became perfect circles when realization dawned, yet the pain seemed to spur him on. When Mona withdrew the knife, he lunged at her again, and she thrust the sharp blade into his neck and withdrew it just as quickly. Blood spurted like a faucet flowing cherry juice. Dazed, he stood for several seconds, obviously uncomprehending until he touched his face as if to stop the flow. But it was useless. He collapsed a second later.

Mrs. Miles, still attempting to stand, was losing blood as fast as Mr. Miles had. But she had more weight, more blood to lose, more stamina. Mona wasn't taking any chances. She thrust the knife into the woman's neck as she had her husband. Mrs. Miles toppled and rolled to her back. Her breasts sagged to her sides and hit the floor. Her body looked as if someone had thrown a gallon of scarlet paint at her. "Sweetie..." she said, looking over at her husband.

Mona, forgetting she was supposed to stick up for women, attacked the defenseless creature again. In and out with the knife, in and out of the woman's belly. Mona figured her efforts were futile since the knife wouldn't reach vital organs through those many layers of flesh. Mrs. Miles continued to breathe, panting like a dog, huffing and whimpering, each breath harder and harder.

Mona loomed over her as Mrs. Miles had stood over Mr. Miles. "How do you like it now, *sweetie*?"

Mona's sugary voice registered with Mrs. Miles; Mona knew it had. The almost-dead woman's eyes glistened. Blood spread from under her and across the hardwood to seep through the hundred-year-old cracks. Mona wondered if the blood would reach the ceiling of the main floor. Would it cause a red watermark on the ceiling? Would the old plaster eventually tear away and fall to the floor?

As if exhaling from a cigarette, the battered woman took one last puff. Mona watched, enjoying the sight. Previously, she hadn't thought she'd enjoy the evening, not after it had been so rudely interrupted, nor had she ever thought she'd enjoy a blood display. But she had. Could she do it again? She wasn't sure. Only if someone bothered her—horribly irritated her—then she supposed she could. Yes, she could. She was sure of it.

Mona hiked her T-shirt over her head, placed the knife on the fabric, and rubbed the damp material over the blade to remove her fingerprints. What else had she touched? The front door. The railing. That was it, wasn't it? She removed her jeans.

"Goodbye, Mr. and Mrs. Miles. I'm leaving. I'll have some peaceful sleep now." She snickered. "So will you."

While retreating, she rubbed her jeans along the second-floor railing and down the stairs. She covered her right hand with the denim, opened the door, and wiped the outside knob after she closed it.

"Funny," she muttered while moseying home, "I still don't know their first names."

Published by Horrified Press in anthology,
I am Woman; I am Man, November 2015

Dickie and Me

Dickie held me close while we danced to a soft samba. No one could see us; we were dancing in a separate area, away from the rest of the crowd. His hands caressed my back, and his lips stole the occasional kiss. I nibbled one of his earlobes while trying to keep time to the music.

"Love you, Dickie," I whispered, knowing my words came from the wine, as had the kisses.

His name was really Richard, but I called him Dickie. He liked the fact I had a nickname for him that no one else knew or used, not that it was *that* unusual a name. Anyone could have addressed him by that, but no one ever did. He had always been called Richard, not Dick or Ritchie or Rick.

In his seventies and suddenly addressed by a nickname was, I think, a form of gratification to him, and he lapped up the personalized attention.

"I've missed you," he said. "Why didn't you keep in touch?"

"Dunno. Just busy, I guess."

We'd had a falling out the previous year, but Dickie seemed unaware of that fact. I liked his wife, Joan, but the four of us never socialized without our spouses. We met occasionally for dinner or the theatre or for afternoon get-togethers to drink and chat. Sometimes we played cards. My husband, John, and I had met them at a senior's dance five years previously.

Dickie had roaming hands and seemed to think he could touch me wherever and whenever he wanted, and he availed himself of every opportunity. If our spouses were in the living room and Dickie and I were alone in the kitchen, he'd strike. He'd plant his soggy lips on mine or grab my boob or clutch my butt. I always pushed him away and laughed it off. We were friends—a foursome—and I wanted to keep our friendship intact. It boggled my mind he took advantage of me like that. Why me? I was positive he never treated his or Joan's other women friends that way, and I was certain Joan was unaware of his actions toward me.

Other times, he was blunt with me, almost as if we had a love/hate relationship that allowed him the freedom to say anything he wanted. He had hurt my feelings on more than one occasion over the years, and I'd gone home numerous times in silent tears from verbal attacks. I couldn't tell my husband; he wouldn't understand. He'd either blame me or accuse me of an overactive imagination.

For weeks after such an evening, I'd want nothing to do with Dickie and Joan. Time passed, forgetfulness interposed, and we'd be together again. They were a fun couple, and John and I enjoyed our times with them.

But get-togethers continued to be never-ending, vicious cycles of Dickie's prying hands and his verbal abasement of me, episodes sometimes more than I could handle. I guess that's what happened the last time the four of us were together, only that time it took over a year before the four of us saw each other again.

Over that period, John would ask why we never saw Richard and Joan. I'd make up some excuse: they were travelling, they had company, they were sick. None of those excuses were lies; those things must have happened to them at some point. They were both world travellers and spent six months of every year in Florida, not to mention other trips, so I only had to cover my tracks for half a year. My husband, a bit naive in the department of life and love, believed whatever I told him.

I'd wonder what excuses Dickie gave Joan since neither of them called us during that period. Maybe we weren't the good friends I had thought we were.

A couple of months after they returned home to Baltimore from their winter down south, I decided to bury the hatchet and invite them out to Dunbar's Dancing Dungeon. It was a place they liked and frequented, so I figured they'd accept our invitation.

And they did.

I loved to dance and so did John. But husband or not, John was too critical of me (much like Dickie was at times) no matter what I did, and his critique of my dancing, the most unbearable. John proclaimed to be one of the world's best dancers (even though he wasn't) and said I should be able to follow his lead. He *was* suave, I will admit, well-versed in moves he had learned over the years (although sometimes too big for his britches), but for three-legged, klutzy me, our moves didn't gel.

Dickie had been a dance instructor in a prior life. (Doesn't everyone have a prior life?) A perfect partner, he knew all the dances: jive, rumba, foxtrot. I was a klutz with him, too, but Dickie never acted as if he minded and even praised my dancing. Although I knew he lied, praise felt good.

Despite my failings, I loved to dance. I tried to stick to familiar music, the kind of tunes everyday people danced to, not the beats requiring specific dance steps one learned in ballroom dance class. Those were the tunes Dickie and Joan danced to.

Slow songs were my forté. Who can't dance to a slow song? You snuggle into your partner and move slowly; that's what a slow dance is. Even John couldn't complain about my slow dancing.

To be honest, I didn't think I was that bad of a fast dancer, either. You simply stood on the dance floor and flailed your arms, hopefully in time to the music. John said that was my problem—I couldn't keep time. According to him, I never heard the beat, or if I did, I didn't pay attention to it. But I danced to have fun, not to win a competition. Why couldn't John understand that?

As a result, I mainly stuck to slow dancing. Besides, once a guy had a woman's breasts smothered to his chest, would he complain?

That night, the four of us met at Dunbar's. After dinner, immediately when the band began, John asked Joan to dance. I was disappointed my husband asked her so quickly, especially for the first dance, but I pretended it didn't matter. Dickie and I remained at the table. I felt uncomfortable, the previous tension between us still floating around although maybe I was the only one who felt it.

"Want to dance?" Dickie asked.

"Sure," I said.

I acted nonchalant, pretending it didn't bother me we hadn't spoken in over a year. We were friends again, that's all that mattered, and I was determined to not let his attitude upset me in the future. And, for certain, I'd make sure he kept his hands to himself.

When the four of us were back at the table, Dickie ordered another bottle of wine.

John seemed enchanted by Joan although I never had vibes the two of them had much in common other than her being a good dancer and conversationalist. With their chairs touching, they were almost too cozy. Enough space existed between my husband and me for another chair.

I slid my chair toward Dickie's. He and I talked while I kept my right ear open to hear what John said. As a result, I couldn't concentrate on Dickie's words. I occasionally agreed with him, hoping I wasn't acquiescing to something untoward.

But Dickie wasn't like that. He loved his wife and would never leave her for anyone. I felt the same way. I'd never leave John, nor would John leave me. We had enjoyed a good forty years together and planned on many more, as many as God would grant us. No, I wasn't the least bit interested in Dickie in that sense, and I was quite confident none of us were interested in leaving our respective partners.

Perhaps the attention we spewed upon each other's partners that night caused things to go haywire. At my age of sixty-two, attention from the opposite sex was almost non-existent. John was approaching seventy, and Joan and Dickie were in their mid-seventies. I'm sure attention given them was even less than that given to me, and at our ages, any attractiveness we once possessed had long been relegated to mere photographs in the past.

"Want to dance?" I heard John ask Joan.

Before I had a chance to comprehend his words, they had disappeared to the dance floor.

Another dance with Joan?

"Guess it's just you and me, Kid," Dickie said.

He always called me Kid, but it wasn't a secret name like "Dickie." I didn't particularly care for the name, but it had a young connotation, so I never said anything. I'd never let the three of them forget I was the youngest of the group, and everyone had laughed when he addressed me as "Kid" that first time. Eventually, the name stuck.

"Yep, you and me," I replied.

"Where do you want to meet?" he asked.

"Meet? What do you mean?"

"You and me. Without the others."

"Without the others?" *What* was he suggesting?

I played along with him.

"Oh, Dickie, you dirty old man, you."

Despite the dim lights, I saw his face redden.

"Sylvia, I didn't mean *that*," he said, with the emphasis on the last word.

It was my turn to blush. But what did he mean, if not that?

To lighten the mood, I laughed. "What? You don't want to meet, you and I, in some clandestine situation, in some seedy motel?"

As soon as the words slipped through my lips, I knew I shouldn't have said "seedy." Dickie had more class than that, and my choice of words made it appear I had none. If, heaven forbid, we ever did meet, it would be at one of Baltimore's finest. Dickie needed and wanted the best—always. He and Joan had unlimited funds, apparently money never an object; their ostentatious house was proof of that, not to mention their other assets. Their foolish waste of money embarrassed me, and I wondered what they must think of John's and my frugal lifestyle.

"Oops," I said, "I should have said the Clinton Arm's Inn or something." The Clinton was one of Baltimore's most prestigious resorts.

Dickie giggled as only Dickie could. His facial expression transformed into elfin-like features, pure and innocent, and his giggle emulated that of a child.

"You can be sure you'd only receive the best from me," he said.

It was my turn to laugh, but with all the wine I had consumed, I laughed too loud.

"Shh," he said. "You're too loud. People are staring."

I glanced around. Everyone was preoccupied with their own business, not with mine and Dickie's.

His admonishment brought back memories of the previous year. Memories of how he had chastised me as if I were a child. I couldn't remember the exact circumstances, but he had belittled me, a feeling almost worse than being manhandled. I was an adult, after all. I didn't need anyone—especially Dickie—telling me what to do. So what if I laughed a tad too loud? The music blared, and no one could hear us. What was the harm?

He was oblivious to my hurt feelings, however, though I sensed him staring at me. I craned my head around the corner, looking for my husband, needing him to dig me out of the hole I had shovelled into. What in the world was I thinking? It wasn't solely the chastising that bothered me at that moment, although that's what had started it; it was the way our conversation had progressed. A lot of it had to do with the wine and my too-free words, but Dickie had already put his ulterior motives in action long before I began drinking.

"What's wrong, Kid?" he asked.

"Nothing." I always replied "nothing"—even to my husband—when I couldn't give the real reason for being upset. "Nothing's wrong," I repeated.

"Come on, let's dance."

"Okay." I didn't know what else to do. Dancing was better than sitting at the table like two lumps.

Dickie crushed me to his chest when the song started. I glanced over to our table several times; it was always empty. John and Joan were still dancing, somewhere that I couldn't see. I scanned the private area where Dickie and I had previously been, but of course, I couldn't see through the thick columns. Were they there, dancing *tete to tete* as Dickie and I had been? Was I receiving a taste of my own medicine?

No, John wouldn't do that to me. Joan was only a friend. We were all just friends. Just couple friends—a foursome. John never saw Joan without Dickie and I being present, just as I never saw Dickie without the two of them.

"Love you, Kid."

"Love you, too, Dickie," I replied automatically. I did love him, but as a friend, nothing more.

Dickie nuzzled against my hair and inhaled. Thank God I had washed my hair that morning, but I did every morning, so no worries there.

"Let's sneak out back."

"What?" I asked.

"Out back. Let's go out back."

I felt claustrophobic on the dance floor. It was getting late, but the crowd hadn't dispersed. Liquor freely flowed; someone was making money. Fresh air sounded inviting, especially when I pictured the lush gardens behind the restaurant. Although an amazing place to visit during the day, at night it was stunning.

I hesitated for a second. "Okay. Let's go."

The refreshing cool breeze brushed against my face the second we stepped outdoors. Small white lights wrapped around tall trees. Similar lights lined either side of the winding pathway leading from the back door down to the shimmering pond and waterfall, where the silky water cascaded from one level of rocks to the next. The sight was breathtaking, even more so after darkness fell when the sprays of water glittered like gleaming gems under glass.

The gardens were everything I had remembered from a visit several months previously when John and I had walked hand in hand down the dimly lit pathway toward the benches, where we sat for a good hour, talking and occasionally kissing.

Dickie and I stood under the shining stars and the glowing moon and watched the water filter down. His arm slithered around my waist, and his hand kneaded my flesh before slyly creeping to my breast. My first thought went to my expanding middle that I couldn't eliminate no matter how often I counted calories or exercised. My second thought was how I could have forgotten all he had done in the past. Was my memory that bad?

As if my body had a mind of its own, I snuggled into him, craving the heat of another human, and hesitantly put my arm around him. He leaned over and kissed me on the cheek before his hand slipped down my shirt and into my bra, where he cupped my breast.

"Perky," he mumbled, just before his mouth found mine and his sloppy tongue tried to pry open my lips.

His probing tongue motivated me to action, and I pushed him away, horrified I had allowed the situation to progress as it had. "Dickie," I said, "what are you doing?"

The stunned look on his face was priceless as if he were God and no one ever said no to him. Well, I had said "no" to him in the past; was his memory *that* bad? And I was saying "no" to him again, albeit a tad late. Apparently, my memory was as bad as his.

Dickie, about my height, was a short, small man, with thinning whitish-grey hair, really too little and much too old for me. Of course, I didn't think of those unappealing attributes at the time. Having someone lavish attention on me excited me since John had ignored me that evening, but things had gotten out of hand.

Dickie was a dirty old man, and I wondered why I hadn't realized that previously.

"Let's go sit down," Dickie said. "We'll just talk. I promise I won't touch you again."

I didn't believe him, but I followed him down the narrow pathway toward the benches.

When we came into the clearing, I saw the occupied bench. Two people sat on it, arms entwined around each other, lips clasped even tighter. The moon shone directly upon them like a spotlight illuminating a solo stage performer.

I gasped when I recognized John. A second later, I noticed Joan.

Dickie recognized them the same time as I had and stopped in his tracks. His arms flew out in disbelief as if practicing to hit someone or something. "What the Sam Hell..."

That was an expression my father had used when something shocked him. As a young child, I had always wondered who Sam Hell was. Did he live near us? How come I never saw him? What a name— Sam Hell.

When older, I learned the original expression was Sam Hill and that it was a euphemism for Sam Hell. I hadn't thought much about those two little words over the years, but I understood the meaning that day. I finally realized who Sam Hell/Hill was. It took me almost a lifetime, but I finally clued in.

My father passed on when I was eight years old, before he revealed what I had always thought to be his secret friend. But that day in the darkened gardens, I realized Sam was everyone's secret. Everyone had a Sam Hell in their lives.

***

On a sweltering day, four years after Sam Hell revealed himself to me, I stood before Dickie's grave. I glimpsed Joan before she saw me. When her eyes caught mine, she looked away.

A lot had happened in four years, not the least of it Dickie's death from a sudden heart attack while fast dancing, probably the jive, a dance much too fast for someone his age. I began divorce proceedings within two days after the night I caught John and Joan on the park bench, and a year later, after over forty years of being one, John and I became two.

Afterward, the suddenness of my action stunned me, but it had been the right decision. Divorce, in hindsight, was something I should have finalized many years previously. John and I were obviously in a rut after that lifetime together, and what love we once had for each other no longer existed. Dickie, without realizing what he had done, helped me see that.

Dickie and Joan remained together, however, and I wondered if Dickie had had indiscretions in the past. I could have been one of those indiscretions, had I not wanted to remain faithful to my husband.

After the burial, I strolled back to my car.

"Hey, Sylvia, wait up," a voice called.

I turned around to see Joan, dressed head to heels in black.

I felt my face turn red, redder than it already was in the God-awful heat. *What does she want?*

"Joan, I'm so sorry about Richard," I blurted.

"Thanks." She wiped her eyes with a tissue, but they were tears from the blinding sun, not tears for Dickie.

"I'm sorry, too," she said. "About John."

"No worries. It's in the past. I've moved on."

"No, I'm serious. I'm so sorry. It didn't mean anything, you know. I was just trying to get Richard jealous. I was the instigator that evening, not John. I tried to call and tell you, but you didn't return my calls. Then I heard you moved away, and I didn't know where to find you."

"Yeah, I left. Too many memories here."

"But you came back for Richard's funeral. How come?"

"Just to pay my respects to the dead." That sounded a bit crass, but Joan didn't seem to notice.

"He always thought the world of you. I knew he fooled around on me, but that's just the way he was. I still loved him. I'm grateful you weren't one of those 'other' women. Thank you for that."

I blushed again, but she was right. I had never been one of those 'other' women and, once I had confirmation they had existed, was glad I had never been. Perhaps I did have class after all.

"Have you seen John?" she asked.

"No, don't want to."

"I hear he's sick, that he doesn't have much time left."

Stunned, I didn't know what to say. John and I hadn't had children, and our families either were long gone or relatives I hadn't kept in touch with, so I had no idea his health had disintegrated to that extent.

"He's not part of my life anymore, Joan."

"But, Sylvia, I told you, it meant nothing."

"See, Joan, that's where you're wrong. I spent forty-two years and four months and six days with John. I deserved more respect than that. He shouldn't have been kissing another woman. I don't care the circumstances. It wasn't right."

Joan's face turned beet red.

Dickie's face flashed. How I had kissed his earlobe that night several years previously. How I had said I loved him, even though the wine talked, not me. And how he had attempted to steal kisses from my lips that were reserved for John. I had never returned the kisses; they had been stolen from me, without my permission. I had only kissed an earlobe and had never asked for the attention he lavished upon me behind his wife's back.

I was innocent. *Wasn't I?*

Was John innocent? No. John had actually kissed a woman. He had his arm around her in a passionate embrace. And he had never danced with me at all that night—not once.

I was right; he was wrong.

"Well, I have to get back," Joan said. "Let's get together sometime."

Joan's remark was a perfunctory one. We had always been a foursome—not a twosome, not a threesome. Joan and I had never

30

socialized without our spouses. John had never socialized with Joan or Dickie unless I was there.

Dickie and I had never socialized without the others, either.

Molly Mulligan

Molly Mulligan watched her four children surround the bed. She recognized the concern splashed across their faces, a worry that was all theirs. She was content with her fate—a fate that came to everyone eventually. Sometimes she wondered why people even bothered living, with an end result of morphing into a pile of ashes or buried six feet under in a shiny pine box.

She had never understood the term "laid to rest." Is that what it was? Resting? She'd much prefer to remain alive and rest at her leisure if the choice were offered to her. Resignation had washed over her when she discovered her terminal illness, and she swore she wouldn't needlessly burden or upset her children.

Of course, best plans are always the thwarted ones, whether by choice or unexpected circumstances, and she'd chalk that one up to the unexpected.

"Mom?" Holly asked. "You okay?"

No, of course I'm not okay. What a stupid question. I'm dying. Who could be okay with death? Except for me, of course. At least that's what I keep trying to convince myself.

"I'm okay. Just tired."

Holly caressed her arm. Jim and Jon observed their sister while she touched their mother. Stan looked elsewhere.

Molly glanced at Stanley and sighed. It was a deep-seated sigh, emanating from the bottom of her soul. *Ah, Stanley. My first-born. The red-headed child who least resembles the others. What temptress—or temper—of fate caused that?*

Holly's long blonde hair framed her fair oval face. The other two boys, darker-skinned, sported jet-black hair. They were twins and the youngest of her children, Jim born two minutes before Jon.

All four children should have reddish hair since they had been spawned from red-headed Irish parents. Molly wondered where the dark hair had come from and marvelled the twins shared the same dark shade. She supposed that was natural, them being twins, and figured Holly's light hair was passable for Irish heritage since many Irish-born had reddish-blonde hair. Holly did sport a shower of freckles, which

Holly hated with a passion, that could be classified as Irish. But black hair?

Ah, Holly. In retrospect, if Molly had been able to change one thing from the past, it would have been her relationship with her daughter. She should have been closer to Holly but wasn't. Holly had a mind of her own, and through the years, disliked discipline, which resulted in bickering and unrest. As an adult, she kept to herself, never sharing her life or thoughts, the result being that they had never bonded. Despite that, Molly had to admit her daughter turned out okay. She just wished they had been closer.

"I...cheated...don't..." Her words were faint. Had she even spoken?

"What, Mother?" Holly asked. "What did you say?" Holly heard her but needed to know that she might have misunderstood. *Cheated? My mother? Or was it Dad?*

For the first time, Stanley shifted his eyes from the illusion of characters prancing across the wall to look at the aged, pale face of his mother. The twins, who sat in the only two chairs, existed in their own world and chatted aimlessly.

"Guys," Holly said. "Ssh."

"What?" Jim said.

Holly put her fingers to her lips and tilted her head sideways: signals for the twins to pay attention. "Mother, what did you say?" she repeated.

Molly looked up at her daughter. Why had they had named her Holly? Oh, because she was born during the Christmas season. The name was also a play on words: Molly and Holly. It was Ainsley's idea. Her husband, Ainsley, who had passed away several years previously.

Molly tried to shut Ainsley from her mind. She missed him so terribly that often it was better to pretend he had never existed, and sometimes it felt as if he never had. Sometimes she actually wished they had never met and that she had travelled another path. An aching heart could be worse than no love at all.

Holly's voice jarred Molly back to the present. "What, dear?"

"You said something, Mom. Something about ch...cheating?" Holly stared at her mother. "What do you mean?"

"Cheating...no...loved him...he loved me. I miss him, loved him so much..." her voice trailed while her eyes wandered to her children. Her dear sweet children.

After gazing at the individuals framing the hospital bed, she closed her eyes. "What? Cheating..." Molly's voice quivered, the rest of her words incoherent.

The children glanced at each other, not daring to voice their thoughts. The same conclusion ran through each of their minds: Stanley, the child who didn't resemble the others even though he bore Molly's trademark red hair, was not part of the family. Stanley's face, at the realization everyone, again, imagined the worst about him, turned a brighter shade of red than his usual pinkish flush.

"But look at them—Jim and Jon," Stanley said, pointing to his brothers. "Look at their black hair and dark skin. Perhaps they're the ones who don't belong in this family. And since when have twins run in the Murphy family anyhow?"

Murphy was Molly's maiden name.

Holly glanced at her twin brothers. She despised the expression on their faces. Stanley loved to goad and make fun of his brothers, continually belittling them.

Jon, usually the quiet one, joined the fight and pointed at Stanley. "Hey, big brother, have you looked in the mirror lately? At least Jim and I look like our mother even if we have dark hair. We have her blue eyes. Who do you look like? It's sure not Dad."

"Leave Dad out of it. He's not here to defend himself," Stanley said, his face even more flushed. Of the four of them, Stanley had been closest to his father.

"Neither is Mom," Jim said.

"Mom's here. She can defend herself quite nicely if she wanted to," Stanley said, staring at his mother. Her eyes were closed, but the slight flicker of her lids belied any pretense of sleep. "She's awake. Look at her. The big fake."

"Stanley!" Holly said. "How could you?" She glared at the others. "Come on, guys, stop it. This isn't the time or the place." Having three brothers who constantly bickered about every little thing grated on her nerves, and over forty years of listening to them hadn't made it easier.

"Hey, you're a fine one to talk, Holly. Look at your hair. Blonde! Who in our family has blonde hair?" Jim said. He looked at his twin for assistance, but Jon barely moved a muscle.

Holly took a deep breath and willed herself to remain silent, thanking the Lord He had made her a girl even if she still harboured tomboy traces. How could she have been anything but a tomboy, growing up with three brothers?

They were each born a year apart, with the last delivery a double-whammy: *Bang, bang, boom-boom.*

"Come on, guys, enough." Holly lowered her voice and changed tactics. Tears welled behind her eyes, and she ensured her siblings saw her pain. "Mom's sleeping. Let her rest in peace."

Rest in peace, Molly thought. *Please, God, let me rest in peace. No matter the wooden crate they toss me in, nor how deep the hole is dug, please let me rest in peace.*

Holly caressed her mother's arm again. "Mom, I'm here for you. Let me know if you want anything." Holly regretted the past, wished she'd been more tolerant of her mother and wished they'd been closer, knowing it was her own fault, not her mother's. Her mother had tried; she hadn't.

After she bent to kiss her mother's cheek, Holly stoically faced her brothers. "Let's go get something to eat."

When the four children converged in the cafeteria, the same thoughts whirled through their heads. Could their mother have cheated on their father? Or had it been their father who'd cheated on their mother? Could one of them not be a full sibling?

All heads veered unconsciously toward Stanley. Even Stanley figured it was him though he'd never acknowledge it. It must be; he was the only one who didn't resemble his siblings in any way. Holly, at least, shared the twins' bright blue eyes, but Stanley's were darker and duller, more sombre. Were they shadowed reflections of what he might not be?

"Cheating? Did our mother say that?" Stanley asked.

"Guys, does it really matter?" Holly said. "We're family. For certain. And we don't even know for sure that's what she said. I was the only one that heard it."

"I heard it," Stanley said.

"Me, too," Jim and Jon chimed in.

Jon added, "We all heard it. Who are you fooling, Holly? Yourself? You don't look like one of us either. We've always wondered this very thing. Mom just confirmed it."

Holly blushed. She had wondered through the years if she had been adopted. She had never felt a connection with her parents, not the kind of connection her friends had with their parents. Most times, she felt out of place, not even close to her three siblings, definitely not as close as the three boys were amongst themselves. Heaven knows the three boys weren't even close. She had attributed her feelings to being the lone female sibling but knew it was more than that. She sighed. Hiding feelings that persistently haunted her was draining.

She couldn't share her thoughts, not even with her best friend. Several times she had almost broached her parentage to her mother but had stopped herself, not wanting to hurt her, perhaps not wanting to hear the truth she so desperately yearned for. Her father had been a distant man, far away in his own little world—much like the twins—and spent almost all his waking hours working. She often wondered about her parents' relationship. Were they close? She never saw an overt sign of love between them, never saw a bond, but her mother, on her deathbed, had declared she'd loved him.

Someone wouldn't lie while they neared death, would they? Wouldn't one want to expose the truth? Get it off one's chest before meeting his or her maker? If one believed, that is, and Holly knew her mother believed—knew she harboured the certainty of a higher being—even if she never admitted it out loud.

Were there secrets? Too many thoughts and feelings were never verbalized by anyone in her family. Too many unasked questions, too many pat answers to asked questions; too many unexplained answers. *Why?* Holly wondered. *Why?* Or was it just her imagination?

And what of her father? The children had never met any other Mulligans, at least not Mulligans related to their father. No relatives, her father had said. An only child, he came from a small family, and his parents and grandparents were deceased. Since her mother had more than enough family to make up for the deficiency on her father's side, Holly had never questioned their lack of paternal relatives. But as she matured, she dwelled more and more on her father's supposed non-existent family.

When had she first realized everything she had ever believed was a lie, that the truth was out there just beyond her nose? Holly felt it in her bones. Whatever that truth was, if it raised enough of its putrid stench, the siblings could be suffocated by the fumes.

"We should call her on it," Jim said.

"Call her on it, Jim? What do you mean?" Holly asked. She had played dumb so long the act came easy.

"Find out the truth. What she meant."

"Maybe it's nothing. She's becoming delusional. I don't think she knows what she's saying," Holly said. "She's our mother. Treat her better than that."

"Our mother! How do you know that? It seems obvious she's not. Or maybe it's Dad. I guess it's more likely that he was never our father."

"Yeah, all these family lies and secrets," Jon said.

"We know nothing of the sort," Holly rebuked. "Our childhoods were normal. Our parents are our parents. We have no reason to think otherwise."

"Holly, you live in a dream world of make-believe and fairies. You wouldn't know the truth if it kicked you to the pavement." Stanley's mouth curled, and he glared at his siblings. "Yeah, I know what you all think. That I'm the odd one out, but you guys need to look in the mirror like Jon said I should. None of us are who we think we are, who our parents said we were."

Stanley gazed out the window. "Maybe we're all adopted. Did you ever think of that? They waited until they were in their thirties to have us." His voice lowered. "Maybe it's all of us. Maybe none of us belong."

"Stanley, stop it," Holly said.

"We need to find out," he whispered. "She owes us that."

Molly knew all about love. And lust. She'd lived it every day when Ainsley was alive. She knew the future would hold love, too—soon—when she was buried deep in some unknown place where she'd rest forevermore, where no one would discover her wanton secrets and lies, where no one would judge—where she wouldn't judge. She would discover love again with Ainsley.

There was that "rest" word again.

The rest of her life.

Molly glanced about the room to find it empty, save for the sterile and expected hospital furnishings and fixtures. She sighed an invigorating sigh that needed to be set free and sucked in a great breath, which made her feel more lucid. She smiled, crinkling more of the creases, which folded like a paper fan on a cold winter day. She patted down her hair and wished she had a mirror to apply her fuchsia lipstick, which would brighten her wan face.

When she remembered the episode with her children, her smile slowly dissipated. As out of the present as her children thought she was most days—which she probably was—she had heard their discussion, heard every word her four children spoke. They didn't seem to care that she heard.

Molly knew their family was made up of all the wrong ingredients, but why couldn't her children let things be? Jim had always been the most vocal of the twins—the most vocal of the four of them—and he, more than any of them, would stir up things. He'd throw cupfuls of words into a huge metal pot, turn up the heat, and thrash the words around with a tough wooden spoon until there was nothing left but burnt reminders of what they once had: a few remaining memories to cherish amidst ugly leftovers and tidbits of their lives.

She'd known, eventually, that those lies and deceits would rise to the surface and overshadow all the good the family had once been blessed with. The heat threatened to suffocate her, but she shivered when a chill coursed through her. Whether they wanted it or not, she feared the truth about to be thrust upon them. Jim would make sure of that. Jim—who knew nothing about truth and untruths.

Molly loved her children, and they *were* hers and Ainsley's children, no matter what the four believed. Her life had been complicated, more so than anyone could have been aware of, except for Ainsley, of course.

The door creaked, and Holly appeared beside her.

"Hey, Mom."

"Hi, love. Where's the boys?"

"They're coming. Stanley's on the phone talking to Debbie. Sounds like she might be over later. Jim and Jon are outside getting some fresh air. The cafeteria air's kinda stale."

"You just ate, then?"

"Yes. We snuck out while you were sleeping. Did you get some sleep?"

"I did, dear."

"Mom…"

Molly glanced at her daughter, knew the questions in her mind, the answers she wanted before it was too late.

"Holly, there's no deep dark secrets. I can't tell you something that's not there." Molly despised her lie.

"But, Mom. Why are we so different? We don't even have the same personalities, not to mention looks." Holly didn't add the unspoken: that questions needed to come sooner rather than later, before the answers were dead and buried forever.

"All children are different. They can take strains from different branches."

"No, it's more than that. We're…different. Too different."

"Holly, don't—"

"Mom—"

Molly was saved from answering when the door opened and her three sons entered. Her head sunk back to the pillow if it were possible to sink any farther than she already had. She had long dreaded the truth that would come out someday and wished, of course, that it could be later than sooner, that the truth would unravel in some mysterious way long after she was buried and not while she lay on her deathbed, lucid enough to field questions and fend off answers.

"Ainsley, where are you? Why did you leave me here to deal with this on my own?" Molly's mouth opened, but she couldn't be certain she had actually spoken.

She drifted back to that night in June of 1958, several months after she and Ainsley had met. She'd never forget the softness of his face and how it had been illuminated by moonlight streaming through the window.

She raised her hand and brushed his imaginary face. She heard his dreadful words once again, remembering how she had thought she'd misunderstood. When he repeated the words, although shocked and offended, she knew them to be true. Things made sense then. She had backed away from him and had turned to flee, but instead had fallen into an imaginary world. Ainsley had caught her, held her, caressed her, and promised he'd love her until his death.

When she had come to, Molly had hoped she'd been in the throes of a dream where horrid demons spewing horrific lies had visited. She had pinched herself to prove she was awake and even told Ainsley to pinch her, as well.

But one can pinch oneself while in a dream, so a pinch hadn't proven anything. She had been thrown into a dilemma, one she hadn't known how to repair, one she hadn't known how to exist in. But Ainsley hadn't been concerned. He said all would work out if she loved him.

Which she had.

Molly adored Ainsley more than anyone on earth. He had entered her life at a time when she needed love, but she would have loved him regardless. A mixed-up twenty-year-old when they had met, she hadn't loved before, nor had she known what true love was. Until Ainsley.

Except his name hadn't really been Ainsley.

Molly shuddered again, transporting herself back to the present.

"Mom, you cold?" Holly didn't wait for a reply but pulled up the second blanket at the foot of the bed. She leaned down and kissed her mother's cheek.

"I love you, Mom. Love you so much. I'm sorry we didn't get along. I've learned, though. You were the best. And my kids are wonderful, thanks to you."

Molly reached for her daughter. "Holly, there's things..."

"It's okay, Mom. Don't worry. We're good. No need to talk."

"No, you guys have the right to know. But...it's complicated. Not sure how to tell you."

"Mom, there's nothing you need to say. Everything's fine."

Molly knew Holly was sincere. Out of her four children, Holly was the most generous and kind. It had taken too many years for Holly to arrive at that place, but she had arrived, which was the main thing.

***

Ainsley glanced away at the sign of Molly's tears, which began after she awoke from her fainting spell and didn't stop for a good ten minutes. For several months, he had known the dreadful day neared but didn't know what to do about it. How did you tell someone you loved that you weren't the person you portrayed yourself to be? How did you tell someone you loved that you were a liar and a fake?

"Molly, I'm so sorry. I love you. I want you. No matter what."

Molly turned. "But...I don't really understand. How can something like that be possible?"

He was aware that Molly was one of God's innocent children—too naïve and trusting, too good at the core to know of bad things or to understand things that didn't make sense. She had been raised in a simple household and had learnt simple things. She was too virtuous for the harsh world that would surely spread out before her.

"I should run. Far away where you'll never find me." His eyes glistened, and he brushed at them with his fist.

"No. No, I don't want that." Molly reached out to take his hand and then thought better of it, wondering if she'd ever want to touch him again.

"Please understand, Molly. God didn't make me the way he should have. It took me a long time to realize that. I've never felt like a girl. Even looking in the mirror I never saw a female. I saw a man in sheep's clothing. A man daring to throw off silly women clothes and shout to the world the truth of who he really was. But I could never do that. I could never hurt my parents that way. But I did, in the end." Ainsley's attempt at being stoic slackened, and his tears escaped.

Molly erased Ainsley's tears with her fingertips. "I'm sorry. I just don't understand how these things can be. You should have told me earlier. At the beginning."

Ainsley stared at the floor. "I know I should've. But at the time, I didn't know I'd fall in love with you. I didn't know I'd feel this way. This is new to me, too, you know. And you would've bolted, had I told you. You know you would've."

"So your name's really Ann?"

"Yes, Ann Matilda Mulligan."

"Where did Ainsley come from?" Molly asked.

"I don't know. It just came to me. I was trying to find something close to Ann. I didn't like Arnold, not that it's closer than Ainsley. I suppose, in the end, it didn't matter what name I picked."

"No, I suppose not," Molly said. Her stomach lurched and her face felt as if it were on fire. She rubbed at the dampness with her sleeve before staring into the distance. "But you asked me to marry you. How can that be?"

Ainsley waved his hands as if swatting at flies and shoved his weight from one foot to the other. "We can marry. I've heard of a doctor overseas who specializes in sex change operations. I'm going to go. Find out my options." His words came out in a rush as if he had to get them out before he changed his mind.

"But...children...I want children someday." Molly's eyes glistened at the emptiness she already felt.

"We can have them." Ainsley's face lit up. "We can adopt."

"But...I want my own children. I want to be pregnant. It's all I've ever wanted.

"Well..." Ainsley hesitated. "I'm sure there's a way around it, that you can be pregnant. I'm not sure..."

Ainsley hadn't a clue what he was talking about but stalled for time, hoping to sway Molly, whom he loved so deeply. At twenty-two, even without previously having dated, he knew she was the one for him. He had known it when he saw her across the room that day six months previously. Molly had known it, too. He had seen it in her eyes that they were meant to be together as man and woman, in spite of his sex at birth.

***

Molly thought back to the day when Ainsley had told her his plan for her to experience the joys of pregnancy, a way for her to have her own children. They had been married for almost ten years by then, and she had become resigned to not ever having her own children. At times, fleeting thoughts niggled at her that they should adopt, but time had a way of disappearing before she seriously thought about it or broached the subject to her husband.

She remembered Ainsley's words almost by heart—and hers.

"But Ainsley, I can't do it. It's wrong. Wrong," Molly told him.

"It'll be okay, Molly. I'll be right there with you."

"But—"

"Molly, if you want children, there's no other way. We don't have money for those fancy treatments. I can't even scrape up the money to get to Germany or wherever it is they do those operations. And I want children, too. We want to be a family, right? I should have come up with this idea before."

She examined his face, hoping a better, less crazy idea would spring from him, but there was nothing more. Ainsley stared back, so she embraced the love in his eyes and hoped all would be okay.

"I'll look for guys that resemble me. Who have red hair and freckles. Who are tall and slim."

Over the next couple of years, they talked and cried and eventually sorted things out. Their secrets would be their secrets. No one would ever know.

Molly abhorred that motel room where she had intercourse with the first man Ainsley had brought to her. A year later, there had been intercourse with another. And a year after that, another. Three shabby motel rooms, three repulsive men, but despite everything, Molly considered herself lucky. At each attempt, she had successfully conceived. Three times to have four children.

Ainsley was present at each episode, spying like a voyeur though he wasn't a sexual deviant. The acts weren't "making love." They weren't even sexual, Molly had rationalized. It was plain old intercourse or coitus or copulation; a means to an end. A necessary act in order to bear children. A necessary evil to fulfill her dream.

Ainsley ensured the men were of Irish descent and resembled him enough so the children would bear Irish traits. So no one would know. Years later, it had been obvious his plan hadn't worked out as well as it should have. The three men either weren't full-fledged Irish or, despite their reddish hair and freckles, other genes had overtaken Irish ones.

Molly didn't care, of course. Her children were her children, whether they were full-blooded Irish or not. And they were Ainsley's children, in spite of him not being their biological father. She and Ainsley had raised them together. They were their children. They were.

Molly knew this day would eventually arrive—her day of reckoning—her day of truth. How could she explain those horrid circumstances to her children? Would they understand? No, they would call her a slut, or worse. Looking back, she wondered what she and Ainsley had been thinking, for there would be consequences, someday.

She continued to rehash the past. How badly she had wanted children, especially after Ainsley had planted his crazy idea in her head. She wasn't getting any younger, and if she were going to have children, it would have to be then or forget her dream forever.

Heck, she and Ainsley couldn't even marry. The two of them were a charade, playing a game of dress-up while they painted a house of lies.

Molly and Ainsley never saw the men again. The men were drunk when Ainsley hand-picked them off the streets of New York City, where Ainsley and Molly first resided. "Drunken men won't remember in the morning," he'd said.

After the birth of the twins, they moved to the country, escaping reminders of nameless slums and gutters where the drunken Irish lived, but Molly never forgot their whiskey breath and their heaviness upon her as they groped and grabbed. They may have been drunk, but they were aroused, and they pummelled and pounded her body until she wished she were as drunk as they were so she wouldn't remember in the morning.

But she always remembered. Their stench stayed with her, no matter how often she showered, no matter how much perfume she splashed over her body. She abhorred motels for the rest of her life.

Molly shuddered. Those three men were etched in her mind as clearly as her three labours, which had been as painful if not more so. Each time in those slummy motel rooms, she had pretended Ainsley was atop her and that it was his penis thrusting in and out and not a dirty drunk's privates filling her most sacred depths. She'd never experience that kind of sexual physicality with Ainsley. They had finally accepted the truth: they'd never afford a sex change operation nor ever legally marry. Raising four kids didn't leave much money for frivolity had marriage even been an option back then.

Ainsley's family had disowned him when, at the age of seventeen, he'd tried to explain how different he was. He had left home then, and a few years later, met Molly. They disappeared for a few days while they carried out their elaborate marriage scheme and returned to Molly's family with the news of their elopement. After that, they left Concord, Massachusetts, and relocated to New York. No one had been the wiser. After the third pregnancy, they moved for the last time, to Williamsville, New Jersey, where they lived in the shadows of their lies.

Molly adored Ainsley's face and body. When they cuddled in bed, they made do with each other as best they could. With his cropped hair, gangly body, and manly features, he passed easily for a male. He spent hours practising his speech so he would sound manlier. He worked hard, and his job as a salesman for Jupiter Corporation often took him away from home for weeks at a time. It was better that way, without the opportunity to socialize and be discovered.

At some point, Ainsley had obtained a new birth certificate and social security card. Molly never wanted to know how he had accomplished those feats. When he died at home in his sleep of natural causes, the coroner waived an autopsy, and Molly had Ainsley cremated without mortuary preparations and services.

***

Molly had known for months her body was failing. When she awoke that morning, in more pain than ever, realization dawned that the end was truly near. Closer than she wanted. Vivid memories invaded her thoughts too frequently, a sign of impending death, but replaying the years with Ainsley brought her joy, and for that she was grateful. She'd always love Ainsley. Their love may not have been perfect, may not have been normal, but it was their love, and they were happy in spite of the challenges.

When she sensed rather than heard Holly hovering, Molly knew she had to either tell the truth or keep it hushed forever. There was no way for anyone to discover the truth if she didn't reveal it.

Holly might understand, but the others wouldn't. Not her boys. They would raise a stink, especially Jim with his quick temper and Stanley with his continual perception of not being a true Mulligan. With their mother gone and not being able to tend to them, the four would break apart. Their bond, what little they had left, would be non-existent, and Molly didn't want that for her children. She wanted them to cherish each other. Life was too fragile not to.

"I...can't do it," Molly said, her voice a mere mumble. She felt weaker than ever and knew her time had drawn to a close. "Sorry..."

"Mother?"

"The boys?"

"They'll be back shortly, Mom."

Holly caressed her mother's clammy forehead, certain there was something her mother was hiding, but—finally—she was okay with her mother's choice. Everyone was entitled to their privacy. She hoped someday her brothers would understand that, too.

Published by Seven Fates Writers in anthology,
Stories for the Dead of Night, July 2013.

Trapped in the Swallow

The warmth spread around her, hotter and hotter, worse than being submerged in a barrel of sweat on a blistering summer's day. Her legs and arms, immobile and numb in the pudding-like mixture, felt detached from her body as if they had been severed before floating into the depths of...somewhere.

Was she in the throes of a dream or awake? Or, despite impending death, sluggishly descending into hell? It was impossible to scream. Even if she could open her mouth—which she couldn't—thick sludge would fill it. Everything had happened so fast. Who'd think a person sauntering innocently along a marked trail would be swallowed up by a sinkhole.

Hell awaited her; there was no question in her mind. Yet, although her skin burned, the heat was oddly comforting. Darkness pressed against her lids. Blackness was all she could see through eyes tightly shut.

Death had a taste like mouldy bread.

***

The early evening was balmy, one of those calm days when one basked in a gentle breeze and relished life. Those days were few for Ruth, who lived in Manitoba, one of Canada's coldest provinces. Several days prior, she and her husband, Ralph, had flown from Winnipeg to Auckland, New Zealand, where they had been enjoying their first few days of flawless weather. Ruth, especially, luxuriated in the tepid climate.

"Your hands are cold, deary," Ralph had said to her a month before their trip.

"Well, take me away someplace warm if you're so concerned." Ruth had laughed and glanced at her husband of forty-one years. Although she joked, she was serious at the same time. It had been over ten years since they had been on a vacation, other than the odd weekend away visiting grandchildren. Disappointment had washed over her when they had to cancel their vacation plans to Hawaii a couple of years previously.

Their only daughter lived a six-hour drive away in Morehead with their grandchildren: ten-year-old Amy and eight-year-old Ethan.

Although Ruth and Ralph tried to visit frequently, Ralph, at sixty-nine, still worked full-time. The recession a few years back had brought his career to an end, and dipping into savings for living expenses, combined with low interest rates, had eaten away at his pension and retirement savings. Ralph had managed to find another job, albeit at half his previous salary, but with Ruth's frugality, a chance existed he might manage to retire at seventy-four.

Ralph had glanced at his wife, knowing she spoke in jest, aware her comment held truth. She had always hated the winter's cold, and Ralph disliked the fact he hadn't made better financial decisions that would have afforded her more luxuries in life.

"Soon," he had replied. He had looked away, a slight smile on his face. At times, he had ribbed how expensive it had been to keep her throughout the years and how much further ahead he'd be without her. "I'd be better off divorcing you and finding a young chick," he'd say on numerous occasions. Ruth knew he kidded, but his flippant references made her feel disposable as if he could easily accept being rid of her.

Once happily ensconced in the Fenwick Motel in Rotorua, one of New Zealand's most-visited tourist destinations, Ruth forgot past problems. She had never seen so many hotels and motels crammed together in such a small area. Wherever they wandered, more and more accommodations sprung up. It was early February; two more months of summer in New Zealand. For once in her life, she gloated—even if in private—that she basked in the sun while her friends and family suffered in sub-zero temperatures. She chuckled at the irony; her two dear friends, Alice and Janine, usually gloated at her.

"What's so funny?" Ralph asked.

"Oh, nothing. Just that I'm here and Alice and Janine are back home in the cold."

"That's mean, you know."

"What they don't know won't hurt them."

"You should watch your mouth."

Ruth thought her husband's tone accusatory. "What do you mean, Ralph?" She wished he'd lighten up. When he didn't reply, she chose to ignore his rebuke and asked, "Did you hear those people last night?"

"What people?"

"The people at the motel when we were sitting at the patio table. They were talking about the woman who sunk into the sinkhole. Well, not really a sinkhole, a bubbling hot spring, although I guess it was a sinkhole if she sunk into it."

"No, I didn't. I don't even remember seeing anyone there."

"Yes, they were there, Ralph. Two of them at the table next to us—a husband and wife, it appeared. You had a beer and I had a wine. They were talking about a couple walking along the riverbank and how the wife slid into the bubbling spring and ended up with burns over ninety percent of her body. Can you imagine? How would that feel, sliding into a hot mass of whatever is down there?" Ruth rambled, indifferent to her own unanswerable questions.

Ralph knew when to ignore her babble. Half the time he didn't listen; the other half he only pretended to.

"I wonder if that poor woman lived. How could you survive with your body burned like that? Must be horrific." Ruth thought out loud. "And what about her face? Did she sink all the way under? And how would someone get her out? Wouldn't they be burned too?"

***

How would she look when someone pulled her out? The thought of her face scarred beyond recognition scared her the most. Would she be blind? Would she be forced to endure painful skin grafts and endless hospital stays?

Would anyone even pull her up? Was anyone up there to know where she was? Was it too late for her rescue? Was she on the last journey to her final destination?

Or was her fate something totally different? Was she mired in limbo forever as a form of retaliation? What horrific deed had she done that she deserved such punishment?

Too many questions. Would she ever know the answers?

***

Ruth and Ralph found the trail by accident when they left the motel to search for the large bursts of steam they had seen earlier in the day. Near the river at the end of the street, they discovered the Maori settlement to their right. The native village was closed though there had been no indication of that when Ruth and Ralph entered. They managed to walk several yards undetected until a figure darted in front of them and screeched for them to leave.

"Closed, closed," he yelled.

Ruth managed to snap several more photographs of the spouting geysers on the way out. She wondered about the temperature of the steam rising from the bubbling holes and whether the almost-clear substance would show up in the photos.

"Jeepers," Ruth said in disgust. "We were just walking. What harm in that?"

"They want their entrance fees."

"Everyone wants money for everything here. Can't believe how expensive everything is. Hey, let's walk this way, along the river bank," Ruth said when they were out of the compound. "It's fun to explore. And look, there's spit holes over there, too."

Ralph was a geologist. "They're not spit holes. They're geothermal springs."

"Yeah? What are geysers then?"

"Basically they're the same. Geothermal springs are formed from the release of geothermally heated groundwater beneath the earth's crust. Geysers are intermittent discharges of water that turn into steam."

"Yeah, whatever."

Ralph shrugged.

"What are sinkholes?" Ruth asked.

"That's when the rock below the surface is limestone or another carbonate rock. Circulating water dissolves the rock over time. As the rock disintegrates, caverns and spaces develop underground. One doesn't know they're there until the support is gone. So, if you step on that area—poof, like magic—you're gone."

"What? That's horrid." Mysteries intrigued Ruth. She liked truths rather than the unexplainable. And for someone to disappear? How unfathomable.

The strangers' conversation of the previous night haunted her. No matter how hard she tried, she couldn't forget their banter.

The couple headed toward the riverbank to their right, and Ruth, ever the romantic, slipped her hand into Ralph's. It had been several weeks since they had made love. Before their vacation started, she imagined sex every night while they were away. Thus far, her vision hadn't materialized, but with two weeks remaining in New Zealand before they boarded the plane for home, she hadn't given up re-kindling their once-sizzling romance. She wasn't sure when things had begun to deteriorate, but their relationship had fizzled over the past several years. What did one expect, though? They had been married for forty-one years, so life and sex were bound to turn mundane or sour eventually. The ever-present green monster had reared its ugly head too many times when she compared her friends' relationships to hers and Ralph's.

Ruth clenched her husband's hand with a vengeance, not wanting to let go. Ralph glanced at his wife as if questioning her sudden affection. Catching a glimpse of his familiar smile, she knew all would be well. She was certain Ralph would keep her warm that evening, just as the sun warmed her by day.

**

Normally, she enjoyed the heat but now found it too warm. Searing. Crushing. Her mind was full of everything—and nothing. She believed what they said: life does, indeed, flash before one when death nears. Death? She'd always hated the thought of death. Not that anyone relished death. Who would? Only someone desiring suicide; not her. She enjoyed most everything about her life.

Why was death taking so long? Death was happening, wasn't it? That's why she was sinking forever into the depths of nothing.

But why was it taking so long? Death should have taken her by now. She should be dead. Shouldn't she?

She wondered again if she were in the middle of a dream. If so, when would it end? Or would it? Was she to exist forever between life and death? Was this her Hell, her punishment for "whatever"? She wracked her brains again trying to determine what caused her to exist forever in a cauldron of heat.

Or had she wished to be warm too often? Should she have appreciated Manitoba's cold weather and not wished for an unreachable goal? She tried to move her fingers, tried to grasp at something—anything—but there was nothing. Nothing but a black void of sludge.

***

"Ooh, look at that," Ruth whispered. "Isn't it amazing? The smell's not that bad either."

She and Ralph stood on a narrow wooden bridge, gazing at the gurgling mud holes dotting the landscape below. The stream, which had meandered unceremoniously through gangly brush and squatty scrubs—save for occasional patches of bubbling springs—spread out when they reached the clearing. Smoke rose from many of the openings and cumulated to form a mass of billowing steam that surfed over pools of water, at times blocking the rock formations from their view. A plateau of yellowish rock, cracked and discoloured by sulfur, spread from one bank and disappeared beneath the shallow murkiness. Miniature cliffs of darker stone framed the opposite side of the widened river. The sulfur smell permeated the air around them.

Ruth had never seen such a wondrous sight, and she noticed that usually reticent Ralph was impressed, as well.

"It is a vision, that's for sure," he said.

She touched his arm. "Look over there. I think those puffs are from the village."

"Yes, likely they are."

"What's the smell from? It doesn't really smell like rotten eggs to me, not like I thought it would. Everyone says sulfur smells like rotten eggs. Is that what it is? I rather like the smell." Ruth opened her mouth wide and inhaled greedily.

"Sulfur's formed from trace amounts of hydrogen sulfide gas. It's poisonous in some areas."

"Poisonous?" Ruth exhaled. "How come we never went to Yellowstone National Park? It's only a sixteen-hour drive or so. We could have seen geysers and stuff almost in our backyard, instead of travelling this far to see them."

"Dunno. Never thought of it, I guess."

Ruth snapped several pictures, zooming in on the bubbling springs, and then changed to wide-angle to capture the full effect. She sensed Ralph's irritation at the incessant *click click*, but for once she wouldn't allow him to ruin their day.

"Come on, there's more ahead." Ruth grabbed his hand as if a small child latching to her mother, and Ralph had no choice but to follow.

They continued on the worn dirt path through brush and clearings, stopping whenever there were more mud springs to gawk at. Ruth couldn't get enough of foreign sights. Occasionally, her mind wandered to the plight of the poor woman who'd fallen into one of the holes. Most of the holes were small holes. Had the woman's body widened the opening so she could be plucked in like an insignificant fly? Or had she wandered on ground that mysteriously softened when it sensed a prey, like a Venus flytrap plant waiting to suck in its unsuspecting quarry?

***

Mud was smothering her. She had slipped and been swallowed up by one of those deceptive holes. She had sunk in a flash and wondered if she'd survive the scorching heat. She relished the heat, but enough was enough. If she could hold her breath and remain coherent long enough to not open her eyes or mouth, she might control the timing of her suffocation. Black sludge surrounded her; she didn't need to open her eyes to see it.

She wondered if some pits were hotter than others. Did bubbles and steam simply appear hot when they weren't? Would it get hotter the farther she sank? Or was she even sinking? Perhaps she had gone down as far as she could and was floating in limbo until—until what? She couldn't touch bottom. Or could she? It was hard to tell with legs stiff and immobile. Her arms felt the same way, too, no matter how hard she tried to wiggle. Even her fingers were numb. Did that mean she was completely red and seared, cooked alive like a twitching lobster gingerly inserted into a cauldron of boiling water? Or was the thick mud clinging to her and pushing against her flesh, molding her into whatever shape it pleased?

She pictured steam rising into the air above her. Was it steam from the hot mud or her body's fumes squalling back into the world? Perhaps each bubbling mud hole contained one slowly roasting human uttering a last breath.

A giant Venus flytrap sprouted before her. She felt like a tiny creature clutched in its leaf. How she had loved those plants as a child. She'd had several over the years, carefully tending each one until death. Once-green stalks eventually browned and bent like an old person shriveled in pain. She wondered if God were enacting His punishment upon her. God was a male; she was certain of that. Only a male god would impose such horrible revenge on women.

How long would she slide before her skin was completely seared off? How much longer would she be able to hold her breath? Her life flashed in snippets. In one scene, her grandfather teased her about digging too deep a hole to bury her dog, Polka, and how, if she weren't careful, she'd fall through to China. She wondered how deep Hell's pit was. Or would she wake up from a horrid dream to find herself entwined in her husband's limbs, suffocated by the heat of him?

But no, he wouldn't do that to her. He loved her, didn't he? She slipped, that was all. Any second he'd pull her out and clean her off. "It's okay, honey. It's okay," he'd say. "I have you. You're safe." And he'd kiss her reddened face and lovingly carry her home.

***

"Watch what you're doing," Ralph shrieked. He yanked her arm so hard she thought it had broken. At the very least, she'd wake up the following morning sporting huge purple bruises. She always bruised, usually at Ralph's hands. Not that he meant to bruise her; her fragile flesh loved to reveal every little tug or pull.

"Jeepers, Ralph."

"You were about to fall. You want me to let you fall down the cliff?"

Ruth rubbed her arm. "It's not a cliff. It's a small hill. And I was fine. You always hurt me when you grab me."

"You're a klutz. If I weren't around to protect you, you'd be dead numerous times over."

"You exaggerate slightly," Ruth said.

"That car almost hit you yesterday."

"It did not."

Ruth hated how Ralph nattered about jaywalking, but she had to admit she hadn't seen the car careening around the corner. Perhaps he had saved her life on occasion, but he didn't have to continually grab her as if she were a child or, worse yet, like she were an elderly woman who couldn't stand on her own two feet. She opened her mouth and then thought better of it. She didn't want to start a fight. As much as she loved Ralph, she had learned to keep her mouth shut over the years. Life was easier that way.

***

She felt herself sliding. The fall occurred suddenly, yet while it happened, the scene played in slow motion. Her feet entered first since she tumbled down the slope on her bum, and she was up to her waist in hot slime before she fully grasped the seriousness of the situation. At first, her arms stretched upward, attempting to grasp at a non-existent hanging vine or tree branch. By the time her head was completely under, her arms had propelled down her sides, tight against her hips. She was unsure exactly when they had changed position. Perhaps she had reached down to her feet to stop the descent. Not that it mattered whether her limbs were up or down; she was trapped regardless.

She should have yelled before she was completely sucked in, but her teeth had clenched together and she couldn't break them apart. Once she disappeared completely under the sludge, it was too late. She felt frozen and helpless, but she tried to keep what little sanity she possessed, knowing she dare not open her mouth.

Would anyone hear her even if she could shriek? Were voices heard from underground? Could she swim to an undiscovered cavern and escape into the river? Surely the mud springs were fed by the river's water.

***

Ruth stared at the bubbling mud springs. What would it be like to disappear into such a hellhole? It must be Hell. And a trap. A trap like a Venus flytrap.

She glanced at her husband, whose eyes were glued to the sight.

"Let's go back to our room. I'm thirsty. It's so hot." Ruth swept her arm across her face. She didn't add how scared she had suddenly become and how she wished she were back home in her own bed, even if Ralph did forget to snuggle with her. "Let's go. Come on."

She turned and headed to the other end of the bridge, not caring whether he followed.

***

The alarm clock blasted in her ear. She moaned before stirring and attempting to shut it off. Her arm was heavy as if she wore wrist weights. Where was her husband? She extended her other arm, which felt as weighted as the right, across the king-size bed. Empty. He must be in the bathroom.

She stretched her legs, which she did every morning before getting out of bed, and felt an awkward sensation. She moved them again. Grit.

Grit? If they had been at the beach the previous night and she hadn't showered off the sand before going to bed, grit might make sense, but they hadn't been at the beach. And even if they had, they no longer swam, so there would be no way for sand to be cemented on her body.

The ignored alarm clock continued to blare.

Grit?

Her hands spread across her slackened breasts that, without the protection of a brassiere, slumped toward her arms. More grit.

She threw off the covers and sat up to find herself covered in a yellowish pale-grey matter. The heavy substance was more than fine grit. Clumps surrounded her in the bed.

"Ralph?" she called.

Silence.

"Ralph?" She whispered.

Silence.

When her feet landed on the floor, clumps fell on the rug. She examined her caked, discoloured flesh.

A figure approached. Ralph.

"What is it, honey?"

"Ralph, what's happening? Look at me."

She scanned Ralph's naked body. Perfect in every way for an older gent. Not covered in the mysterious substance as she was. Clean. He had come from the bathroom. Had he showered?

"What's wrong, honey?"

"Look. Look at me." Tears formed in her eyes. Hot tears. She wondered what her face looked like. Was it covered, too? Would tears dredge a clean trail down her cheeks? She touched her face but couldn't tell if it was covered with grit. Her skin was taut as if she hadn't applied her nightly face cream. When she glanced at her fingers, she noticed the substance adhered like Krazy Glue.

"Ralph?" She held out her hands for him to see.

"Honey, what's wrong?"

"Look at me. Look!"

"Ruth, calm down." His eyes bore into hers.

She saw his eyes. Dark. He made no move toward her. Why wasn't he coming to comfort her? To give her one of his big hugs?

"Ralph?"

"Honey, calm down."

She detected exasperation in his raised voice. He was angry. He would turn his back on her and retreat, which was what he did when something didn't go his way or when she said something he couldn't face.

"I am calm. I am. I just woke up." She wanted to rub her eyes to remove the sleep clogged in the corners of her eyes, but her eyes would fill with the unknown crust if she did.

Tears rolled down her face. A drop landed on her arm. The watery blob disintegrated into the jaundiced matter and immediately dried, leaving no evidence of where it once had been.

"Go back to bed. You're dreaming. Calm down."

"I'm not dreaming. Look at me! At this! What is it?"

"Honey, you're acting strange. It's not morning yet. Come on. Back to bed."

***

Ruth slept.

A donut lay before her. She bit into the cream-filled confection and sweetness spread across her lips. Her tongue darted in and out, lapping up the excess. The smooth, warm texture slipped down her throat.

Yellow balloons waved above her while she ate another donut. She reached to snatch the dangling ribbons. Despite stretching as far as she could, she couldn't reach the illusive swaying strings.

She lingered below them, watching them fly away.

Published by Seven Fates Writers in anthology,
Stories for the Dead of Night, July 2013

Tart Thorns Among Silken Threads

(beware, you husbands: past, present and future)

Spiders produce silk from their spinneret glands located at the tip of their abdomen. Each gland produces a thread for a special purpose – for example a trailed safety line, sticky silk for trapping prey or fine silk for wrapping it. Spiders use different gland types to produce different silks, and some spiders are capable of producing up to 8 different silks during their lifetime. (Wikipedia.org)

Rose eyed the last drop of clear liquid as it plopped into the glass of orange juice and disappeared. Maurice loved thick orange juice, the pulpier the better, and he'd finish it without hesitation.

"Maurice, are you awake yet?" She entered their bedroom, as excited as a child on Christmas morning instead of a seventy-seven-year-old woman in the throes of murdering her husband. One of the twin beds was neatly made while the bedclothes on the other lay in a tangled heap.

"Oh, Maurice? Where are you?" Rose drew out her words in a sing-song manner, her voice soft and lilting, poetic, yet with a controlling undertone.

Maurice stirred when Rose lifted the sheet. His pleading eyes almost begged her to put him out of his misery. Rose was disgusted to find the sheets drenched with sweat and urine. Unable to get up on his own, he had peed the bed through the night.

"Rose, sweet..." Maurice's voice faltered. "Help me..." He raised his trembling hand.

"Maurice, drink this." Rose leaned and slipped her arm under his head. "Here. Just one sip to start."

Feigning a gentleness only a loving wife could feel toward her partner, Rose patiently ensured he finished the contents. "One more sip. That's good. Another."

She eyed the clock, and a sigh escaped. Fifteen minutes to dump the juice into him.

Drat you, Maurice. Die. Now! You're taking up too much of my precious time.

"It won't be long now, Maurice," she said. "You'll soon be fine."

"Rose, come lay with me."

"Maurice, I have work to do."

Rose's knotted fingers brushed wayward strands of coal-black hair from her face and rubbed her unlined forehead. She glanced in the mirror, something she did on a regular basis, not to brush her short curly hair or apply her bright red lipstick or draw the dark eyeliner across her almost non-existent eyebrows, but to admire her beauty. She prided herself on taking care of her face without the aid of fillers or plastic surgery, grateful she didn't look a day over sixty.

She and Maurice had married nine days previously. She never had a problem attracting the opposite sex, but she had been selective in her partners over the past several years. Her men had to be elderly, and more importantly, they needed to be rich. Those requirements were necessary to secure her future. People only lived once, and she wanted the good life and everything it entailed.

Men were immaterial. A means to an end.

***

Rose, reclining on the couch and reading the latest romance novel by Sally Finchblood, jumped when the doorbell buzzed.

"Doorbell, go away." She grasped the book tighter. She rolled on her side and yanked the quilt to her ears, hoping to drown out the insistent intrusion.

She had reached chapter nineteen. One chapter left. Did Jamie snare Rebecca? Of course; the hero always ended up with the heroine in sickeningly sweet romance novels, but she still read them. She was an avid reader, and once immersed in a story, she'd morph into the lead female character and experience juicy love scenes as if the men were in the room with her. Almost nothing could take her away from reading, especially when in the thick of sexual fantasies.

The buzzing finally ceased, and Rose once more became Rebecca, who caressed Jamie's toned abs and leaned in for a lingering kiss.

***

Rose, still in her bathrobe, stood at the kitchen counter and fixed herself a cup of tea, ignoring the ringing of the telephone and the peeling of the doorbell. A half hour later while she sat in the living room nursing her second cup of tea, the front door crashed open.

"What the hell—" She dropped the cup and turned to find herself face-to-face with two policemen.

Rose's arms flailed in the air. "What are you doing here?"

"Where's your husband?"

"Maurice? He's in bed."

One of the policemen sped down the hall. Rose stepped to follow, but the other officer snatched her arm.

"Hands off of me," she shouted. "You can't disturb him. He's sick! He needs rest!"

"Calm down, ma'am."

Within seconds, Rose had decided he was the good cop. He was the one with the brooding blue eyes that slowly undressed her. She moved closer.

"Sorry, ma'am," he said. "We wouldn't have come in the way we did had we known you were home. You didn't answer the phone or the door."

At that moment, the other officer—the bad cop—returned. "I called 9-1-1. He's unconscious."

"No, he's not! He's sleeping. I just checked on him a second ago." She glared at the bad cop, hoping her face hadn't turned too red.

"Ma'am, he's unresponsive. "I think you better come to the station with us." The bad cop grasped her arm.

Rose cringed and grabbed the wooden arm of the recliner. "No! I've done nothing! And I'm not dressed. Just go. I'll take care of Maurice."

"Sorry, ma'am, I have my orders."

Rose glowered from one cop to the other. "But…why…how?"

"We had a call from your husband's daughter. She was concerned. Hadn't heard from him when he said he'd call. Plus your neighbours said they hadn't seen him out and about lately."

"We just got back from our honeymoon. We were on a four-night Miami cruise. He caught a bug. He'll be fine in a couple of days."

"I'll give you a few minutes to get dressed," the nice cop said.

***

Rose slammed the front door, thankful to be away from the Eleventh Precinct. The interrogation had taken five hours out of her precious life.

In a high-pitched voice, she mimicked the officers: "We'll be in touch. Don't leave the state. We'll have someone watching." She threw her purse to the hall table. "Blah, blah, blah."

She entered the bedroom, which smelled like a latrine, and tore the blanket and sheets from Maurice's bed.

"Drat you, Maurice. Why didn't you die like you were supposed to? I'll give you an A-plus, though. You lasted longer than I expected."

She threw the soiled sheets into the hall. If only she could throw Maurice somewhere—somewhere deep.

Her thin lips curled in distaste. Maurice was older than her usual prey but healthier. She prayed she wouldn't be stuck with him until he died a natural death. If she attempted poison again, she'd be discovered.

She donned her thinking cap. *I'm a smart woman. I can come up with something else. Another method. Something I haven't already used.*

She remembered her past husbands—all seven. Maurice was her eighth and last. Everything had gone according to plan once she'd coerced him to change his will the day prior to boarding the cruise ship. His previous will had left everything to that dratted daughter. She hadn't been aware he had a daughter until after their marriage.

The new will left everything to Rose. There would be no more wills. Maurice was weak and ill, in no position to draft a new one.

She was safe—or had been until that damned daughter stuck her hawk-beaked nose into lives that weren't her business, stirring up nonsense, causing trouble. Heck, Rose had almost landed in jail thanks to her.

Maurice was the least attractive of her husbands. When they met, she decided she could endure jutting bones and sagging skin and a head that looked as if crows had attacked it. He was frail. He wouldn't last long. And if something untoward happened to him, who would care? He hadn't mentioned relatives. He had most certainly never mentioned a daughter. Rose must have misunderstood his reply because she was certain she had asked those questions.

"Ah, Maurice, you make me ill." She spit a thick wad of phlegm on the soiled sheets before ambling to the den to confront her roll-top desk. Her hands caressed the shellacked surface as if it were her greatest love. The desk had belonged to her mother and was the one piece of furniture she cherished above all. No one had ever understood her like her long-departed mother had. Her mother had seen through Rose and her wanton ways, even at an early age, but hadn't been too wise when Rose forced her to drink a specially-prepared glass of orange juice.

Rose's laughter filled the room when she remembered her dying mother telling a twelve-year-old child to "be good" and the expression on her face when she said, "I'll love you forever, Rosie." Tears ran down her mother's face, but Rose's eyes remained dry. She had stared at her mother, willing her to hurry and breathe her last so she could go outside to play.

Rose shivered, not from memories or cool air, but to bring herself back to the problem at hand. It didn't help to dwell in the past. The past was the past, and the future was the future, but the current situation was what mattered at that moment.

The future was, by far, the most important to Rose, but she first had to deal with the present and tie up loose ends.

***

Rose pulled the grey silk shawl tighter over her head, completely covering her hair and letting the ends dangle down her shoulders like long hair she had as a child. In normal circumstances, she much preferred colour, but she had dressed to be inconspicuous. Her eyes darted up and down the hall, noting with distaste the pale green walls and beige tiles. Hospitals were always the same: green, cold, and sterile. The nurses, busy at the counter area halfway down the hall, ignored her, and the rest of the hallway appeared deserted. Rose clutched her purse to her side and slipped into room 454.

Without lively breath to keep the room bustling with truth and lies, the room was dead. Maurice lay motionless in the bed, fed and fertilized by tubes and wires fanning out like spiny spider legs.

"Maurice?" Rose knew he couldn't hear. She wished she knew how bad his condition was, whether it was even necessary to put herself into further peril to finish him off.

When she touched his hand, she avoided the mass of bruise and blood that surrounded the needle dangling from a lopsided vein. His skin felt like death—damp and forgotten—although his forced, even breathing belied the fact he lived. Rose, familiar with death, estimated he wouldn't have much time left in her world, but even an hour was an hour too much.

How lucky she'd been with her previous husbands. Although she was naïve when she married her first husband, Richard, both of them barely eighteen years old, she'd had the foresight to know she needed him—or someone—to drag her away from her sordid life. Fortunately, he had been killed in Vietnam and left a large insurance policy. She giggled. No one could blame her for his death, even though his body had never been recovered. "Missing in action," they'd told her.

Seven more husbands followed Richard. Seven husbands in the span of fifty-nine years wasn't too bad. Math had never been her forté, but she figured it worked out to approximately eight years per husband although she hadn't spent nearly that long with any of them. Five years was her absolute limit.

David, who lasted almost two years, had died a mysterious death the authorities had ruled accidental. Back then, of course, medical technology hadn't been nearly as sophisticated. Plus, she had been young. No one had suspected.

Bob had suffered a massive heart attack after a little over four years of marriage, and no one could blame a heart attack on her.

Peter—ah, Pete. Pete had been a good-for-nothing cheater who disappeared a month after their marriage. The entire town had pitied her. She moved shortly after Peter left, once she'd sold their million-dollar home, which she had previously connived to have transferred into her name.

She made a fresh start in small-town Milton, Alabama, where she'd changed her name and met Jerome, a hulking black man, who had been the hardest to dispose of—and the messiest. Although he had no relatives, which left no one to care about his death or money, he had been stronger and healthier than her previous husbands and younger than the others except for Richard. She had managed to stage a home invasion that resulted in Jerome's horrid death. No one had been the wiser, and she had easily collected the insurance policy purchased several months before his death. Although she shuddered every time when she remembered the mess associated with his death, it had been the simplest of her planned attacks.

After Jerome, she had lain low. She moved to Nevada for the warmth, where Anthony and another husband named Robert had followed in quick succession. Both of those gentlemen had been many years her senior, extremely well off and sickly. They had been easy prey—easy to snare, easy to squash—and despite parting ways with a portion of their estates, she had received the bulk, to the chagrin of grown children, none of whom had contested their fathers' wills.

Rose's happiest years had been those in between her marriages. She loved men in general and had allowed numerous dates to treat her to vacations and other extravagances. She'd always luxuriated in a lucullan lifestyle until the money ran out, which then forced her to find a new target. Whenever she searched for new prey, she built webs of lies and deceit. Once a trap had been woven, her prey had always been snared, entangled in fine threads of supposed love and, ultimately, death.

She had cast Maurice's net shortly after the death of the second Robert. Eight husbands. Although Maurice was supposed to have been her last, she would continue to enjoy the company of men who flocked around her.

As much as it repulsed her, Rose touched Maurice's wrinkled hand again. She received no movement in return. She glanced about the room and peeked down the hall. Even for a hospital, it was unusually quiet. Joy and laughter obviously didn't dominate an ICU.

She dug in her purse for the vial of liquid. After careful consideration, she had decided to continue with her original plan. One more dose would be all Maurice needed.

Her several months of volunteer work in hospitals, where she had hovered close to nurses while they administered medications and assembled IV packs, would finally pay off. The IV bag, down to its remaining one-quarter of liquid, hung innocently in front of her.

At the last second, instead of slipping the needle into a vein, she decided to put the syringe into the IV liquid.

She steadied the bag in one hand while the needle poised in her other, a fang ready to inject its deadly venom. When the needle pierced the plastic, two policemen burst from behind the closed bathroom door. Rose's hands were forced behind her back and cuffed before she knew what hit her.

"Whatever you say can and will be used against you," one voice said.

Another said, "We've had the goods on you for several years. Just waiting to catch you in the act."

Rose recognized the good cop's voice, the one with the roaming eyes.

She glanced at Maurice, surprised to see his eyelids flutter, and she giggled at his lust. His eyes would stray down her backside as she exited the room.

The cops turned her toward the door.

Published by DIVA in anthology, Crime Gone Wrong, *January 2013*

Footprints in the Snow

G ranny, will I ever get as old as you?" Five-year-old Charlotte asked.
"Not right now, Charlotte, but you will someday. A long time from now."

"I don't want to ever be like you, Granny. Your skin is so wrinkly and you're always too tired to play. I want to be young forever, like Peter Pan."

***

"Mom, Kathy's mother died yesterday."

"Oh no, Charlotte. That's too bad."

"Does that mean you're going to die, too?"

"Not right now, sweetie, but I will someday. A long time from now. Kathy's mother had been sick for a while, I think, so don't worry about it."

***

"Jack, Maria died last night," Charlotte said.

"Really? That's too bad."

"I don't even feel sad. Awful to say, I know. She was only in her seventies but so crippled up with osteoporosis and arthritis. Bed-ridden for years. What kind of life is that? Don't let me live when my quality of life is gone. I don't want to be fed by tubes and all that."

***

When had Charlotte been a child? Or a teenager? Too long ago for her to remember despite segments of her life constantly bombarding her thoughts, even mundane and nonsensical events, such as one from second grade when a classmate picked her nose and wiped the booger on Charlotte's new sweater, or another when she had been taunted and called "fatso" and "lardo" and other not-so-nice names. Many instances she hadn't recalled for eons—nor wanted to—were as fresh as if they had happened the previous day rather than in another lifetime.

Charlotte stared at the ceiling—characterless creatures—ghostly, white, and unreachable like Heaven. Ceilings rarely collapsed or needed to be repainted, for they were similar to clouds—untouchable, hanging over life and death.

When had she aged to awake in a nursing home? Hadn't she recently knitted a shawl and crocheted a sparkly evening bag? Had she even had the opportunity to wear them?

"Don't let me survive on feeding tubes and artificial means," she had told her husband, Jack, a few years previously. She had never made a living will—neither had Jack—so her wishes weren't in writing. Jack was elderly, too—if one called seventy-seven elderly—but he still lived in their home, capable of taking care of himself.

The last day she had been home, she felt suffocated. Not suffocated as if someone were asphyxiating her or not having adequate personal space, but suffocated as in lacking the basic ability to take in air that everyone took for granted. Who would remember the time of day one breathed? Could anyone say with precise accuracy, "I took a breath on February fourth at two o'clock in the afternoon," or "I remember breathing on November twenty-fourth at five in the morning"? Of course one could, but no one would because the action was common and ordinary, continuous and automatic; one could state one took a breath at any time of day, for breathing was a given, akin to trees shedding leaves in fall.

But Charlotte remembered her last breath that day, the last one she had taken on her own before the paramedics arrived. Since then, she had used a breathing tube off and on, and for the most part, had been bedridden. She shuddered remembering the promise she wanted Jack to keep, glad he hadn't acted upon it before the breathing tube had been inserted.

Granted, she was ill, but she was still young. Similar to those dried, withered leaves, old age was a given, and she was aware she didn't possess special powers to prevent time from overtaking her. Even if the emphysema hadn't preyed upon her, she lived with a death sentence as did the rest of the world. She simply hadn't been prepared for the end to arrive so soon.

Or had it? If Jack had his way, she'd live forever, no matter what form she morphed into. She figured it had more to do with his own fear of death than his love for her. If death didn't claim his wife, then he, as her husband, might reign forever, too. Jack had never vocalized his "end of time" wishes as she had, but she had been adamant: "Don't let me survive without quality of life. Don't keep me alive with tubes and wires."

Jack had concurred with her wishes. Of course, agreements can be unconsciously consented to during conversation, especially when it's an unwelcome topic. Promises are separated from lies when that actuality arrives—that moment of truth.

While she lay in bed waiting for Jack's daily visit, she pondered how their life might have been different had they chosen a different path. They had discussed retirement often, even talking about leaving

Ontario to relocate full-time to a better climate. They had thought Florida was the place since everyone seemed to retire to Florida.

Their good friends and previous neighbours, George and Sarah, had discovered their paradise in a Mexican village. Within a month of visiting Nuevo Vallarta, George and Sarah had sold their house and furnishings, gave away items, packed personal possessions, and moved. From all accounts, they were happy and on several occasions had even conversed with Charlotte and Jack on Skype.

"Come for a visit," Sarah said. "We have lots of room. You'd love it here. The weather is gorgeous. Get away from the snow."

"We'd like to, but what about the crime?" Charlotte said. "Every day we're hearing reports of murders and the like."

"Oh, poo! It's all exaggerated. Our community is extremely safe."

"I'm not sure that—"

"Do you know people live longer here?" Sarah said. "We have way more friends here than we ever had in Toronto. Lack of stress and warm weather keep us young."

"I suppose so," Charlotte said.

"We walk everywhere, and that gives us way more than the thirty minutes of exercise a day that everyone needs. There's a calmness here that we didn't have in the States."

"It does sound glorious," Charlotte said. "But—"

"Talk to Jack. We haven't any company coming for the next couple of months. Think about it, okay? We miss you guys."

Charlotte missed George and Sarah, too. They had been friends and neighbours for almost thirty years. Their children had grown up together. Even their grandkids had played together on occasion.

But Mexico? So far away. If someone asked if she could leave her children, she'd probably answer yes, but toddlers were a different matter. Sam was barely four and Jessica, two. Charlotte enjoyed quality time with them and couldn't survive a week without seeing them. Being in close proximity and having access to them on a whim were requirements as necessary as her caffeine in the mornings.

Jack enjoyed travelling and had been excited about the prospect of a trip to Mexico. Charlotte liked travelling, too, but Mexico? The many reports of violence, in particular the recent discovery of five headless bodies not twenty kilometres from where George and Sarah had relocated, scared Charlotte from wanting to venture from her own home let alone travel to a foreign country.

What would have happened had they visited their friends in Mexico? Would they have eventually relocated as Sarah and George had? Would she have given up her grandchildren for her own selfish reasons?

More importantly, would she be in such a dire state health-wise had they moved? In the condition she found herself, she regretted they hadn't given Mexico a try.

Sarah and George were approximately the same age as Charlotte and Jack, yet if one believed them, they were in perfect health and would be for many more years. Sarah's recent words haunted her over and over: *no stress, warm weather, socialization keeps one young...*

Despite Sarah's claims, however, Charlotte had not wavered from her stance regarding a visit to Mexico. Easy-going Jack hadn't seemed to mind at the time, but she figured he was a tad disappointed.

She feared death. And knew it neared. *It's the harsh winters. It's the lack of friends.*

Once more, she envied Sarah and George, but did their reality exist within their spoken and written words, or was it camouflaged between truths and lies? Who was ever one hundred percent truthful? Charlotte had fibbed to Jack and was positive he had been less than forthcoming with his little white lies, especially after she discovered he'd had a mistress for several years.

No, she didn't trust Jack at all. Could she depend upon him, her husband of fifty-two years, to carry out her last wishes?

Jack entered the room just as she was about to doze off.

"Hi, dear," he said and leaned down to kiss her.

Charlotte reached up to caress his face. She had forgiven him years previously for his dalliances, but she'd never forget. Despite that, she wished he'd come clean and acknowledge his wrongs. She had proof but had never called him on it.

"How are you feeling today?"

"The same as ever," she said. "I look like hell. I'm sure of it."

"You're beautiful. You'll always be beautiful to me."

"Jack..."

"What, dear?"

"Do you ever regret we didn't go to Mexico to visit Sarah and George?"

"Sometimes, I guess. But you were the one who wouldn't go, remember?"

"Yes, I know. Don't remind me. Perhaps it's a regret of mine. One of many."

She coughed, and Jack handed her a tissue. She didn't add that she might be healthier had they followed their friends' lead, but who could have foreseen she'd become ill so quickly, and who could definitively say she'd be healthier had they moved? And what about the grandchildren? They were her light through the tunnel of life, her joy, the one constant in her day.

She sighed.

"You okay?" Jack asked.

"I'm fine. Don't forget our pact. I don't want to be kept alive unnecessarily. If I'm brain-dead, then let me go, okay?"

"Yes, dear. We've discussed that before."

But when the time comes, will you heed my wishes?

Despite the pain when she moved, Charlotte needed to cough, but it was as if concrete blocks compressed her chest. She could barely open her mouth to speak. When she was in the final stage of her disease, she'd be a shell of her former self if she weren't already—a hollow crab washed upon the beach, the fruit within eaten away by coastal parasites.

"It's okay, dear," Jack mumbled. His voice sounded far away. He touched her arm. "You're cold."

"I'm...okay...not cold."

He massaged her arm and pecked her cheek. His moist lips were warm.

She clutched his arm, terrified if she didn't hold tight, she'd drop twenty stories to the pavement.

"It's okay," he said. "It's okay."

His words were a wasted breath. A higher force was at work, one neither could thwart. No amount of money or time could save either one of them.

But it was her time, not his.

Jack stared down at his wife of fifty-odd years. Drool congealed in the corners of her mouth and dribbled down her chin no matter how often he wiped.

He read her expression, her saucer eyes pleading for him to save her, even though they both knew it was hopeless.

Would he hold her back if he were able, or would he let her go? He pictured himself gripping a balloon's flimsy string, releasing it, and watching his wife soar to Heaven.

Disappearing forever.

If their roles were reversed, he'd be petrified, too.

Charlotte sensed Jack hovering beside her. Tons of mortar still weighted her down. She raised her arm so she could acknowledge his presence, but her entire body was stiff and immobile.

Was she dead already? No, she lay in the hospital bed.

She could see straight ahead but couldn't move her head enough to see him. Or was he even there?

A faraway voice. "Charlotte, it's time. I think you're gone, sweetie. This is what you wanted, right? Let me know if you've changed your mind. Just nod your head or shake it. Something." Jack's voice cracked.

She heard his tears. The pleading.

The halls were quiet at night. If Jack were to follow through with his wife's last wishes, he must do it when no one was about.

For several days, Charlotte had been unresponsive. She stared straight ahead, never closing her eyes. Her mouth was half-closed—or half-open, depending upon his mood at that particular moment. When he held her hand or massaged her arms and legs, she remained motionless. Life support would be next if she didn't soon pass. He shuddered at images of more weedy wires and twiggy tubes entering and exiting to and from every orifice of her body.

The time had come; he was sure of it.

He touched her hand. Cold. But Charlotte always had cold hands, and the old cliché "Cold hands, warm heart" must have been written with her in mind, for she had the warmest heart of anyone. He didn't want her to die, but dragging himself to the hospital every day was taking a toll on him. Not that the situation was about him; it was about his wife. But he had to think of himself, too, didn't he?

A few days earlier, his son had asked: "Why do you keep going in every day, Dad? She doesn't know you." "But I know *her*," he had replied. *I know her. I love her.*

Shame washed over him that he classified visiting his ailing wife as a chore.

He slipped his hand under the sheet and touched her warm, sunken chest. *Cold hands; warm heart.*

Her lips, once too moist from drool, had become so chapped they seeped blood. Every day, he faithfully applied the prescribed cream—which hadn't helped—and wondered if he was the only one who administered it. To reinforce his suspicion, he performed a test. Each day after using the cream, he placed the tube in a specific position in the drawer, and every day when he opened the drawer to apply the cream, the tube had never moved. No one cared but him; her time was near. What did chapped lips matter?

Painstakingly, with all the gentleness he possessed, he spread the ointment over his wife's lips, remembering better days when she carefully applied ruby-red lipstick.

"Charlotte," he whispered. "You there?"

***

Charlotte floated higher and higher every day, her mind full of too much—her past, her family, her interests. With so much left to do, she desperately wanted to get better. She was only seventy-five. Was it her time? Most people held out into their eighties and nineties, didn't they? What ages would George and Sarah attain? Probably one hundred and twenty-five if their stories were believable.

Her grandchildren hadn't been in for several weeks, and she missed them terribly. She had overheard her daughter, Ann, explain to Jack that it wasn't good for little ones to see death, and Charlotte wanted to scream that she was alive. She could hear and think. She wanted to see her sweet darlings.

Despite Ann not allowing the grandchildren to visit, she and her husband continued to visit. Charlotte had lost track of their last visit, but she was aware of Jack's constant presence.

Dear, sweet Jack. Fifty-two years they had been together, but there wouldn't be any more years, only weeks; perhaps months if she were lucky.

But no, that was a dream. A wasted wish. Only days remained; mere hours in a day. With her memories and her mind intact, she would enjoy and treasure these precious minutes.

She wasn't ready to go—didn't want to go—despite the promise she had wrangled out of Jack. But she wasn't worried. Jack didn't have any gumption. The other day she had thanked God for that.

By the time she realized she wanted to be kept alive as long as possible, with whatever available means, rather than be snuffed out like a quivering candle at night, her lips had frozen and left her unable to speak.

***

No, Charlotte screamed. *No.*

Jack hovered over her, fiddling with the bedclothes.

What's he doing?

"I'll take care of you, Charlotte. Like I promised. I hope you haven't suffered in the meantime. Please forgive me I didn't do it before, but you know me. Mr. Wimpy."

No... No... I'm still here...

She could still think. Could still reminisce. She had entered another phase of living. She was a gigantic humanized puzzle, able to pick and choose pieces of her life and put them in order.

What's he doing? He's huffing and puffing. The exertion's too much for him. What's he doing?

"It's okay, sweetie."

Jack stopped and stared at her.

Oh, good. He hears me.

"I made that promise. I'll live up to it now. I'm sorry."

No, you don't understand. Not when I'm alive. Not when I'm lucid. Only if my memory is gone. I'm still here. Still here...

She opened her mouth to scream, but it was filled with cotton. She frantically yelled with her eyes, forcing them to dart here and there, pleading. Were they moving? Could he see the tears?

Jack, I'm here. Jack...

Charlotte spied the white cloud floating above her. The object hovered and slowly descended toward her face—lower and lower—until the soft yet unyielding object embraced her.

Bathroom Fixtures

Although the mirror reflected the image of a middle-aged woman, Edith had no idea how she had reached the age of fifty-two so quickly. Of course she knew, though: years added up too fast, and birthdays came and went. She had celebrated her last birthday the prior month; a woman remembers her last birthday unless she's demented or in the throes of Alzheimer's, and Edith was quite sane and normal. Memory loss hadn't hit her yet, and if she had any say, it never would. But no one can control the effects of time.

Despite her age, she was young and spirited though she didn't feel that way every day. Her hair used to be an unbroken blonde until a hellish grey streak struck one-half of her bangs, turning her into part skunk. In recent years, the youthful shade had come from a package of *Colour Me Easy,* but dark roots too often and too soon seeped into her chicken-yellow hair—proof positive she wasn't a natural blonde any longer. The upper part of her head, the crown, being the most prominent, was the first area she studied every morning and the first thing people noticed about her. Were they gossiping about her? Commenting on her hair?

She grew tired keeping on top of the hair situation, but after the first time she coloured her hair, she couldn't quit, the result being she didn't actually know the true colour any longer or how much dark or grey was camouflaged behind the blonde.

She gave up examining her hair and other faults, none of which she could alter, and scanned the room. The bathroom, though cluttered, seemed empty with only one towel and one facecloth on the rack. On the counter, two tiny jars of liquid makeup sat beside a cover stick, eyeliner, brow definer, brush, special tangle-free comb, hair dryer with its cord dangling into the sink (could she be electrocuted?), hairspray, toothpaste, floss, and toothbrush protruding from a cloudy glass—all female essentials—not to mention the plastic basket containing the rest of her cosmetics and necessities. It's hard work being a woman, especially in the mornings. And no way would any human glimpse her before she'd showered, brushed her teeth, and applied her makeup.

Greg—now that was a different matter. Greg was Edith's husband. At first, she didn't think she'd ever let him see her true, blemished self, but gradually time passes and guards are let down. You think: well, he married me; he must love me for who I am, imperfections and all, for better or worse. One can't hide behind hair colour and makeup and girdles forever. In the end, it truly didn't matter, for Greg never saw her age spots, or the occasional adult pimple or blackhead, or the dark circles under her eyes. He never even saw the extra ten pounds that had crept upon her, not even when she'd mentioned how fat she was— at least, that's what he had said on numerous occasions.

"I love you the way you are. You'll always be beautiful to me," he'd said. She never believed him since he rarely volunteered praise, and she disregarded his comments as someone blinded by a routine, every-day love. He did love her, didn't he? He said so; it must be true. And she loved him, too. She married him, didn't she? They married when she was nineteen, and she remained true to him for over thirty years.

Thirty-three years of marriage.

Her eyes darted about the bathroom again. It was the bigger of the two, quite a bit bigger since it was the en-suite bathroom. Greg had taken over the tiny guest bathroom, which allowed barely enough room for one person, but it contained the requisite shower, vanity, and toilet.

At first, they hadn't realized there was another bathroom. They had been busy *oohing* and *aahing* over their rental, which would be their home for the next month, as they wandered room to room. Edith entered the master bedroom first and kept walking and walking— through the large bedroom, by the gaping walk-in closet, and then into the bathroom.

"Look," she had screeched. "Another bathroom! I had forgotten there was a master bathroom." She had seen pictures of the condo before booking it, but time passes and memories fade.

"Goodie," Greg said. "We can each have our own."

"I don't think so!"

Greg ignored her sarcastic tone.

Since when do we not share? she thought, until she remembered there were lots of times they hadn't. "Look at all the space! There's more than enough room here for both of us."

"Yeah, you're right. There is plenty of room," he said.

They unpacked and laid out their toiletries. "I'll take this side of the counter," she said. "You have that side."

Edith hung up towels and facecloths.

"I'll use the toilet in the other bathroom," he said. "It's closer to my side of the bed." They had already determined she'd have the left side of the bed and Greg, the right.

"I might use that bathroom at night," she said, referring to the guest bathroom that he had mentioned using. "It's closer than this one."

"Not really. It's closer for you to use the master."

"Well…maybe," she replied.

"Oh, no," he blurted, "there's only one sink in this bathroom."

She hadn't noticed.

"I'll use the sink in the other bathroom." He shoved his shaving cream, toothbrush, and toothpaste into his travel bag and disappeared.

The next morning before she stepped into the shower, he said, "I might as well shower in the other bathroom. Then we won't be fighting for the shower every morning." He snatched a towel and washcloth from the rack.

"Since when have we ever fought over the shower?" At home, on weekdays, so as not to disturb Greg while he readied for work, she usually stayed in bed until she heard him shut off the shower. Often she didn't get out of bed until he had traipsed down the hall and was in the kitchen.

"All right, then," she said a few minutes later. "You want your own bathroom, fine! But it's yours. You clean it. I've got enough to do without cleaning two bathrooms. You clean your own toilet. Shower, too. I'm not stepping foot in there."

That same afternoon, he had taken his clothes, which she had neatly folded and placed in the dresser, to the second bedroom. Next to go were his slacks and shirts, which had been hanging on the hangers. "More room for both of us if I use the other closet. Our clothes won't be all jumbled together."

"Gee, you might as well sleep in there, too," Edith had said.

"No, I don't want to sleep there."

"Why not? There's two twin beds. You can have your pick."

"No, I don't think so."

The master bathroom was a normal bathroom, with all the amenities, but missing something: a man's touch. No shaving cream, no Philips shaver, no double toothbrushes, no double tubes of toothpaste (though different brands because Greg had his favourite flavour and Edith had hers).

Edith felt lonely having her own private bathroom. She'd never had that luxury except for two weeks when she had been a teenager and her sister had been at camp. She supposed every married woman dreamt of bathroom privacy, but she wasn't just any woman. She enjoyed the closeness of her husband—the early morning scuffle on the weekends when she and Greg rose from bed the same time and shared the bathroom, the late night sharing before they hopped into bed to snuggle under the linens. To her, that's what togetherness was—sharing a special joy of oneness that only happens through marriage or commitment. Isn't that what marriage and love are all about?

At first, she didn't know what to do with herself in the bathroom. She missed bumping into her husband in the close quarters. She missed eyeing him while he brushed his teeth and shaved. She missed the wet sheepdog look of him stepping from the shower, his head of hair slicked back, and his chest hair matted to his skin. She might have passed him the towel. Other times, she'd have dried him. Occasionally, she would have joined him in the shower.

Suddenly, she and Greg were occupying separate bathrooms. Although he said he'd never sleep in the other bedroom, Edith wondered when they'd be relegated to separate beds. After that would come separate bedrooms. She had always pondered married couples who didn't share the same bed or, worse yet, the same bedroom. Years previously, she and Greg had discussed that topic and agreed it would never happen to them.

But everything's a progression. Change begins slowly. Before you know it, you have more change than you had ever wanted—or imagined. Was that the start of a change in their marriage? Would it continue after they returned home? And what was happening with their vacation that they'd be spending quality bathroom time apart?

She shook her head at their silliness. No biggie. But a bit strange, don't you think? Especially when he removed all his clothes to the next bedroom, almost as if that was the last straw.

The laundry hamper sat in the closet in the master bedroom, which meant Greg conveniently forgot its existence. Edith would pass by the spare bedroom on the way from the master and couldn't help but notice Greg's mounting stack of dirty laundry on the floor. The pile began with dirty underwear, the first pair landing there after about three days since he never changed his underwear daily, never one to have listened to his mother with her advice (much like other mothers) about never wearing dirty underwear in case of an accident. After another two or three days, he'd add the second dirty pair and on and on.

Edith had long ago given up trying to change that disgusting habit of his. Once upon a time, she used to snatch his shorts (boxers not briefs) every evening before bed and toss them into the hamper. The following morning, he'd mumble about his missing underwear. After a few years, she'd grown tired of picking them up, and she'd let him wear dirty underwear as many days as he liked. If he wanted to wallow in filth half the week, that was his prerogative. Such uncleanliness wasn't for her, though. She wore clean panties every day of the week, thank you very much. Greg thought her a bit of an upstart regarding clean underwear and never ceased giving his opinion.

Having separate bathrooms made her feel as if she were single though she hadn't ever had that experience since she had married Greg right out of high school. Thus, she relied on him for everything, never having had the opportunity to fend for herself. She couldn't survive without him. Life was hard—going off to work every day, ensuring enough money for bills, paying bills on time before interest accumulated. Greg was efficient; he had the accounts paid almost as soon as the envelopes dropped down the mail slot. Cheap was more like it. When was the last time he had bought her an unexpected gift or given her a decent present, something other than baking pans or an egg beater?

Edith had an inkling single life would be better in one respect—no scrunched-up, cap-less toothpaste tubes; no globs of toothpaste on the counter; no puffs of shaving cream around the edges of the sink; no lopsided towels on the rack or heaped on the floor. She should be grateful for the luxury of two bathrooms, but save for sharing a bed and three meals, Edith felt alone, unsure of her perceptions.

Dynamics had changed.

After a week or so, Edith relished her newfound freedom. She could leave the toilet unflushed if she liked, for she'd be back within an hour; she didn't need to waste water. No more fighting with toilet seats that didn't stay down or toilet lids that remained up. She could position the toilet paper in the "under" position instead of the "over" position even though she was quite aware the 1891 patent for toilet paper states that the paper should be hanging off the exterior. Also, her preferred way made it harder for toddlers and cats to unravel the whole roll—not that she and Greg had toddlers or cats, but if they had, life would be much simpler without toilet paper cluttering the floor. She didn't have to pick up wet towels or dirty clothing from the bathroom floor. (On occasion, he tossed his dirties into the hamper, but that was likely because he ran out of clean clothes.)

It was pleasant without a male voice yanging about using too much toilet paper. "Two folded squares should do nicely," he'd say. But he'd tell her that hours later, not when they had been in the bathroom together, pretending to not see her. Did he spy on her when she wiped herself? He must have; how else would he have known she used more than two squares?

And him continually complaining about the "gunk" she plastered on her face as if he knew the goings-on of a woman and what she should or shouldn't do.

But Edith kept mum because that's what dutiful housewives do. They listen to their husbands—and obey them.

She enjoyed the solitude of the dressing room, too. She didn't have to listen to Greg's scolding about changing her clothes one too many times. What gave him the right to dictate what she wore? Shouldn't she have the right to cover her body—or not, not that she'd ever traipse around naked; no decent God-fearing woman would do that—with whatever clothing she desired?

Not sharing the closet, she didn't have to adjust his droopy clothes on the hangers or pick up those that had fallen to the floor. When she folded laundry, she placed his clean clothes on one of the twin beds.

He'd put them away or let them remain. His choice; it didn't matter to her.

After the shock wore off of having her own private bathroom, not to mention a walk-in closet that doubled as a personal dressing room as if she were a famous movie star, she began enjoying the solitude and found comfort in the peace that prevailed in her private area of the house.

***

One Saturday night, with guests invited for drinks, Edith entered Greg's bathroom to see if he had been cleaning it as he had promised. The counter, cluttered with his shaving items and toiletries, none of which he bothered to put in the drawer or cupboard, confronted her. Drops of yellowed piss lay on the toilet seat. Tiny dollops of dried poop clung to the bowl near the rim. A used tissue littered the floor.

"Oh, it must have fallen from my pocket," he said.

"Tissues don't fall out of pockets, and tissues don't magically pick themselves up off the floor either. You were playing basketball with the tissues and the waste can, weren't you?"

"No, not I."

"And you said you'd clean up after yourself!"

Despite Greg's promises the day they had moved into the unit, Edith knew she'd end up cleaning the second bathroom. It was the guest bathroom, after all. Guests couldn't be traipsing through the master bedroom and by the open closet before reaching the bathroom. No, guests had to use Greg's bathroom, which meant Edith had to clean it. Even if Greg cleaned it, he couldn't clean up to her standards; no one could clean as well as her.

Disgusted, she flushed the toilet, threw cleanser into the toilet bowl, and scrubbed. She wiped the lid before tackling the sink spotted with granitelike toothpaste and scattered hairs and globs of shaving cream.

***

Edith and Greg returned home after their month away. Although sad their vacation had ended, Edith was glad to be home in their own house and with their own possessions. A year was a long time to wait for another vacation, but with the most recent one still fresh in her mind, she wasn't too concerned. Besides which, she wasn't sure if she'd ever want to rent another vacation home. Hotels and motels, though smaller, of course, had the added advantage of built-in maids instead of Maid Edith. What kind of vacation was that for her—or for any woman?— when she had to wash dishes, vacuum, and clean those dratted bathrooms?

73

Truth be known, who—man or woman—would admit to enjoying those jobs unless one lied? She pitied the poor maids with toilet cleaning being part, if not the main part, of their job description. Edith performed maid duties when home, as well as when away, while Greg lolled about, getting the house dirtier and dirtier, what with peanut shells discarded on the floor and tissues fallen from his pockets. Yeah, right! Drat him! Never again would she vacation without the certainty of a maid at their destination, at least one to clean the bathroom. For that was the most disgusting job, wasn't it? No, she'd not do that again. Life was too short to work while on vacation.

If Greg had lived up to his end of the bargain as he had promised, the situation wouldn't have bothered her as much. And he had promised! It wouldn't have mattered to her if she had to clean a bathroom they shared, which they had always done in the past, but no, he had to mount his high horse, think he was better than her, and move into the other bathroom and bedroom. Sure, he hadn't slept in that bedroom, but he used the dresser and closet, dressed in the room, laid clothes on the beds—both of them—which meant another room to be cleaned. If it weren't for him, they could have closed the doors to the spare bedroom to keep out the dirt and dust, and the room would have remained as when they had moved in. But no, he had to dirty not just another bathroom but a bedroom, as well.

Never again! For sure, next time—perhaps there'd not be a next time—she'd put a stop to those shenanigans of his. She would have done so that last time, but everything happened suddenly and gradually, and before she had a chance to realize what had transpired, the deed had been done.

She sighed and looked around her house. Their house. Glad to be home, even if she had to succumb to full-time maid duties, she unpacked. Greg had to be at work by eight the next morning. Despite being the owner of his own business, he couldn't be late, not after taking a month off, even though Neil Dillingsworth could handle the firm quite nicely without him. No, Greg had to arrive precisely at eight o'clock. And good old Edith respected his wishes.

The next morning, she lay in bed while the shower gushed. She pictured water spraying over Greg's lean body and drawing suds from the top of his head down to his feet. It was Monday, and as per their routine, she would remain in bed while he readied for work and not enter the bathroom until his stockinged feet padded down the hall.

Away from her.

She sighed and rubbed her eyes, debating whether to get up and invade his space. Heck, it was her space, too—her bathroom, as well as his—at least until he packed up and retreated to the second bathroom. No, he wouldn't do that; the only other bathroom was at the far end of the house. Too inconvenient for him.

Edith sighed again. Four more days until Saturday rolled around when she could freely brush her teeth and shower while the two of them shared the room. Four more showers before she would see his figure through the frosted glass doors and watch him step from the stall, his thick hair matted to his body and water dripping to the floor. He never remembered to move his towel closer to the shower, but that was okay because that was their routine and what they always did, and Edith picked up after him without complaint because that's how she had been programmed by her mother (and soon after her marriage, more programming by her husband), for if she didn't pick up after him, no one would.

But not on vacations. No more.

They hadn't had children. They'd wanted children, but Edith apparently was barren, or perhaps Greg shot blanks when they had sex because no babies came. And neither had questioned why. Just God's will. No one had ever asked why they hadn't had children. Had no one cared? Had no one thought it odd? Or had people figured they'd be better off without children, that they'd not be good parents? Had everyone known something that Greg and Edith hadn't? But by the time Edith had mulled over the situation, it was too late. She was in her late forties then. Too late to ponder any longer.

So there was no one to pick up after Greg but Edith. And no one to pick up after Edith but Edith.

The shower stopped and the door clanged open before banging shut. He'd towel his face first, buff his hair, and dry his face. He'd bend over to dry his feet, drag the towel up over his legs, and pat his arms and chest dry. Edith pictured his motions, which never changed.

The towel bar rattled when Greg positioned the towel, not a delicate motion but in a rough manner. As heavy as the wet towel was, within seconds it would land to the floor. Even from the bedroom, Edith heard the thud. If by some miracle he hadn't heard the dull whump, he would surely glimpse the fallen towel on his way out of the room, but whether intentional or not, he never replaced it on the rod. No, that was a job for Maid Edith.

Edith didn't work, and never had, so according to Greg, she had plenty of time to clean up. "Edith has nothing to do. Edith can do it." And she would.

When he padded down the hallway—away from her—she waited a few minutes to ensure he wouldn't return. But he didn't. He never did, not even to throw a kiss or spew "have a good day" or "don't work too hard"—not that he ever cared how hard she worked because, according to him, she didn't; his words were sarcastic jest. She never spouted "have a good day" or "hurry home," either. He'd leave the office when he was ready, and not before, which was at five o'clock. Nine hours at the office—nine hours away from her—plus the twenty-two minutes each way for the commute. Almost ten hours a day for five days a week, but never on weekends, for the weekends were theirs to share, bathroom and all.

When the front door slammed, Edith waddled into the bathroom. He always used the front door, whether he entered or exited. She picked up the towel that was in full view of anyone who entered or exited the bathroom and draped it across the rod. She pulled the edges across the length of the rod, ensuring the towel was stretched taut so it would dry wrinkle-free. Greg requested fresh towels every couple of days, but he never remembered which colour he last used. Once the towel was dry, he was none the wiser, so she left him with the same towel as long as she figured she could get away with it. She replaced hers twice a week, for she deserved clean towels more than once a week. Didn't she?

After removing her nightgown, she turned on the shower and stepped in the stall. The bar of soap lay on the floor. The bottles of shampoo and conditioner leaned on their sides. Thick white drooled from the conditioner bottle, and apple-green foam seeped from the other bottle. It was always the same with her lazy husband—too lazy for this, too lazy for that.

She lathered her hair, taking her time to rub her scalp. Standing under the nozzle, she let the shampoo wash down the length of her body as Greg had minutes previously. She placed dollops of conditioner strategically on her hair and let it soak. Water rolled down her large breasts—breasts she considered pretty firm for a fifty-something—and down her softly protruding belly that, despite the lack of pregnancies to disfigure her shape, wasn't as nice as her breasts. She dipped her head under the sprayer to wash out the conditioner. She ran her fingers over a body soft and smooth from soap and conditioner, imagining Greg's fingers massaging her flesh instead of hers, and tried to remember the last time he had touched her. The last time he had *felt* her.

She gave up, slammed the shower door as Greg had, and dried off, ensuring her towel hung neatly from the rod before she left the room. Back in the bedroom, she dressed in her favourite slacks and a tight sweater before returning to the bathroom to dry her hair and apply makeup.

She stared at herself for several minutes, scrutinizing her face and hair. Her hair was perfect, a different shade of blonde than she usually used, one not so chicken-yolk-glaring, but she was pleased the dark roots were covered, for sometimes the dye didn't take, or perhaps on occasion, she didn't leave the dye on long enough. Forty-five minutes was the required time, she had discovered.

From the closet, she grabbed the largest suitcase and filled it with several outfits, shoes, and whatever else she thought she couldn't temporarily live without. She stuffed her makeup and toiletries into a smaller bag and placed that into the suitcase, which she zipped and rolled to the front door.

She ambled back to the bathroom, her stockinged feet not unlike the sounds of her husband an hour previously. She yanked open the shower door, threw the bar of soap to the floor, and set the shampoo and conditioner bottles upside down on the metal wire rack, with the lids open, of course. The liquids slowly cascaded, the white melding into the green, which despite being void of red, made her think of candy canes at Christmas. Red was a colour she had never cared for and decided next Christmas she'd decorate in green and white and ignore Greg's must-have red.

Leaving the shower door open, she snatched Greg's towel from the rod and threw it across the room, where it landed by the toilet. For good measure, she grabbed the end of her towel and let it fall to the floor. At the bathroom door, she hesitated, returned, and tossed the bar of soap that had been by the sink (not the one on the shower floor) into the toilet, where it sunk to the bottom. She dropped Greg's toothpaste (the lid nowhere to be seen) by her feet, stood on it, and watched the blue and white wavy peppermint stripe squirt on the tile. When she was satisfied the tube would be of no use to him, since he never bothered fighting with the tube to get out the last dollop as she did, she snatched his toothbrush from the counter and dropped it into the toilet, where it hit the soap and bounced back to the water's surface.

Her eyes bulged. Staring at Greg's items in the toilet had provoked an idea; it wasn't something she would have thought of on her own, and if she hadn't had that second glass of wine before going to bed the prior night, she might not have been able to follow through with the plan, something she'd never tell anyone about—ever—for it was a most unladylike thing to even think about, much less do. But she did it.

She sat on the toilet, after lowering the seat of course, for don't all men leave it up? And she peed. It was a refreshing relief. She was unaware until then that she had held her bladder as long as she had, for she suddenly realized she hadn't peed since she woke up, what with her mind too full of deeds if she dared follow through. And she had: dared—and peed. While urinating, she peered between her legs, wondering how she aimed so precisely onto the bristles of Greg's toothbrush as if she possessed a penis for the first time in her life. No doubt it wasn't her aim but the fact the toothbrush happened to be floating in the right position.

But she liked to think she had aimed perfectly, that her newly-discovered penis had its premiere audition. Bull's-eye!

She yanked at the toilet roll, wrapping wads of connected squares around her hand, and wiped herself. For extra good measure, she pulled the dangling tissue. And pulled and pulled. And pulled. She smiled at the pile of white and noted the almost empty roll. What? Two tissues left? She snickered.

Before leaving, she glanced around the bathroom one last time, eyeing the upheaval. She didn't think it mattered. Greg hadn't seen her for years; he wouldn't notice the bathroom, either. Sure, he looked at her, noticed and commented on what he didn't like, but when had he ever cast gracious comments, such as "Nice shoes you're wearing today," or "Did you get your hair cut? If you did, it sure looks pretty," or "The house looks spotless." No, she received none of that—ever.

Why did she bother?

She needed a vacation. Alone.

Edith skipped to the front door. She picked up her suitcase, opened the door, and slammed it behind her as loud as she could, not that the statement mattered. No one was there to hear.

Mother's Siblings

Mother, having grown up as an only child, always wanted to know about her siblings, those two unfortunate babes. One died before it could take its first breath; the other lived for a day or two. Mother wasn't certain of the details. Her parents wouldn't answer her questions, or so she said, but knowing my mother, she likely never asked.

Her need for answers became greater after my father died at sixty-five. When we returned home from Father's funeral, my sister, Maxine, and I led our mother upstairs to her room. We weren't halfway up the stairs before Mother, two years younger than Father, wailed about our father and how he had deserted her and left her all alone. I guess me and my sister didn't matter as much as we had thought, nor did her five grandchildren, three belonging to Maxie and two to me.

My sister was happily married, or so she said. Me, I was happily divorced. Marriage had never agreed with me—or perhaps it had been my husband choice, not that I had any desire to try again.

We comforted our mother but weren't much help. Maxie, the baby, had been the favourite, and I had never been as close to Mother as my sister had been. I had an extra two years to bond; you'd think I'd have been closer.

Mother wailed and wailed, her voice raspy. In between gasps and gulps, the tears flowed. "I'm an orphan now. I'm an orphan." Maxie tried to console her, but Mother continued to moan, her voice echoing throughout the house as if we lived in a cave or some such eerie place.

When Mother sobbed and spouted about being an orphan, I almost reminded her that children are orphans, not adults, especially not adults in their sixties. Besides which, her parents had died ten years previously, so if she were orphaned, it would have been then. Somehow though, I didn't think she'd appreciate comments about word meanings, not the day of Father's funeral, at any rate.

Maxie managed to calm Mother down enough to get her to bed.

Ironically, my parents had been harshest with Maxine despite her being their darling, but Maxie harboured no grudges against them. At least, I didn't think she did.

"I have to get home now," Maxie said after Mother was asleep. "Tony's waiting."

Tony was Maxie's husband, and what a farce of a husband he was. Had to have the house spotless, couldn't get their kids to bed without her, always upset if she went out with friends. Very possessive, he was, but Maxie never seemed to mind. If she did, she never let on. Perhaps she kept her secrets. Everyone has secrets.

"Okay," I said. "No problem. She'll be fine in the morning, I'm sure."

Me and my two kids had moved back home after my divorce. I couldn't handle finances on my own, not with the wages Mr. Penney paid me.

"I'll call you. Bye, sis." Maxie hugged me tight, almost as if I might disappear as fast as Father had. My cheek was wet when she moved away from me. "Love you," she whispered.

"Me, too." And I did; of course, I did. She was my sister. I loved her dearly. Death has a habit of bringing out repressed emotion in people. She had never before told me she loved me; neither had I told her.

I locked the door after her. I shed a tear for Father, one of many over the past several days. I knew I'd spill more when I crawled into bed. Father had been ill, what with heavy drinking and smoking, but I don't think any of us expected him to die this soon.

I was glad Randy had taken our two boys for the week. Although our love had waned fairly quickly after our marriage, Randy loved our boys as much as I did. (Why I stayed in the relationship as long as I had and birthed two kids in the middle of chaos was beyond me.)

I loved my children more than life itself, but the day would come when they'd want to live permanently with their father. I wasn't that naive to think they'd stay with me forever. Don't most boys of a certain age want to live with their fathers? I shuddered at that thought and wondered what would become of me then. Mother wouldn't live forever, maybe not much longer now that Father was gone, but perhaps longer with me and the boys living with her. I didn't figure Mother could survive on her own without her husband.

Pondering about Mother made me wonder about my well-being, for how would I exist when my boys packed up and moved out? Where would I live once Mother passed on? I couldn't afford Mother's house (all hers now that Father was gone), not with my measly salary from Creighton's Groceries, but it wasn't fair blaming old Mr. Penney. I should've stayed in school as Father said, not dropping out at the end of tenth grade. Surely I could have hung in for another two years. Maxie, now, she finished high school, even went on to a year of secretarial school at Timberview College over at Gainesville. Did real well, too, and now works for Mr. Dudley Jones at Gleeson & Jones, the largest law firm in this area. Makes me jealous when I look at moth-eaten Mr. Penney five days a week while she gets to stare at her hunky lawyer boss.

I had sworn to Father that I'd go back and finish, but I never did. Promises like that are hard to keep, once life takes over. The local high school offered night classes, and if I had some gumption and ambition, I could get my GED. It would only take me a few months, I've heard. That would make Father proud, even from his perch high in Heaven— whenever he arrives there, which I'm sure he will. And when he does, I'll hear a bird chirp outside my window, for I once read a human could return as a blissful bird when someone accomplishes something great. "Come back to sing praises," or some such phrase.

I could go back to school when the kids were older, but by then will I care? When—if—I ever finished, I'd probably be so old no one would want to hire me. And no doubt, my kids and their friends would make fun of me. Mr. Penney, I think I'm stuck with you and you with me until one of us gets tired of the other—either I get sick of your roaming fingers or you get good and tired of me throwing them back in your face.

Mother thought I should accept Mr. Penney's advances. "He has money. He likes you, and he'd take care of you and the boys."

I retorted, "I don't need taking care of. And Randy will take care of the boys if I can't. And I don't love, or even like, Mr. Penney. He's too old for one thing. And ugly, with that scrappy hair that hangs over his eyes. And greasy."

"Francine! Watch your mouth," Mother had said. "You could do a lot worse. And have."

Mother never did like Randy, but she had to admit he was a good father.

***

The phone jarred me from my sleep the next morning. It was Maxine.

"Fran, is Mother up yet?"

"No, she's still sleeping, but I wouldn't be surprised she's awake now, thanks to you."

"Sorry, just worried about her. It's after ten. Not like it's early, you know."

"Is it that late?" I rubbed my eyes, thankful it was my day off. But with Father's passing, Mr. Penney would have given me the day off anyhow, without pay, scrooge that he is. "I better check on her, but I'm sure she's fine. She needs sleep. She was exhausted. Want me to call you back?"

"No, that's okay. I'll stop by later. When do you get the boys back?"

"They're gonna stay 'til Monday. Randy will drop them off at school. They'll come home on the bus." Once again, I was grateful my ex helped me out with the kids. They were a bit rambunctious, as boys are, and Mother needed quiet time.

"Good. Well, if I don't get over today, I'll stop by tomorrow."

Gee, one second you're coming over today. Now maybe not 'til tomorrow?

As if she read my mind, she said, "Depends on what Tony has planned. I think he has to see Mr. Langille about the roof."

"Good enough. Catch ya later." I almost added "alligator" like when we were kids, but we weren't kids any longer.

I grabbed my robe and peeked into Mother's room. I didn't hear anything and was about to enter when a snort came from beneath the covers. A hump of something, which I assumed was Mother, moved. The snort confirmed it. She and I were alike in that respect—covering our heads with the bed linens when we wanted to escape. Our snort sounds were similar, too, something like a cross between a donkey and a pig. Not at all flattering for females.

Mother was downstairs putting on the coffee when I appeared after my shower. "Morning, Mother." I put my arm around her shoulder and kissed her cheek, something I've rarely done. "You okay?"

Dumb question. Of course she wasn't okay. She had just lost her husband. Would I ever gain couth? She didn't look well either. Despite my thinking she'd had a good night's sleep, it was obvious she hadn't. Her dark circles were more pronounced than usual, her face as pale as the refrigerator. She hadn't showered nor made any attempt to brush her hair. From the whiff when I neared her cheek, I didn't think she had brushed her teeth, either, which was unlike her. Since I had never lost a husband—can't count losing Randy since he is still around—I couldn't put myself in her slippers, which she wore that morning, and fathom how I'd act were I in her position.

"Maxine called. She might be over this aft. If not, tomorrow. Did the phone wake you?"

"No, I heard you in the shower."

Mother always had a way of making me feel guilty.

"Sorry."

"No, I'm sorry. It was late. I should have been up before now."

"She woke me up," I said.

"Like I said, it was time we were both up."

I knew she'd stick up for Maxine somehow, some way. I wasn't disappointed.

"Want me to get breakfast? Cereal? Eggs?"

Stupid question. Mother never ate eggs for breakfast or any time, for that matter. She had a thing about baby chickens. And to think she and Father had forced me to eat foods I hadn't wanted. Both Maxine and I had to sit at the table until our plates were clean. Maxine had even fallen asleep at the table one night, her face smack in the middle of peas and mashed potatoes. Mother took pity on her eventually and carried her to bed. Father wouldn't talk to either of them for three days. Maxie hadn't cared. Neither had I; I thought the whole thing rather hilarious, especially our parents' rant: "Them children are starving in China, you know." I didn't know how eating every morsel helped starving kids the other side of the planet, but our parents insisted it did. Maxine had been braver than I. "Okay, take my food. Mail it to those starving kids in China," she'd say. "Maybe they'll send me Chinese food in thanks." Maxie loved Chinese food. Me, not so much. A lot of it had to do with hearing about that starving race.

"I'll get something," Mother said. "I guess I'll have to learn to take care of myself now. Not sure how—"

"I'm here, Mother, I'll always be here for you. You know that."

She placed two mugs on the counter and turned to look at me. "But you have your own life, Francine. Or at least you should. You and the boys. And a new man someday."

"They won't be around forever. Kids grow up. And I don't want a man."

"You're still here. Your kids will be, too. And someday, you'll change your mind about men."

***

A few days after Father had been buried, Mother said, "I would like to find my brothers."

Brothers? You mean I have uncles I don't know about? Why didn't someone tell me before today? Seconds later, I realized, she meant her dead brothers.

I vaguely knew of them, but their existence had rarely been discussed. My grandmother, my mother's mother, once bemoaned that her two babies hadn't survived. Mother had said to her, "But you have me. Aren't I enough?" She said it in jest, of course, probably to make Grandma feel better, but I saw the faraway look that accompanied Grandma's watery eyes. I wanted to yell at Mother to shut up. Why did she want to upset an old lady, especially one so dear to her? And, of course, Grandma was dear to her. Grandma meant the world to Mother. She had lived with us after Grandpa had died, and Mother shed many tears at their deaths.

"What do you mean, Mother? Your brothers?"

"I want to know about them." She paused and looked at me. "I don't know much about them, you know. Did they have names? I don't even know for sure when they died. Or how. Or even if they were boys. Perhaps I had a sister."

How much can you know about two dead babies? Not like they ever had thoughts or lived a life to brag about. And that was over sixty years ago.

"I want to know," Mother repeated. "How old were they? Were they boys? And are they really buried in Evers Cemetery?"

We had been told they were buried in the old Evers Cemetery down in Pocksville, a good five hour's drive away, but who knew? No one had ever gone looking for them.

She glanced away and then back at me. "No one would talk about them. My father thought my mother too frail to know the truth. Whatever the truth was. Will we ever know? And now that I'm an orphan, I need to know them." She gazed out the window as if a magical forest stretched before her into which she might escape. "I need to know."

"How will you find out?"

"I'll have to go to the records office. Check old files."

"That would be here in Portersville, wouldn't it?"

"No, it wouldn't, as I'm sure you know. If you won't help me, I'll ask Maxine," Mother said.

It was as if I wasn't there, that I wouldn't offer assistance, that I wasn't important enough for her to ask me for help. Forget about old Francine and rely on dear, sweet Maxine who couldn't care a fig's ass about the past or anyone but herself.

"I'll help, Mother. Besides, Maxie's too busy with her career and Tony and the kids. She'll never get time off, not if we have to travel any distance."

"Okay, fine," Mother said. "But I think we'll have to go to Ogdensburg. That's where we were born, all three of us. I had to send papers there to get a copy of my birth certificate when I couldn't find it, remember? I tried here first, but they told me I needed to contact Ogdensburg."

"That's five hours away, Mother. Over five hours."

She glared at me. "I said I'd ask Maxine if you won't go."

Exasperated, I said, "Mother, I never said I wouldn't help. I'm just stating facts."

Genealogy had always fascinated me, and I wished I had delved into our past years ago, at least before Father died. He has no relatives left now, so his life and stories are dead and buried with him. Too late for any of us.

"I would have asked about my brothers when I was there, but that was years before I was an orphan. It didn't bother me then." Mother rambled, on and on, as if she were centre stage and held a rapt crowd.

I wanted to tell her yet again she hadn't become an orphan because of Father's death, but I bit my tongue as hard as I could, afraid I'd lose my temper, especially at her comment about asking Maxie over me. Was I that inconsequential, that much of a wallflower that no one saw me?

Mother came back down to earth. Maybe my sudden silence and the look of consternation on my face jolted her from her ranting.

"I'm sorry, Francine. Would you like to accompany me?" Her syrupy voice carried sarcasm.

"Yes, I would, Mother. I'd be glad to help. We could make a little trip out of it, stay in a motel. We can't drive that far in one stretch."

"Yes, I suppose I could manage that." She paused. "It's set then. You and I."

"Or we could telephone, Mother. Save the money."

"I said if you didn't want to go, I'd get Maxine. Or I'll go alone."

I should have kept my mouth shut. "Mother! That's not what I meant."

She calmed down. "I need to go in person. They'll tell me more with me staring down their faces. Besides, I want to know now, not months later when they get off their fat butts and do some work. You know how those government employees are."

"Okay, it's set then. We'll go, you and me. Randy will watch the kids. When do you want to leave?"

***

We drove to Ogdensburg exactly two weeks to the day after Father died. Whether Mother realized that or not, I don't know. It was a Friday. I had switched days at the grocery with Lorraine so Randy could have the boys on Saturday, his day off. I booked Mother and me a room at the Highcrest Inn for $29 a night.

Mother hadn't talked about Father much, not since she started her brother kick. I probably should have put the trip off for another couple of weeks until she felt a little better, but she'd have found a way to chastise me and bring up Maxie again.

I saw flashes in Mother's eyes, little snippets of anger, for as much as she missed him and wanted him back, she was mad at him for deserting her, but when she spoke, her love for him showed. Deep down, she knew he couldn't have controlled fate. I often heard her sobbing in the bathroom, where she thought she was safe from prying ears. I left her alone. She needed to deal with her grief in her own way. I'd be more of a burden if I intervened. Would have prolonged the agony, so to speak. I very rarely mentioned Father at all after he died, not knowing how Mother would react, not wanting to upset her.

The trip to Ogdensburg was uneventful. The sun shone brightly all the way there, a feeble attempt at lightening our mood. After numerous washroom breaks and a gas stop, we arrived too late to go to the records office. We headed straight to the inn, which I didn't have any trouble finding. After we checked in, we picked up sandwiches and milk from the corner store and ate in our room.

We woke early the next morning. Mother wanted to be first in line at the office to beat the rush as if there'd be a mad dash of people seeking information on the dead. Barring a sudden fire that destroyed the records, the information would remain, no matter if we arrived at eight o'clock or ten o'clock. And somehow, I didn't think office hours began at eight.

Mother insisted though, so away we went before eight in the morning. The government building, four blocks down Garden Avenue, with a right turn on James Street, would stand before us when we reached the corner of Hitchcock and James, or so the innkeeper said. Her directions were accurate. We arrived at 8:13.

"See, Mother. I told you so. Doesn't open 'til nine."

"No matter. We'll wait."

Of course we'd wait. We were hardly going to return to the inn or drive home to Portersville. "Let's walk to the park, Mother. The one we passed. It's only a block away."

It took some persuasion, but I convinced her.

Sitting on a park bench, we chatted.

"You know I'll want to check out the cemetery before we leave. I'd like to see where they're buried."

"Hopefully the office will have that information. Are you even sure it was Evers?" I asked.

"That's what Pa always said. Two little white crosses, high on the hill overlooking the water."

"When's the last time you've been back here?"

"Oh, it was years ago. Too many years for me to remember. I only lived here for a couple of years, you know, until we moved to Portersville. Pa never wanted to go back. Neither had Ma. Too many memories, I suppose. Pa thought eight hours away was a good distance. Of course, it only takes five hours now, with the new highway and all."

Mother paused and stared at a tree. "I'm an orphan now, did you know?"

I clasped her hand. Was she demented? That's all she harped on: orphans and dead people and cemeteries. She was only in her sixties. Wasn't that too young to go off the deep end?

"Mother, yes, you told me. It's okay, don't worry. We'll find them. We won't leave 'til we do." *Except I have to get back to my kids. We have to leave tonight*, but I didn't voice those thoughts.

A couple of people were in line when we returned. After about fifteen minutes, it was our turn.

"I need information on my two siblings. They were born between 1920 and 1925. I'm not sure exactly. Last name of Clements."

The woman reached under the counter and produced several papers. "You'll need to fill these out. It's $15 for each certificate."

Mother looked puzzled. "Oh, but dear, I just want their death dates and where they were buried so I can visit them. They're my siblings, you know."

"Ma'am, you still need to fill these out. We'll mail the information to you within three weeks."

Aghast, Mother said, "But I'm only here for the day. I need it now. And I don't need no certificate."

And the battle began.

I was hesitant to intervene. The fight was hers, not mine. Mother could hold her own when necessary; I'd seen her in action a few times. There'd be more words and raised voices. Next, the tears would stream, and no one would be able to say no then. A tear had already formed. It wouldn't be long.

The Department of Health in Ogdensburg didn't cover much of an area, only as far as Cronin and down to Clearmarsh. The facility was small and not at all prestigious, not a monstrosity as those I would imagine finding in big cities. I eyed the map on the wall while listening to the babble between Mrs. Sneedle and Mother. I almost intervened several times when Mother faltered, but each time she rebounded like a boxer in a ring.

"My husband died two weeks ago yesterday. I can't afford the money right now. And I've driven all this way..."

That was the fourth time Mother brought up the car trip. And the money? She couldn't afford it? Had Father not provided for her?

Mrs. Sneedle glanced around the room. Although several people milled about, no one was in line but Mother.

"We just got our records computerized. I'm not supposed to do this..." The woman stared at the computer.

Mother sported a smug look of satisfaction.

"Baby boy Clements, born March 6, 1920. Died at birth. Buried Evers Cemetery." Her fingers flew across the keys. I was amazed at her skill. She peered at the screen. "Baby boy Clements, born January 27, 1923. Died January 29, 1923. Buried at Evers Cemetery."

"I'm the middle child. And they *were* boys." Mother whispered, in awe of the knowledge. Her eyes glowed.

I suppose it was good news, in a way, since it was information she had wanted and never figured she'd have, despite the fact she had only desperately wanted it for the past couple of weeks.

She looked at me. "I had two brothers like Pa said. I'd be the middle child, Francie, if they lived. Do you believe it? Think of the fun the three of us could have had." Her eyes clouded over.

I touched her arm. "Mother, I think we should go."

She was rooted to the floor. I couldn't budge her.

"Thank you so much for your help," I said to Mrs. Sneedle. "You don't know how much this means to my mother."

Mother perked up. "Yes, thank you. Forgive my manners."

Mrs. Sneedle smiled, but not a regular, happy smile. More like a grimace, like a *who cares?* She was glad to be rid of us.

"If we're going to the cemetery, we better get going." I grasped Mother's arm. Despite receiving the news she had wanted, she seemed to morph into a fragile flower that would fold at the slightest breath upon it. I wanted to gather her in my arms, to protect her from the evils of the world, evils that were out there, waiting for a desolate soul.

***

Evers Cemetery, in Pocksville, was twelve miles from the Ogdensburg Department of Health. We walked back to the inn to get the car.

We stopped at the caretaker's hut just inside the cemetery.

"Records were never kept properly. Records were destroyed over the years. Someone will have to do an inventory someday," the grizzled old man muttered.

The work wouldn't be done by him was my first thought. Would he be buried in Evers, the cemetery he sort of looked after, for how could one individual possibly oversee that many dead people? Or was it easier taking care of the dead than I thought? Definitely an easier job taking care of the dead than the living.

"Check up at the top of the hill," he mumbled. "That's where the older part of the cemetery is."

"That's where Pa said they were buried." Mother grinned as if she had already found them.

We thanked him. Mother immediately wanted to check out the hilltop, which looked as if we'd have to trek up the side of a mountain—a gradual climb to Heaven, apropos for a cemetery—but we took our time so we could check out headstones along the way because who knew for sure where the babes were buried. I was glad she had worn her old walking shoes.

Mother continually harped on her brothers. "What if one—or both—are still alive? What if Pa had given one up for adoption? Or what if one had been kidnapped? Unlikely it could have happened to both of them, but one could be alive. Right, Francie? The records could be wrong. They could have been faked."

Too many "what ifs" for me. Mother wouldn't give up and continued her ridiculous rambling about kidnapping and adoptions and faked records.

Because Evers Cemetery was a large and sprawling area, we traipsed it for hours. The scorching sun beat upon us, but Mother was unflinching. The brambles bit through our slacks. The bugs swarmed about our faces, and we forever swatted at them like two crazies in a loony bin; perhaps we were. The task was more daunting than finding a sane person in a mental institution. No real headstones existed for Mother's siblings. Grandpa had said there were only two small white crosses—or so he had thought. How long would wooden markers last? Wouldn't they have disintegrated over that period? Without anyone managing their plots, who'd take care of them? Vandals could have come along, as well. Thieves and vandals always want something, and

I'm sure they wouldn't have ignored crosses, no matter how insignificant.

Who cared about the dead anymore anyhow? Did anyone?

We reached the top no problem, but no wooden crosses were to be seen. Sweat poured down Mother's face, and strands of hair matted to her cheeks. She huffed and puffed as if she were about to blow a house down.

"Look at this headstone. It's the same year, 1920. My brothers must be here somewhere." Mother walked to and fro, reading headstones, searching for her siblings. "Maybe someone bought them a new headstone," she said. "The two could be sharing one."

"Who would do that? Wouldn't Grandpa have known about it?"

"No, not necessarily. The church could have done it."

I thought that highly unlikely but didn't want to dissuade her. So then we searched for one old stone with two names, without success.

When she found a small clearing void of any headstones, she said, "Maybe this is it. Maybe I'm standing over them right now. What if that were so, Francie?"

She didn't want an answer, at least not one in the negative, so I didn't give her one. What do you say to someone who has so obviously lost their mental facilities, even if it's your own mother?

She moved a few paces, where she looked out over the water. "Isn't it peaceful here, Francie? I feel vibes they are here. I can feel them, I really can. Their little voices call to me."

That was enough for me.

"Come on, Mother. Time to go or we'll never get home before dark."

She smiled and stood straighter, like a top-heavy sunflower overshadowing wispy baby's breath that I had once likened her to. Her cheeks crinkled, spotlighting dimples either side of her mouth. I couldn't remember the last time I had seen those small indents. Maxie, when she was young, used to stick her fingers into them, which had made Mother laugh. The sun highlighted strands of white in her grey curls. For an instant, she appeared as I had remembered her many years previously when she was the age I was that day, when the sun glistened through her long blonde hair and the wrinkles on her face hadn't yet appeared.

"Yes, we should go." Mother perked up even more as if infused with new life. In her heart, she had found her brothers' final resting places, high on a hill, overlooking the water, as Grandpa had said.

Arm in arm, we strolled down the hill. My preoccupation with rushing home waned. My boys would be fine until I returned.

*(Based on a story about my mother and I searching for
Her two deceased siblings in Bermuda.)*

The Dinner Invitation

Many years ago, I killed a woman. It hadn't been intentional; at least I hadn't pre-planned her death, so there was no way they could try me for premeditated murder. I can't say I was too upset over it, though. I didn't shed tears. I slept like a baby the night it happened—and have ever since. I didn't go to her funeral, either; actually, no one did since her body was never found. Hard to have a funeral without a body though I suppose it's done on occasion. Can't have family grieving forever; must have closure. As a result, the woman is still technically missing though I'm sure her file has long been relegated to the dungeons of cold cases, in amongst cobwebs and creepy crawlers feasting on mould.

I used to tell that story to my two granddaughters, April and July. Yes, my fine daughter, Lisa, actually named her daughters after their months of birth. July was born two years after April. Lisa almost had another child—a boy—who would have been named June, but he died at birth. Stillborn, I guess, is the correct term.

I like to think the baby died on purpose, that the kid-to-be knew his fate and didn't want to grow up being ridiculed with a name like June. For sure he would have heard the Johnny Cash song, "A Boy Named Sue," that Lisa sang to him while he was ensconced in her belly. Lisa and her husband, Grant, are big country music fans, not to mention their great adoration of Johnny Cash. Had almost-baby-June been born in August, his fate might have been different. After all, there are many Romans called Augustus. August could have been lengthened to Augustus. If names can be shortened, they should be able to be lengthened.

I told Lisa that baby boy June didn't want to be born into this cruel world of ours where there's already enough bullying as it is without creating more. Of course, I waited until after July was born before I shared my opinion. She might not have taken kindly to my words until she'd had adequate time to mourn.

I adored the two little girls, April and July. Granny's Girls, I called them. I'd often keep them on weekends so Lisa and Grant could enjoy quality time together. They worked hard through the week and deserved a break.

Children should be read to, so when Granny's Girls were young, I read to them from the many books that survived my childhood. I couldn't recite the stories in my head to them, not at that tender age, though the volumes of nursery rhymes, fairy tales, and fables—all classics purporting to be suitable for children—weren't much better, what with tales of wolves eating (heaven forbid!) grandmas and witches forcing beautiful ladies to eat poisoned apples and townsfolk drowning disabled women. (All misbehaviours against females, in case you didn't notice.) Little piglets running to market to steal wares, bad boys sticking thumbs into fruit pies to annoy their mothers and ruin dinner, and siblings wasting commodities by dumping pails of water down hills were more my style back then when April and July were innocent and impressionable.

I'm not privileged to enjoy Granny's Girls anymore. Teenagers aren't interested in spending time with old folk. They want to chase after boys, play on their cell phones, and hang out at malls. Even if April and July wanted to visit, which they don't, Lisa won't let them. She says I'm a bad example, that my stories were horrid and that I used to scare them to death so badly they had nightmares for days—but that had lasted only until another weekend rolled around when Lisa and Grant wanted couple time.

Regarding the so-called offensive narratives I supposedly spewed, I only told Granny's Girls my scary stories, like the dinner invite one, on those occasions when the youngsters were particularly evil. The girls seemed fine at the time, even laughed uproariously and begged for more. Something must have happened between the time they left me and returned home. Or perhaps it was those cruel classics and those unknowns "that go bump in the night" coming back to haunt them.

The last time, which was a couple of years ago, that Lisa brought Granny's Girls over to my home, one of them said I stunk, that my home smelled like old people and oh, how disgusting it was. I do believe April spoke the words, now that I think back. My dear sweet daughter never bothered to stand up for me—her very own, one and only mother. She'll be old someday—they all will—let's just see how their gilded years unfold.

To hell with them all. I'm quite content here in my cozy home, with my rocking rocker and my memories. Their loss, not mine. My rocker comforts me as no human can, often lulling me to sleep, and I spend those evenings deep within my own world. I'd be back in time when I was a young mother with a swaddling babe in my arms; but in reality, it was just me—a world-weary woman existing with her many memories and pondering what merriment she might enjoy inflicting on kin who rudely want nothing to do with her.

I fall into my rocker, pull my afghan around me and drift off, remembering a dinner invitation many years ago...

***

Using the fanciest script I can muster, I carefully address the envelope:

Miss Harriet Williams
139 Willow Lane
Halifax, Nova Scotia

I want to write a poem, sort of a double entendre, but I never was good at rhyming.

Come for dinner
Don't be late
I'll have plates
Food to sate

No, that's no good. I ponder another.

Come 'round for dinner
Don't be late
For a dinner date
Be a winner
Stomachs we'll sate
Laying on the plate

I want to substitute "sinner" instead of "winner," but that sounds a bit too ominous, don't you think? Something like "thou shalt not eat of thy flesh." After several tries, I give up and scrawl a plain dinner invitation on a sheet of bright pink paper.

There will only be one invitee.

Heehee. Harriet will get a kick out of this, at least I hope so. I only pray she'll accept. If not, my lovely plans will be ruined. Such fun I have planned. I'm as excited as a piglet with its teeny curlicue tail.

I don't trust the post office to deliver the envelope in a timely manner, so I hand-deliver it. Besides, she lives a mere two blocks away. After I drop the invitation in the front door mail slot, I return home and begin with preparations.

Thankfully, I hear from Harriet on Tuesday, the day after the delivery. And she accepts.

Saturday dawns bright and sunny though by the time evening rolls in, dusk nears. The night has always intrigued me. Dastardly deeds and unknowns that go bump come alive then. I come alive then, too. I've always been a night owl.

Dinner is scheduled for Saturday, six o'clock sharp. I believe in punctuality.

I'm wearing my best dress, the blue patterned one with splashes of pink and red roses across the bodice. I wear my white high heels. I don't much care for stockings, but the evening will be a special occasion, and I want to look and feel my best.

I take one final glance at my coiffed hair and fuchsia lipstick before heading to the front door. I'm so excited; I want to be waiting for her. Mustn't keep guests waiting.

It's two minutes of six.

Two minutes later, Harriet raps the brass lion-head knocker.

"Come in, come in." Am I too gushy?

Harriet looks scared. She's made up well, but rouge can't camouflage her pallor. Her sparse grey hair is pulled back into a tight bun, but there are several wayward hairs I long to brush back with a bit of hairspray.

"What's wrong?" I ask.

Harriet's eyes dart about the room.

"What's wrong?" I ask again.

She continues to scan my small home, what she can see from the foyer, which isn't much: just the short hall leading to the kitchen and the parlour on her right.

"There's no one else coming for dinner. Just you and me."

"Just us?"

"Yes, just us." I pause. "You scared?"

"No,"

Yet, she appears scared. Why did she agree to come if she feels this way?

I note her outfit—the length of her dress, half-way between her knees and ankles. Harriet is a bit of a prude. I like to be daring, though I never expose my knees.

"No, I'm fine. I just thought there'd be someone else here."

"We're dining alone, you and I. Oh, dear, where's my manners? Come in." I lead Harriet to the kitchen. "Have a seat. It's six o'clock, and I'm hungry, so let's eat. You hungry?"

I pull out one of two chairs for my guest and wait for her response, but she says nothing. Perhaps she's hard of hearing.

The table is set with my good china, sterling silver cutlery, and crystal glasses. Only the very best for my guests.

"Here's a napkin. Wouldn't want to dirty your clothes now, would we?" I hand her a freshly-pressed, twelve-inch square linen napkin. Harriet delicately places it on her lap. She rubs her hands over it several times, flattening it out.

I don't like Harriet much, never did. I don't think she likes me either. We tolerate each other, and we must put on a good act because none of our friends realize we don't particularly care for the other.

We're God-fearing women who attend church every Sunday and spout the graces of our Lord God in Heaven and remain on track with our niceties. But let's put it this way: I won't shed a tear if she dies, whether from a freak accident or murder. Or perhaps due to one of those many mysterious, unexplained disappearances, an unresolved death where a spirit hovers in that strange, unknown space between that of life and death, waiting for a peace that never arrives. Peace never will, not if the body is never discovered.

"Let me get organized. Are you hungry?" I ask again.

She must not have heard me the first time because she replies now. "Yes, somewhat. What are we having?"

I ignore Harriet's question as she ignored mine and head to the sink.

My dining room is part of the kitchen. The table is small, adequate for four guests if they squeeze in tight, but I moved two chairs against the wall so there's more room.

I pick up the carving knife and, brandishing it in the air, face Harriet. "We're having meatballs."

"Meatballs?" she eyes the knife. I glimpse her eyes, see the glassy orbs.

I walk toward her. Her face glistens under the glare of the fluorescent light centred exactly above the table. Up close, dilated pupils gleam.

She raises her arm to fend off an attack.

What! You think I'm going to gouge your heart out? Slice off your head? I giggle.

"I forgot to fill the water glasses." With the knife still in one hand, I snatch her glass with the other.

"Ice cubes?

"Yes, Agatha, please." Her voice is weak, barely a whisper. She doesn't dare decline ice cubes. I could ask for anything at this point; she'd deny me nothing. I smell her fear, mingled with the meatball aroma seeping from the oven. And what a luscious smell it is.

I place the items on the counter, return for my glass, fill the two glasses with ice cubes and tap water, and set them back on the table. Harriet seems to have calmed down, but her face is sweaty and flushed, her eyes still watery.

"Let me check the meatballs." I open the oven. Ah, the smell. The tomato sauce bubbles around the balls. Onions and spices meld in with the tomatoes; all in all, a heavenly aroma. "Smell them?" I ask Harriet.

"Smells good," she says.

"I have boiled potatoes, too. And peas. Just a few more minutes and I'll start plating."

I pull out the empty chair and sit. I'm not really sure what to talk about besides the upcoming meal. "So what have you been up to, Harriet? Have you been on altar duty lately?"

"Next week is my turn. Reverend Munden is away this week, so there's a substitute for Sunday. I'm glad it's not my week. I'd be afraid I wouldn't do things right, not knowing how someone else likes things done."

Harriet is too timid. It's a volunteer job. All Saint's Episcopal should be happy to have us women to take care of minute details. "I wouldn't worry about it."

The silence is deafening. Harriet stares off into the distance. I glance where she's looking, but there's nothing. My stomach growls and interrupts the quiet. The meatballs must be ready. I realize I was so excited for this evening that I haven't eaten all day. Not even one nibble.

I pull out the tray of meatballs. Once they're out of the oven, the fragrance is even stronger. "Smell it, Harriet? Yum, yum."

I grab the large spoon and ladle out several meatballs for each of us. I hear Harriet in the background. "Not too heavy on my plate." I ignore her. She'll eat what I eat. I drain the potatoes and add a few to our plates, then spoon out the peas.

I hesitate. What's with all the rounds? What in the hell was I thinking: round plate, round meat, round potatoes, round peas. The conglomerate is colourful at least: white, green, red. (The small pink flowers gracing the plates are well hidden beneath the food, thank goodness. Pink would clash.) Looking at the food-laden plate reminds me of Christmas. Oh, the stories I could tell of Christmas. I had a distant relative (long-deceased now) who disappeared at a family gathering one Christmas. As the story goes, his wife, Winnie, apparently killed him and added his body parts to the stuffing, but no one knew for sure. Who would do that? Meatballs, with their mixture of breadcrumbs and onions, are similar to stuffing. I snicker and glance again at the balls. So perfectly round. Heavenly.

Harriet watches me when I approach the table with the plates. She eyes her food. "Looks good. I didn't realize I was as hungry as I am."

We delve into our food. Despite the odd appearance, everything tastes scrumptious. "Good, eh?"

"Yes, I must admit, it is." She chomps on another meatball. "What's that prominent flavour? I can't quite determine what it is."

"Oh, I can't give out my cooking secrets. Suffice to say, it's something you'd never imagine eating in meatballs. Quite healthy for you though, at least I think it is. A necessity of life, something all bodies require to stay alive."

I finish what's on my plate, soaking up the savoury sauce with the bread slices I belatedly put on the table. When Harriet sees my uncouth manners, she does the same. "Good to the last drop, eh?"

She nods.

I place our empty plates on the counter. The long serrated knife still sits there, alone, unused, gleaming from the ceiling light. Meatballs are soft; I didn't need to use it. I glance out the window. Harriet and I had such a good time, the evening passed before I knew it, but there can still be more fun. Night will soon fall and blackness will descend. The time for ghouls and, if it were Halloween, goblins and witches though I suppose those creatures can appear at any time.

I grab the knife and charge to the table as if I'm going to battle. "I have no dessert, I'm sorry to say. It took me longer than I thought to prepare the meatballs and then I had no time left. I wanted to be ready for six o'clock, and I wouldn't have been had I spent more time on dinner."

When I sit down, Harriet glares at me. "What are you doing with the knife?" She glances around the table, but she knows all the food is gone.

"I don't know. Perhaps I need some dessert."

Her face turns white, but otherwise, she is calm. "What do you mean?"

"Oh, I don't know, really. I enjoyed those meatballs so much I'm thinking something else along the same line." I belch before apologizing. Unusual food does that to me.

"I'm full, actually. Thank you very much for dinner. Perhaps I should go now."

"You don't have to run away so fast. The evening's young."

She glances at the knife. "I still don't understand." She burps then. Not an unladylike one as I had produced, but a dainty burp. "Sorry. I don't usually hiccup."

It's not a hiccup, I want to say. It's a belch. I knew she'd copy my cue.

Harriet covers her mouth. Was another coming? "I don't know what's come over me. I can't stop hiccupping."

"No worries. You're in good company. Belches are a sign of a delicious meal, did you know that?"

"No, I didn't. But I've the hiccups. Belches aren't for women."

But I just belched, I think. "It's okay. It's the meatballs, methinks. My secret ingredient. I never made them like that before. I may try them again sometime. We were pigs, you and I. We ate them all."

"Really? I didn't eat that many."

"Yes, you did. I gave us seconds, remember?" I barely remember that myself, but I did indeed fill our plates a second time. Upon reflection, I'm mad at myself for doing so since Harriet ate what I planned on having for lunch the next day. Drat that Harriet and her big belly—and, of course, my niceties in offering my guest an additional helping. But no worries. I can make more meatballs. I have all the ingredients, just that it takes precious time to mix the components and mould them into those precise, individual balls.

I pick up the knife. I notice the silvery sheen, how the light dances off the razor-blade edge. Earlier, I soaked it in bleach to remove any traces of blood. Just in case. All meat contains blood. One can never be too careful; one never knows when police might knock on the door.

After belching again, Harriet jumps from the chair. "I really must run now thank you for dinner I'll see you in church."

I'm pondering knocks on the door in the middle of the night and still savouring the exquisite flavour of the meal, the meatballs in particular, that I don't hear the front door slam. Her seat is empty.

"Oh, Harriet," I mutter. "Do you really think I'd use this knife on you?"

I'm suddenly hungry and craving dessert, some sort of delectable round thing dipped in melted chocolate or stuffed with chewy hot caramel. Maybe with dollops of whipped cream.

But she's gone, disappeared from my kitchen without a trace.

I belch.

***

The next morning, I wake in my chair. Having dreamt of my world-famous meatballs causes my stomach to growl though breakfast, even for me, is too early for meat. Yet I can almost smell those delectable meatballs from long ago.

I have a brainstorm: I should call Lisa. Perhaps she'll reconsider our relationship. Maybe she'll allow the family to come for dinner tonight. It's been a long time since I've seen Granny's Girls. I just hope Grant doesn't accompany them. Grant's a hefty man.

I won't be able to serve meatballs. That meat is long gone from my freezer, and I'm too old now to find that secret ingredient. Besides which, the prep work is much too difficult at my age, but I'm sure I can come up with another fancy treat.

Who knows, I might even make dessert. Dessert slipped out of my grasp that night many years ago when Harriet was my guest, and I've regretted that unfortunate circumstance ever since.

But I'm getting ahead of myself since I don't know whether they'll accept. I'd better call Lisa now. Just in case I have to prepare for dinner guests.

Published by Horrified Press in anthology,
I am Woman; I am Man, November 2015

Diamonds and Roses
and Everything Nice

Elsa stood in the kitchen fingering the silk scarf. "It's lovely, but you can't keep buying me things. The money you're spending—"

"Don't worry about the money," Kelvin said.

"But—"

"I worked overtime, remember?"

"Yeah, I remember, but the ring last week must have cost a fortune." Despite agreeing with her husband, she wondered if he were having an affair. Were the scarf and the previous gifts given out of guilt? For the past few weeks, there had been many such gifts though none as extravagant as the ring, which had been the biggest surprise.

He smiled. "I worked more overtime that week, that's why I spent more."

She eyed the large, sparkling solitaire diamond on her left hand, a stark contrast to the thin gold band nestled beside it. When they had married, gold bands were all they could afford, but she had been happy with the exchange of plain bands. She would have been happy without a ring as long as she had her husband.

"Don't worry about the money," he repeated. "All's good. I don't mind the overtime. Plus I got a raise, too."

"Really? A raise?"

"Yes, really." Kelvin beamed. "That scarf goes perfect with your blue eyes and blonde hair." His eyes shone like the diamond flashing from her hand.

Elsa wrapped the sumptuous silk around her neck. "Feels delicious."

She could get used to these luxuries. But could they afford them?

***

Kelvin heard the door reverberate behind him though he wondered if he had imagined it. He didn't bother taking the time to look since it was vital he disappear as quickly as possible. He wasn't too worried, however, as he had finalized the plans days previously.

Every heist was basically the same. He needed only to ponder small variables and implement minor adjustments. After the deed was done, he would speed down the street and turn at the first left or right, continue down a block and cut across to another block. He crossed streets at every corner. Cops would never successfully tail him. At an opportune moment, he would casually saunter into a mall or a grocery store, where he would linger until the situation had cooled.

Thus far, he had lucked out though he didn't consider himself lucky. Planning took foresight; he simply concocted foolproof plans and followed through. He had no reason to think success wouldn't continue.

After leaving the bank, he veered left on the first street and performed his usual zigzag pattern until he found himself on the waterfront, facing the ferry terminal. He had never taken the ferry back to Dartmouth when in getaway mode from Halifax, but in a flash decided he could be on the other side before the police knew anything untoward had happened. The plan had been to return to Dartmouth by bus, just as he had taken the bus from Dartmouth into Halifax several hours previously, but a sight deviation shouldn't matter.

He purchased a ticket before the whistle blew, having timed it perfectly. He walked on the ferry and plopped into the first empty seat. The ferry heading in the opposite direction to Halifax passed by. He almost waved, but that was a gesture for kids. Adults didn't wave at travelling passengers, especially not on the Metro Transit Ferry.

The ferry lurched when it docked. He exited, caught the bus coming up the street, got off on Jackson Street, and ambled to the parking lot where he had left his car.

He tossed the backpack on the front passenger seat and jumped in. After revving the engine, he drove to another nearby parking lot, where he stopped and dumped the bills from the backpack on the front seat.

He smiled. Almost three thousand dollars! The First Citizen's Bank had been an easy heist. He looked at his watch. Not yet four o'clock. He had determined, after spying on the small branch of the bank, that the later in the day the better.

He couldn't wait much longer, not with rush-hour traffic and yokels punching out from daily grinds. He had to be long gone before they were let loose.

He shoved the bills back into the knapsack and headed to Micmac Mall where he'd buy something special for his wife. At five o'clock, he'd head for home. Elsa would be none the wiser!

Kelvin's days had been slashed from five to three a week. How Farmington Foods could expect an employee to work three days a week and support a family was mind-boggling. For six years he'd been a valuable and faithful employee in the accounting department. How could they do that to him? Times were tough, but to cut two days from his week was more than unfair.

Had his hours been cut because Joe, the supervisor, knew he was childless? None of his co-workers with families had suffered his fate—except him and Ted, who was single. Weren't layoffs supposed to be in order of seniority?

And how would he ever fess up to Elsa? She kept him high on a pedestal though, unbeknownst to her, he had never measured up. He'd told so many lies—little white fibs—that he feared she'd see through him one day.

He wasn't sure how he had begun stealing. The idea had probably sprung from a television show or a movie. It wasn't like he accosted little old ladies on the streets or murdered or maimed. No, he simply walked into a corner store or a small branch of a large bank or a flourishing restaurant. He spent many days planning; nothing had been on the spur of the moment nor had he once veered from his original plans except for riding the ferry that day. Once he had his two days reinstated—which his boss indicated could be feasible once the economy picked up—he'd stop. The money was necessary for the short term. He had to continue to appease Elsa. He couldn't lose her.

He wanted his wife to have the best of what life could offer, and until recently, he hadn't been successful. Deep down, he harboured enormous guilt about his inadequacies and worried she'd leave him. She was forever commenting on Jane's fashionable outfits or the expensive jewellery Bill bought Alice or Grace's new sports car. What could Elsa brag about to her friends?

Nothing—until recently.

***

Elsa noticed the change in her husband. She wasn't sure exactly when; perhaps it had been so gradual she hadn't picked up on it until it was too late. She brushed aside thoughts of him cheating. Cheating would be so obvious she was certain she would have known from the start. No, something else bothered him; something else was happening. She wasn't sure what.

On Thursday, Kelvin left the house as usual, outfitted in a newly dry-cleaned dark suit and navy print tie and shoes that shone so brightly Elsa was certain he could see his face in them.

She slipped into her red Honda Civic and followed his black Camaro. She stayed far enough behind he wouldn't notice her. Then again, he'd have no reason to look in the rearview mirror to search for her.

He parked in the work parking lot and disappeared into the building.

Thus far, all fine, she thought, *but it'll be a long day if I have to sit here for eight hours*. Despite that, she was determined to stay. She had her tablet, so she read and doodled on a notepad. At eleven o'clock, she drove the short distance to the nearest Tim Hortons for a sandwich and coffee. She returned to find his vehicle hadn't budged. The rest of the afternoon was uneventful. She drove away at 4:30, knowing he'd be finished at 5:00. Kelvin was always home by 5:15.

Elsa followed her husband again the next day, Friday. Puzzled, she wondered why he veered to Halifax and not Dartmouth, where he worked. Perhaps he had a dental appointment? Or a doctor's appointment? No, he always informed her when he had personal appointments. And both offices called the home phone for confirmation, so most times she knew of his appointments before he did. No one had called. And he hadn't mentioned any appointments.

Kelvin took the exit to Halifax Shopping Centre. Shopping? For her? She was confused about the weekly gifts. She glanced at her watch to see it was 8:15 a.m. The mall didn't open until 9:30 a.m. She followed slowly, watching while he drove toward Winners and parked at the side of the mall by the Bay. At that hour, the parking lot was almost empty.

She stopped behind a parked car. Time passed slowly. She didn't dare pick up her tablet or notepad. Her husband was positioned within eyesight. When nine-thirty neared, the parking lot filled. Still, he remained in his vehicle.

What's he doing? She wanted to return home to her routine but felt possessed to remain.

On the dot of nine-thirty, Kelvin exited the car.

She debated following but decided to remain in the car. He'd notice her for sure if she went into the mall.

While she waited, cars pulled up around her. Close to noon, Kelvin reappeared. She almost missed him and didn't notice if he carried packages.

She followed when he pulled from the parking lot. He headed down the highway toward downtown Halifax, where he drove around the busy streets for a good hour. With the hectic noon traffic, Elsa had trouble keeping him in view. Her stomach growled, and she glanced at her watch. One twenty-nine.

What in the heck is he doing?

Finally, he parked in front of the Early Bird Café. *Great, he's getting lunch and here I am stuck in the car.* He got out of the car and entered the restaurant.

Not knowing what to do, she drove around the block. When she returned to the street where her husband had parked, she slowed and slipped behind a vehicle a few car lengths from Kelvin's car.

Just when she had shut off the engine, Kelvin raced to his car and disappeared down the street. Enough time hadn't elapsed for him to order a meal, let alone eat it.

Most concerning, despite the warm weather, he had worn a ski mask. And what was with the backpack?

Before she had a chance to restart the engine, two individuals emerged from the restaurant and scanned the street. She waited for several minutes. When distant sirens drew closer and closer, she drove away.

Kelvin pulled into the hospital parking lot and drove along the emergency entrance. He stopped in an empty spot, removed his backpack, and flung it to the passenger seat. He rummaged inside and withdrew a fistful of bills. He'd be lucky to have escaped with a hundred dollars. No one paid with cash anymore, everyone wanting to earn points with credit cards. He dumped out the rest of the money and counted the bills, surprised to find almost four hundred dollars.

He folded the bills and jammed them in his pocket. He plopped the coins into the ashtray. Smiling, he drove toward a mini-mall where he entered a fast food restaurant, ordered a six-inch sub and pop, and sat at a table. While eating, he read the *Metro* newspaper. The recent heists baffled the police, but if he read between the lines, they'd be on to him soon. He couldn't continue forever; eventually, he would mess up.

He mused about executing another robbery that afternoon. He had never attempted two in one day, and of course, he didn't have one planned, but an impromptu heist might be beneficial. That would really fox the cops, who were probably still busy at the café.

He stared at the sole sandwich maker/cashier. With lunch hour over, the restaurant was empty. The till should be full since most fast food patrons used cash—he hoped.

On the way home, Elsa noticed Kelvin's car parked in the mini-mall, around the corner from Fast Subs. She parked at the other end of the mall and glanced into the picture window on her way to the door, where she had a perfect view of Kelvin's backside. The ski mask, looking more like a toque, was rolled up around his head like a turban. His motions indicated he was demolishing his food.

She marveled at her luck. She hadn't expected to find him, not with his head start.

The blood drained from her face when he rolled down the toque.

After Kelvin pulled the ski mask over his face, he approached the counter. The oblivious young man was startled when Kelvin said, "Hand over your cash. I have a gun. And no funny business."

Kelvin walked around the counter and stopped at the cash register. He removed his backpack, and the younger man, his pimply red face sweating, dropped bills into the open pack.

Kelvin closed it and raced from the restaurant.

Elsa had moved beside a trash can, but when Kelvin exited the building, he brushed by her, so close his hot breath wafted over her.

He raced toward his vehicle. By that time, the restaurant employee, talking on a cell phone, had exited the restaurant and scanned the lot. He glanced at Elsa.

She forced a smile.

When he returned indoors, she sauntered down the parking lot. Trying not to draw attention to herself, she walked as slowly as she could, but she was sweaty and nervous and hoped she wouldn't faint. Kelvin had already disappeared around the building. The employee hadn't seen him go there.

When she reached her husband, he was sitting in the front seat, the door wide open. The knitted hat and backpack lay on the passenger seat.

She yanked on his sleeve. "What the hell you doing?" she screeched. "I saw everything. Everything!"

Kelvin grabbed at her arm to release her grip. "Leave me alone. I gotta go." He was calm, not surprised to see her. He closed the door, revved the engine, and was gone.

As previously, Elsa heard sirens advancing. She plugged her ears; she didn't want to hear, didn't want to believe what she had just seen. She continued around the parking lot to the rear of the building, where she slumped against the wall.

Elsa couldn't prepare dinner; she just couldn't. She had vomited twice since arriving home. She kept glancing at the clock and its frozen hands. At one point, she wondered if the batteries had died. But, no, the hands had moved; the hands were simply too slow.

When seven o'clock arrived and Kelvin hadn't returned, she began to worry. He was her husband, and she loved him no matter what. But what was he thinking? Stealing? They shared the same values. Stealing wasn't in her repertoire, nor was it in his.

So what had happened? Why hadn't he gone to work?

And then the door slammed. She raced from the living room into the kitchen.

"Hey, honey," he said. He held out a dozen red roses as if nothing was wrong.

Of course, she didn't know there were a dozen, but who'd present eleven or ten roses? Or thirteen? Thirteen was too unlucky. No, there were twelve.

"What are these for?"

"Roses for my honey," Kelvin said.

"I'm your honey?"

"Of course you're my honey."

She stared at her husband. Her heart beat so fast she thought it would burst.

"What's wrong?" he asked.

"What's wrong?" Elsa felt her face flush. "What's wrong! You tell me."

"Here, take these."

She ignored the proffered roses. "Tell me what's going on."

Kelvin glanced away. He threw the roses to the floor and stood rooted to the linoleum.

"Kelvin? Tell me. What's going on?"

He was silent for several long seconds.

She watched the clock hands. Perhaps the battery was dead after all. No, one hand moved.

Elsa moved, too. She caressed her husband's chin, feeling stubble on her fingertips. Had he gone to work without shaving? No, he hadn't gone to work. "Where were you today?"

He remained silent.

"Kelvin? What's going on?"

He looked at Elsa. "I brought you roses. Who brings you roses?"

She stomped one foot. "I don't want roses. I want honesty. I want my husband." Her voice echoed, louder than she had intended.

"I'm here."

"I know you're here. In body. But not really, are you? Where did my husband go?"

"What do you mean?" He glanced away as if pretending something important had caught his eye by the window.

"What was today all about?"

He sighed and was silent for several seconds before looking back at her. "Do you love me?"

"What a stupid question! Of course I love you."

"I did it all for you."

"Did what for me?"

He glanced at the window again.

She grabbed his head and twisted him around. "Look at me."

"I'm looking."

"No, you're not. Tell me. Please. Now!" She shouted the last word.

"Stop yelling."

"I'm not yelling. But you have to talk to me. I'll scream my lungs out if you don't talk."

"I did it all for you," he repeated.

She examined his face, seeing weary, defeated eyes welling with tears. One plopped to his cheek. She had never seen him cry.

She dabbed at the drop and made it disappear.

"I love you, sweetie. I love you so much." Kelvin dropped to the floor beside the roses. Two stems had escaped from the wrapping.

Broken petals resembled splashes of blood. "I'm so sorry. I wanted you to have nice things. I'm such a failure."

She knelt beside him and smoothed wayward hairs. "You're not a failure. I love you so much."

"I'm worthless." He gulped. "I lost my job. Like months ago. Well, not really the entire job. Two days a week. They cut me two days. How are we supposed to live on three days?"

"What? Why didn't you tell me?"

"I wanted you to be proud of me."

"I am proud of you. Jeepers, Kelvin, it's only a job. You can get another."

Kelvin sobbed and swiped at tears. "I can't. The economy's caput, you know."

"It's okay." She snuggled into him, crushing him to her chest. She kissed his moist cheek and rubbed his back. "This isn't so comfortable, you know. Let's go to bed."

He sobbed, ignoring her request.

"Come on," she repeated. "I'll give you a back rub."

"A back rub?"

"Sure. Don't I owe you one?"

Kelvin laughed. "Yeah, you always lose our bets." He raised his head. "Look at the roses. Do you realize how much they cost?"

At the mention of money, she remembered the day's happenings, forgetting the back rub. "I don't understand how you could resort to stealing."

He hung his head like a chastised child.

"I'm stunned. I still don't understand."

"I know," he said, tears again rolling down his cheeks.

She kissed his lips. "Are the cops after you, do you think?"

"I don't think so. I'm sure I'm in the clear. I've been very careful."

She laughed. "I don't hear them at the door."

Other noises buzzed around her. Her world had collapsed, but she'd wake up from this dream any second and her life would be back to normal. Normal? What was normal?

He husband sobered, not that he had consumed a whiff of alcohol. "I don't know what I was thinking. I just wanted you to have the best of everything. This was the wrong way to do it. I know that now."

"Yeah." She averted her face from his. She loved him so much. He'd always be her husband.

She gazed at the wall. "Was it hard what you did?"

"Not really. I was careful. Methodical. You know me."

"Yeah, I know you. That's what accountants do. But this isn't something I'd ever think you would do. But you succeeded, didn't you? Was it luck or your plan?"

He waited several seconds before he answered. "My plan, of course."

"What's it like?"

"What do you mean?"

"Doing it. The stealing. What feelings did you have?"

He glanced at her. "I never really thought about it before. I guess it's kinda like climaxing, an adrenaline rush." He raked his fingers through his hair and sighed. His blue eyes, glazed over, stared into the distance.

"It was like I was sixteen when I smoked Marijuana for the first time. Too much, actually. I had to run then, too, before my parents found me. But these past weeks, with the money in my backpack, it was like I was running away from my parents again. But it was the cops. And the wind against my face felt so good. I don't know..."

Elsa was afraid she'd lost him to the past, yet he was sitting beside her. He couldn't run again, not with her cupping his face. He was home, in their house, and she loved him. She always would. "I just don't believe you'd do something like this."

"Me, neither." Tears streaked his face.

Why was she continually harping on his actions? Stealing, having nice things without money worries—who wouldn't love that?

He averted his face before looking back at her. "But I did it for you. So I could buy you things. I was afraid you'd leave me."

"Leave you? God, Kelvin, I love you. More than life itself. Money isn't so important that it would ruin our marriage if we didn't have it."

He leaned over and kissed her. His lips were salty as if he'd been swimming in the ocean.

She broke away. "Kelvin?"

"What?"

"Do you have more plans in the works?"

"What do you mean?"

"More plans to rob?"

"I—yeah, I guess so," he said.

"Maybe I could go with you next time. Or you could teach me."

"No, I don't want my wife stealing."

"Why not? We could be like Bonnie and Clyde except I don't want us to be shot. We'd have to be extra careful." She kissed his cheek again and tasted more salt.

When he didn't answer, she said, "I trust you. Your plans are always perfect."

Her husband grinned. He picked up a rose and inserted it behind her ear.

The Final Countdown

While living, we're unaware we live on the edge though, of course, we know death will come eventually, but we don't know if we will be hit by a car or be murdered by a crazy.

Or, perhaps, develop a lump, and be told, "All is fine. We got it all." Then, a month later, be told your life is almost over. The doctors were wrong. They didn't get it all.

We live on the edge. The edge of today leaning on the edge of tomorrow.

We are on loan to the world. At death, we're relegated to a six-foot-deep plot we'll own forever. Or we're scattered by warm breezes, our ashy specks floating through the air to meld with the atmosphere where we'll exist throughout time, for where else would ash go except endure forevermore, whether in air or falling to earth.

Every part of us remains forever, for all of eternity, though not in our earthly form.

None of that consoles me.

***

I watched a crisp leaf scurry toward the trees as if a human running from a pursuer.

Perhaps that pursuer was life.

Or death.

Are life and death the same? You can't have one without the other.

When the leaf disappeared between two trees, I longed to chase after it, crush its frailty beneath my feet, put it out of its misery. Leaves live for a season: brown, dry, and meld into the soil, morphing into fragments to nourish the earth and produce foliage. In reality, that one leaf lives forever.

Onward, ho!

Humans are similar to leaves. We live for our season—whatever number of years that may be. We age and disappear into the soil. Memories survive for our family and friends. We live forever—as long as we are remembered.

I brush away tears. Grief overtook my joy several days ago, and I'm still digesting the news. What *do* you do when you're told you have six months left?

You ask, "Are you sure? Can't be!"

But, yep, you heard correctly, and the doctors can't do anything. Six months! What do you do?

Do you grin and bear it as cliché as that is? You can rant and rave, scream to whatever god is out there and hope for a reprieve, even a few more weeks of breath. Or a mere few days.

Anything!

You can crawl into bed, cover up with the linens, cower from a world you'll no longer be a part of. You can harangue at a universe that caused your demise in the first place (most probably my untimely death is environmental), holler at doctors and others who can't save you. You can hide, praying death forgets you. You can hope you'll wake after shedding tears to happily discover you've endured a horrific dream. Or you can sleep and dream of a better life—another life—that you'll enjoy, if only for a few hours, and pray to die in your sleep so you never awake from that dream.

You wonder of your family, how they'll feel. How will they cope? Will they miss you? Will they think of you for a long time, or will you eventually fade to less than a memory, one to be conjured on occasion whenever something jogs their memory?

And your spouse. Those fights and disagreements. Does he really love you—really and truly love you—or will he forget you as quickly as the next love interest appears?

Should you disappear? Would you save others untold grief if you vanished into oblivion by suicide? Should you end it now?

In the end, is painful, horrendous suffering worth it to gain a few more days? Everyone dies eventually. Even you!

And me.

We're all doomed for death.

Life throws harsh bullets, spews hatred in between the good. Where is God in these times?

No one knows how much time we have. We live our lives as if we have forever, which in reality we don't. And now, with the devastating news of cancer spreading through my body, I ponder life.

I remember that scurrying leaf. I don't want to be crushed underfoot. I want to live life. I want to be here forever: for my husband, my children, my grandchildren.

For me.

***

Despite being a plush armchair, the chair is hard. My back is sore. I desperately yearn to lie in bed, but my family thinks I'm better off in the living room where they can pretend, more or less, that everything is okay. How would everyone fit into the bedroom, anyhow? Even if they did, they wouldn't stay.

So we sit in the living room: Chad and Bruce from out of town, and Dylan, who lives down the street. Ed, my husband of forty-five years, sits here, too. He's a basket case. I can't alleviate his pain. I have too much of my own.

Everyone chatters about this and that. I'm listening, yet I'm not. How can I listen to drivel when my life is ending? How can I sit and pretend?

How can they?

But they do, of course. It's their coping mechanism. They don't know what else to do, so they don happy masks and pretend nothing has changed.

But everything has changed. Everything!

My three children haven't been together in over five years. Two of them live a thousand kilometres away, and it's not a normal occurrence for them to be gathered together, visiting me. But I'm dying, so they've made that last effort. I applaud them, but wouldn't it have been better had they visited when I was alive?

But no one knows what the future holds. No one knows when death will approach.

Cancer struck me eight months ago—at least that was when I knew something was wrong. I didn't know then it was cancer; no one did. The doctor said the lump in my jaw was nothing. "Go to Florida. Enjoy your vacation. Come see me when you return. We'll deal with it then."

I trusted the doctor. Why wouldn't I?

But it was cancer. I think I realized that before the diagnosis when the pain increasingly worsened and the lump quickly enlarged.

Even when I returned from vacation and had a biopsy, the doctors—several of them—told me not to worry. Later, when tests revealed it was malignant, they assured us that radiation and chemo and surgery would take care of it. "Don't worry," they said again.

And again.

How many times had I heard "Don't worry"?

Don't worry.

Easy enough for you bystanders to spout those words. You're not going through a life and death situation. You're not in pain, wondering how you're going to eat your next meal—or even if you're going to have one. Your life doesn't flash like endless old-time movie reels that drone on and on.

Chad talks about his job and about Alana, his ex-girlfriend who could have been his wife, and how she's threatening custody of twelve-year-old Bethany. Chad has had custody of his daughter for the past three years, ever since Alana went to rehab.

Bruce has a new job with Lincoln Construction. He's going to move up in the ranks and own the company someday despite the fact it's a family conglomerate that'll never release control. They'll never let an insider into their business affairs. What the hell is Bruce thinking?

Where's Dylan? Dylan, my middle child, is my favourite, the one who is always here for me. Of course, living nearby makes it easy. His wife, Claire, and I are close. Where the heck are they?

As if reading my mind, Chad pipes up, "Mom, Dylan will be along shortly."

I ignore him. It hurts to move my head. *Please take me back to bed.*

My respite worker has left for the day, leaving Ed in charge. He thinks I want to be up and about. He hasn't faced reality that my days are numbered. He hasn't faced the fact I can't help him anymore. I don't want to; I can't.

Leave me alone. Let me die, God, oh God, let me die. No one should face this agony, endure the dwindling dregs of life. I'm barely here. Even though I haven't had as much as a whiff of alcohol, I'm drunk and out of it.

Give me a glass of wine. Maybe that'll help my disposition and make me livelier. I might answer you then.

But no one thinks to offer me a real drink.

Death hides on the back burner until it hits home. Death doesn't normally give notice, but when it does, it's too late, and if you have time, you do nothing but muse over regrets: should have done this, should have done that. In retrospect, I didn't live my life how I wanted, the way I should have.

***

"You okay, Mom?" Bruce asks.

No, of course I'm not. But I can't tell him that. As much as I want to rage at the world, I can't be rude to my own son, and so I ignore him.

I can't talk. I can't eat. I'm sick of the feeding tube invading my stomach. Truth be known, I don't want to eat. I have no appetite. And oh, how I used to love food.

Bruce touches my hand.

Through slits in my eyes, I see him staring at me.

Kill me now. Kill me. God, let me die. But I don't want to die. I really don't.

I miss my grandchildren, Ally and Allen. They're six and four, but I don't want this to be their last remembrance of me. I want them to remember me when I was lively and vibrant, when we enjoyed sleepovers, when I made hot chocolate and baked cupcakes and we scooped icing into four bowls and added red, yellow, blue, and green food colouring. After icing the cupcakes, we sprinkled them with silver-coloured sparkles. Each of us ate one—or two—sneaking the second from the table so the others wouldn't see because that was the rule: one cupcake each. We saw each other do it, though, and we laughed.

And it was okay.

I miss them already: Allison with her big blue eyes that inquire about everything. And Allen, quieter than his sister, yet smart and inquisitive. Both of them sporting flaming red hair.

The door slams, jarring me to reality. It's Dylan. As much as I want to see him, I pray he didn't bring the kids.

***

Though three months isn't a long time, it can be an eternity. I have friends who vacation for three months. How does that compare to someone left with three months of life? I have to cram twenty years into twelve weeks, for shouldn't I live until at least eighty-five?

I don't want sympathy. I don't want pity. Or do I? I don't know what I want.

***

The glare. I can't see. What are you doing, Ed? Turn off that light. Let me sleep.

I sense him watching. Am I drooling? Does he see bloody scars? Is he wishing death would hurry?

Put me out of my misery. How I want to die.

I can't talk; I don't want to. I want to be left alone. I'm miserable, yes, but wouldn't you be, too? Family and friends tell me to embrace my last few weeks.

Such a cliché: Live life to the fullest.

Obnoxious noise pounds against my head, so close as if someone is screaming inches from my ears. Perhaps senses are magnified as death nears. I want to screech, *"Shut up. Someone's dying, don't you know?"* But they're children—my grandchildren—and what do children know of death?

I want to call them over, so I can see and touch them. So I can kiss their chubby cheeks and tousle their thick hair and give them great big bear hugs. I won't complain about sticky fingers or too-sweet slobber. I'll lap it up, kiss dirty faces, hold squirming hands. Sit, talk, stay with me. I want to be near. Just for a little while. Just until I go.

I can't keep rambunctious grandchildren still for as long as I'd want to keep them near.

***

I'm prone on the bed, an available guinea pig for inquisitive eyes. Tear me apart. Make fun of my desiccated body.

I don't want to die. Does anyone? Yeah, sure, there are suicidal maniacs and females aborting babies. Why can't God make the world an even field? Let those who want to die, die. Let those who don't want children to never become pregnant and allow those who desire children to experience the miracle of birth.

I haven't rationalized my demise yet. Not in my mind, not as it pertains to me. At one time, before the cancer, I thought I'd live forever. After the cancer diagnosis, I envisioned a magical cure to miraculously materialize to save me from this scourge. But doesn't everyone feel that way when their time nears?

Some things are beyond our control. Life isn't fair. I've heard that numerous times: an endless broken record.

I'm dying. The words roll on my tongue and through my head. Over and over, and there's nothing I can do about it. No way to stop time; no way to stop the cancer that's ravaging my flesh, destroying cells and eating me alive until it's won the battle.

When your life's about to end, do you know? Do you have a sudden inkling and inhale, knowing that it's your last breath? Or do you breathe normally, realizing a second too late that you don't have another?

Or do you gulp that last breath and dare death to suck it away?

***

The end of the last month approaches. I'm worse, so my time is limited despite hope that maybe—just maybe—God will grant a reprieve.

My head pounds. Fire demons rush through my veins. Never letting go. Burning. Raw. Intensifying. High doses of morphine are shoved into me. But I still feel.

I still know.

***

The countdown begins though it truly began at diagnosis when I was given six months. A week after that, six months morphed into three when the doctors informed us they'd made a mistake: three months, not six. And just like that, I had lost three months!

The end becomes more real when life's down to the last week. Seven days. One Hundred sixty-eight hours. Ten thousand and eighty minutes.

Or will I not last that long?

I'm going back into the hospital tomorrow.

I heard them talking. Ed and the children. "It's for the best," one of them said. I don't know which one. They all sound alike.

"She won't come home again," another said. I'm not sure who said that, either.

All voices sound alike. Everyone looks the same.

The pain is worse. It's hard to catch my breath. My body's weighted down as if I've been dumped into a massive hole with a high rise constructed on top. Buried for all time, to never see the sun. To see nothing but darkness and suck in snippets of mouldy air and breathe miniscule dust particles.

Other than our parents and grandparents, Ed's never been around death before. Not someone he's been sleeping with for the last fifty years. He's awkward in this new situation. I see his agony; it seeps out of him and enters my pores. He gives me shivers when I'm warm, and I can't remember the last time I've been warm. He drapes blankets over me, tucking the edges under each side of the bed and leaving the material bunching in the middle as if the thickness will protect me. Don't bother; don't waste your time. I'll soon be gone, and your efforts will have been for naught.

In retrospect, when I received the deadly diagnosis I should have swallowed a bottle of pills or dug a hole I couldn't have crawled out of. Death would have found me faster. I could have prevented Ed's pain. I could have saved my children's pain. Everyone could have resumed life earlier. Heck, they'd be walking the mending path by now.

And what difference, in the end? Time passes too fast, gone before we know it, and in the end, nothing really matters. Passing time disappears along with the dead.

He's choking me. No, not Ed. Ed loves me. Not him; someone else. Someone or something is covering me with that infamous shroud of death, suffocating me, pushing down on me so hard I can't breathe. I can't cough. Drool seeps from my lips, trickling down my chin and coating my neck. Thick. Blood. I smell iron, the metallic rustiness of a car rotting at the bottom of an ocean, the salt corroding its metal skin.

The glare prevents me from opening my eyes. When had I closed them? I'm lightheaded, drunk, but I haven't had a drink in months. Alcohol interferes with medication, either rendering it useless or making me sicker. Neither seems detrimental in the long term.

The stairs loom in front of me, a long and winding staircase like the Beatles' *long and winding road*. I can't climb. I'm facing Mt. Everest, a mountain few have mastered. The stairs are deep, deeper than normal steps. I'll have to take two strides on each tread. I look down at my feet. I've shrunk to half my size; my feat would be quadrupled. It's not worth the effort.

I turn to leave before I realize there's nowhere else to go. The end sprawls in front of me, the long and winding road spiralling into dark clouds. Menacing clouds, yet after I pass through them, I know all will be fine. I'll live in peace.

We all will. In the end.

The Pill

Hey, listen to this, Jennifer. It's a pill that'll make people twenty years younger."

Jennifer, concentrating on her needlework, almost stabbed herself with the needle at her husband's outburst. "What?" She eyed him across the room.

"A pill that makes a person younger." Tony skimmed the article. "It's out now. Trials are done, and it's deemed safe. But it's only available when you've reached your seventieth birthday. Can you imagine? A pill a day will erase twenty years. And it's only a dollar a pill. Three hundred and sixty-five dollars a year! We can afford that." Tony, who would be seventy in seven months, lowered the newspaper. "Wouldn't that be wonderful? I'll be your age."

"What's with your math? I'd be older than you then."

He laughed. "Nothing wrong with that. I like older, experienced women."

She frowned. "I thought you liked younger women."

"I do, but you look way younger than you are. I'd have the best of both worlds."

Jennifer glared at her husband. Before she could throw something, he ducked behind the newspaper.

"Only kidding!" he said, lowering the paper.

She groaned. "Where are your glasses?" Though she used to receive compliments that she looked ten years younger than she actually was, her appearance had finally caught up to her age. Despite that, and without an egotistical vein in her body, she still considered herself prettier and more youthful than other fifty-eight-year-olds.

Tony, too, had looked younger than fifty-seven when they met, and she marvelled at his attractiveness despite thinning hair, sagging jowls, and deep facial furrows. His libido had gradually slowed after their marriage, as had hers. She had read that a man's sex drive remained stronger than a woman's of the same age. Because of their eight-year age difference, she figured their desires had equalled out and that they had reached a mutually adequate and satisfying stage.

She loved him dearly the way he was and didn't want a younger, supposedly improved man. Sure, if a pill existed to maintain healthy lives or to prevent diseases, she was in agreement. But a "fountain-of-youth" pill? She wasn't in favour of medication, or even surgeries, to alter appearances simply for the sake of vanity, and after only five years of trials, how could the drug be touted as safe?

"You don't look like you're nearly sixty," Tony said, interrupting her thoughts. "You still look like you're in your forties, and now I can look fifty."

She thrust the needle into the linen. "You like younger women, and I like older men. I'd be eight years older than you if you do this, and you wouldn't be happy then. Besides, I don't want some foreign substance in your body."

"But the article says it's safe. The FDA wouldn't allow it on the market if it weren't."

She sighed. "It's a government agency, Tony. You know bureaucracy. Who can trust them?"

Tony scowled at her. "I'm sure it's fine. I'm going to check into it. I'd give anything to be fifty again."

"In theory, you might look fifty but not in actual fact."

"If I look and feel fifty, I'd be fifty. And what's wrong with that?"

She set her needlework on the coffee table. What was the sense in arguing? He knew more than her—or thought he did. She envisioned their future if he took such a pill. She would be eight years his senior, and that spread, the opposite of their current situation, would present challenges for them both. Other than the odd movie star, not many men wanted cougars. He would desire a woman younger than she was—maybe not at first, but eventually.

Her chest tightened. "Tony, we're happy as we are. Why change us?"

"This won't change us. It's just going to make me look better and add years to my life, which means I'll be with you longer. And if I look better, I'll feel better and I'll be happier."

"I thought you were happy now."

"I am happy. But everyone can be happier."

Tony had been a confirmed bachelor—his words. Neither he nor Jennifer had been previously married or had children. How amazing was that in a world of out-of-wedlock children, partners instead of spouses, and multiple marriages and divorces? It was as if they were meant to be together and had unconsciously waited until they found each other. And without baggage, their life together was perfect. She didn't want their happiness jinxed. She wanted Tony to stay as he was.

She changed tactics. "But how is it fair that only seventy-year-olds can take it? How's it fair that I have to wait?"

"I suppose they have to draw the line somewhere or the world would be in chaos with too many young people. And if you make it until seventy, maybe they figure you're healthy and entitled to look better and live longer."

"I hope they have the same rule in twelve years when I turn seventy." She stared at the wall for several seconds. "What if they keep raising the age? I'll never have a chance to catch up."

"I don't think there's any worry. The age has been set. They can't be changing it nilly willy."

"I suppose. But all this is new. Never tested."

"The trials are done." He walked across the room and thrust the newspaper in her face. "Here, look how young this guy looks. He's seventy-four but looks even younger than fifty. Honestly, Jenn, we'll be a better match if I do this."

"We're a good match now."

"Oh, you know what I mean." He returned to the couch.

Jennifer twisted her long blonde hair. "No, I don't know what you mean." But she did and didn't like it. Why should her husband be able to shave years off his life so effortlessly and not her? She worked hard at staying young. She exercised daily. Every six weeks she had her hair professionally cut and dyed, and she visited a manicurist each week. She applied makeup so flawlessly no one noticed she wore any. And she was extra careful to select clothes that camouflaged a not-so-perfect body.

She hadn't known Tony when he was fifty. When they met, she was forty-five and he was fifty-seven; they married a year later. She had a thing for older men. Still did. She would never have dated—let alone married—a younger man, and now the powers-that-be could alter, with a container of pills, the age of the person she had decided to spend the rest of her life with?

She had heard of the pill Tony referred to. She had read about it weeks previously but hadn't mentioned it. She had been frightened of his reaction if he discovered such a pill existed, and her prediction had come true. He was too eager and excited over a supposed fountain of youth. How could researchers definitively declare there'd be no long-term effects? In a way, she was glad she was forced to wait twelve years. After that period, surely any serious side effects would be discovered and rectified.

She glanced at Tony. He was too quiet. She had to say something—anything. Fight for what she believed was right. Their marriage would be doomed if he followed through.

"There should be a rule that husbands and wives take the pills as a couple, no matter their ages, so they progress together. It's not fair altering what already is," she mumbled.

He ignored her and continued reading the paper.

"I really wish you'd wait a couple of years, just to ensure it really is safe. You know how I feel about pills." She swiped her hands across her jeans, wishing she could pick up her needlework to calm her nerves, but her fingers were too clammy.

He lowered the paper. "I told you already. I'm not worried. The FDA says it's safe."

Despite the heat, she shivered. "But that sort of stuff has happened before. Look what happened to that drug they brought out a couple of years ago. Mesi...mesatil—whatever it was. It altered brain matter in certain people. They went berserk, remember?"

She didn't want to lose her husband, not to divorce or death, most certainly not to deformities or death because of a frivolous pill, and she also didn't want to lose him to another woman. Tony was a handsome guy and would be even more so with twenty years eradicated.

"Besides, I like you the way you are."

Tony threw her a dirty look. "You know what? I think you're jealous. Why can't you be happy for me?"

"What's that supposed to mean? Happy for you? I'm happy, but I also care about your health. And us. Will we be as happy with you twenty years younger?"

"It's only my looks. I'll still be me."

She shrugged. "You don't know yet that you can even take the pill. Maybe they won't give it to you.

"You're allowed to apply at sixty-nine, so I'm going to do it. I can't imagine why they'd turn me down."

Tony got off the couch again, crept behind the chair, and wrapped his arms around her shoulders. He leaned and kissed the top of her head. "I love you. I always will."

She leaned back. "Promise? No matter how old I look?"

He laughed. "Of course."

"Even if I don't want to take that stupid pill when it's my time?"

"Even if you're a hundred and I'm fifty, I'll still love you."

**

Time sped faster than Jennifer had expected. She worried constantly about the effects of the drug on Tony's system—on anyone's system— but he couldn't be dissuaded. Other seventy-year-olds had begun treatment the previous year, without reports of ill effects.

Despite that, she continually fretted. If not about his health, about their relationship, certain Tony would seek out a younger woman. Tony constantly reassured her that their relationship was safe, but she had her doubts. Women didn't improve with age. When they first met, he had professed his preference for younger women, and it had always been fodder for banter between them. It wasn't only Tony she worried about; it was younger and more attractive women who might vie for his affections.

A month after Tony turned seventy, they drove to Millwood Clinic, about an hour's drive from their condo. Three weeks previously, Tony had received an information package in the mail, along with a ten o'clock appointment. He had already completed the first batch of forms, along with the requisite blood tests, and had received preliminary approval. All that remained was to be assessed and examined by the assigned psychiatrist and medical doctor, respectively.

The psychiatrist asked mundane questions. Jennifer gauged his reactions to their answers, both hers and Tony's. Neither Tony nor Jennifer confessed to Tony's recent memory issues, for that would be grounds for immediate disqualification. She could very easily have revealed his memory lapses, but she loved Tony enough that she had no desire to quash his wish.

They must have handled themselves well, for the psychiatrist signed off on the forms and told them to proceed down the hall to Dr. Gregory Garth's waiting room.

Dr. Gregory Garth took Tony's blood pressure and checked his heart, vision, and ears. "Perfect health," he exclaimed, scanning the paperwork.

Tony threw Jennifer a "told-you-so" look.

"One a day." Dr. Garth handed him a slip of paper. "The prescription gives you dosage for thirty days. Don't take more than one a day because you'll run out. Accidentally lose them, you don't get replacements."

"Are there any side effects?" Tony asked, his prior seriousness turning into a smirk that was solely for her benefit.

"None," the doctor replied. "None except for thieves. Guard the tablets. Lock your doors. I fully expect a future of break-ins. And worse."

"Break-ins?" Jennifer hadn't thought of that, but it made sense people would steal—even kill—to regain youth, especially if denied due to ill health or lack of years. And she found the doctor's declaration of no side-effects hard to believe. What prescription drug didn't warn of at least one ill effect?

The doctor nodded. "You never know what might happen. This is all new, you know."

"I'll guard them with my life." Tony laughed.

"And remember, the change will be gradual. It'll be at least six months before you notice any results."

On the walk to the pharmacy, Jennifer grasped her husband's arm. "Don't broadcast what you're getting. We don't want to be robbed." She scanned the street. "And when we leave, we better be careful. We don't want to chance being followed and carjacked."

When they arrived home, Tony swallowed the first pill. "Perhaps I should put the rest in the safe."

"Good idea." She giggled, a nervous action, for the situation wasn't at all funny. The doctor's comment had unnerved her. She envisioned home invasions and attacks on seniors. Perhaps it wasn't far-fetched to hide the pills. She had read that once the process had started, one couldn't quit. She had forgotten to ask the doctor what would happen in that case. How could that have been determined in the short trial?

Despite her happiness for her husband—if he was happy, she was happy—she was glad she hadn't reached the requisite age and wondered if she'd want to enroll in the program when that time arrived. Rumours had swirled that the medication might one day become mandatory. Would messing with the ecosystem cause the world to become more off-kilter? Global warming had caused enough damage. Perhaps nature had a reason for aging. Sure, she'd love to look younger and perhaps live longer than destined—who wouldn't?—but at what cost? People shouldn't play God. Nature should run its course.

***

Six months passed. As Dr. Garth had stated, the effects were so gradual neither noticed any change until one day Tony appeared refreshed as if he'd returned from a long, relaxing vacation or had a facelift. Tony's words proved correct: they did look closer in age.

Though he sported several strands of silver at the temples, his sparse hair had thickened to a dark brown. Facial crevices had lessened into fine lines. He had lost fifteen pounds, and two buckle-notches less in his belt allowed his slacks to settle where they once had. His arms and legs were more muscular, which could have been the result of working out more often since he possessed more energy.

He was also more alert. What Jennifer had prayed was merely simple forgetfulness—but worried might be a sign of dementia—had disappeared.

Tony stared in the mirror. "Amazing! It's happened."

She examined his face and body. She tittered. "Now I see how you looked before I met you. Women must have been after you like bloodhounds."

Tony's face glowed and his eyes sparkled like champagne on New Year's Eve. "Nope, never had women chase after me."

Jennifer scowled, not believing him. "Well, don't let them start now."

"Oh, Jenn, you're crazy. I have eyes for no one but you."

"But you've changed. You look so different." He wasn't the man she had married, but she kept that thought to herself.

"Only on the outside. I'm still me. And you haven't changed."

"Of course I haven't changed! I haven't taken the pill, remember?"

"Jenn, quit. I see the wheels turning in your head. I love you. That'll never change." He grasped her to his chest. "I love you so much."

"I love you, too. Don't ever let me go."

He wiped the tear sliding down her cheek. "Hey, stop it, I said."

Weeks later, she supposed it made sense his personality would change along with his appearance, for a youthful outer skin provoked youthful feelings. Despite his words of undying love, she constantly worried he'd seek out a younger woman.

She didn't feel older than him, but she counted recent crinkles around her eyes and deeper creases from her nose to the corners of her mouth. Her ruffled neck distressed her the most. *Gobble, gobble*. If he hadn't already, it was inevitable he'd soon notice her flaws.

The medication—for her—existed too far in the future. Could their marriage survive until then? She made up her mind she would take the pill when it was offered.

Days melded into weeks. Weeks into months. A year.

Those twinges and tingles that had once coursed through her veins whenever Tony touched her disappeared.

She knew why. She'd always been drawn to older, mature men with craggy, worn features that proved they had lived. Her husband didn't look like her Tony—or even act like him anymore. She had enjoyed running the tips of her fingers over his wrinkles, pretending to flatten them, and she missed spooning against his padded body. She had adored his reserved attitude, his mellowness, his maturity. Weren't those the reasons she had fallen in love with him in the first place? She had deemed him perfect—the father figure she'd dreamt of.

She laughed at the irony before tears rolled down her cheeks. Oh, how she had fretted that after he returned to fifty he'd leave her for a younger woman. But Tony appeared happy: happy with himself, happy with her.

She had warned him the pill would change their relationship. Why couldn't he have listened?

To Be Startled

He wants me to be executor of his will," Kelly said, "he" being Fred Snyder, her next door neighbour in the trailer park.

"Really? That's an honour," I said.

"Yeah, he says he'll be leaving everything to me."

"Wow, you serious?"

"Yeah, but he doesn't have much, and I'm not sure I'm going to accept. Although I did say yes."

"Why not?"

"He's a bit strange."

"But you always liked him."

"Yeah, that was when Isabel was still alive. I dunno. He's changed."

"He's already given you a ton of stuff. I can't believe you'd say no."

"He hasn't given me much."

"You have all Isabel's good China, her silver, her doll collection. Even her jewellery."

"But Isabel gave me that, not him. And it was mostly stuff for the girls. She had no children, so she kinda adopted mine."

Isabel had been giving items to Kelly's children, six-year-old Ava and four-year-old Emma, for over a year. Who would give away dolls from a cherished—and obviously expensive—collection? And her exquisite jewellery: a fourteen-karat gold pendant necklace to Ava and a charm bracelet to Emma, among other lovely pieces. Even as astute as I was, I hadn't clued in, but it all made sense later when Kelly told me Isabel had terminal cancer.

"I still can't believe you'd turn him down."

"I'm just thinking about it. But I'm not sure I want to be around him anymore. He's drinking too much. Comes over too much."

"What do you expect? He just lost his wife. You said he had no relatives."

"There's no one around here, but I think he has a daughter somewhere with his first wife. Isabel told me she didn't want her to have anything of hers, that's why she started giving things to me."

Kelly grunted and pointed out the kitchen window. "Speak of the devil. Look at him, drunk again."

I peeked out the window, which overlooked the Snyder property. Fred, unsteady on his feet, weaved toward the front of his trailer where he disappeared.

I'd been introduced to Fred and Isabel though I hadn't had much contact with Fred other than casual greetings. Isabel, a lovely woman, had popped in a few times while I'd been visiting Kelly. There had been something sad about Isabel, a resignation. A faraway space veiled her eyes, perhaps a place she retreated to when life became too difficult. I had mentioned my observation to Kelly, but she said she had never noticed. Later, I figured Isabel's broodiness had to do with the cancer diagnosis.

"And look at that trailer. It's pitiful," Kelly said. "The inside isn't as bad as the outside, but the inside is still pretty gross, and the furniture is old and worthless. Not sure when Isabel ended up with all that great stuff. That doll collection is something else."

"She likely had it all before marrying Fred," I said.

"Yeah, that makes sense."

Fred and Isabel had been neighbours ever since Kelly and her husband, Mark, purchased their property. "It's not a trailer," Kelly had emphatically stated when I exclaimed how spacious the trailer was soon after they moved in. "It's a mini-home. There is a difference. Besides, it's only temporary until we can save the down payment for a house. Three years is my plan." Kelly always had a plan. She wore the pants in that household.

Kelly and Mark's mini home was larger, newer, and nicer than Fred's. Their neatly mowed lawn and colourful flowers bordering the walkway contrasted sharply with Fed's scraggly, brown grass and the sad remnants of flower gardens that Isabel had lovingly tended. The yard had gone downhill the last couple of years of Isabel's life. She must have known her illness was terminal. Why else would she allow flowers to wither to a cruel death and give away cherished possessions to a neighbour she had only known a year?

Kelly friended everyone. She had that way about her, made you feel as if you were her best friend and that she'd do anything for you. But Kelly was merely Kelly; Kelly out for Kelly.

I'd felt sorry for Isabel, caught in Kelly's clutches, but as Kelly had confirmed, most of the items Isabel had given her were designated for the girls and had been safely stowed into each girl's respective hope chest. Isabel had been genuinely fond of Ava and Emma. The girls, without grandparents nearby, had even adopted Isabel as their surrogate grandmother. Fred as a grandfather? Not so much.

I had been shocked when Kelly didn't attend Isabel's funeral. The least she could have done was support Fred in his time of grief and pay final respects to his wife, who had been so kind.

"Wasn't Fred upset you didn't go to the funeral?"

Kelly shrugged. "He understood."

"Really?" It boggled my mind that Kelly could be so heartless.

"His own daughter didn't show up, so why should I?"

I had no words.

Kelly glanced toward the girls' bedroom. "Sometimes I feel they're upset Isabel's not around anymore."

"Might have been closure for them had you taken them to the funeral." I couldn't bite my tongue.

"Oh, no, they're too young. I couldn't have."

I disagreed but stuck my tongue between my teeth and clamped down while I silently counted to twelve.

"I gotta go." I couldn't bear to hear any more from thoughtless Kelly. I had more compassion for Isabel—even Fred—than Kelly had.

A couple of weeks later, Kelly telephoned. "I signed the papers today."

"What papers?" I asked.

"Fred's papers. For his estate."

"How come you had to sign? I never heard of that."

"I don't know. I had to agree that I'd handle his estate."

That seemed odd, but what did I know?

Months later, I dropped by Kelly's home to retrieve my sewing machine that she'd borrowed.

"We're moving soon, I hope," Kelly said. "Gonna put the mini home up for sale."

"You have the down payment this fast?"

"It's been over three years. That was my plan." She leaned in to me. "Don't tell anyone, but Fred gave me an envelope of money the other day. Five thousand dollars exactly. With that and what we have saved up and the profit from the mini home, we'll have enough for the down payment."

"What?"

"Yeah, so the agent is coming to list our place tomorrow. I hope it sells fast. I need to get out of this dump. And away from Fred. He's starting to come over more and more. I have to pretend we're not home sometimes. He's weird."

"But he just gave you a whack of money. How can you desert him like that?"

"Oh, it's okay. I think his daughter is coming soon. He wasn't sure when, but soon he thought."

I felt my eyes expand into circles as large as my mouth, but Kelly didn't notice and continued rambling.

"I hope she doesn't wonder where all Isabel's stuff went. But she probably didn't know what she had. I'm sure she's just coming to see what she can get. At least that's what Fred thinks."

"Wouldn't she have come before now if that was the case?"

"Fred told me he just let her know of Isabel's death. So that's why she didn't come before."

"That's weird."

"That's what I said. The whole thing is weird."

"No, you said Fred was weird, not the situation."

Kelly peered at me. "What are you, a lawyer?"

Before I could answer, she added, "Which reminds me. I went to my lawyer and had my name removed as executor."

"I don't understand why you'd do that after all they've done for you."

"You've seen their trailer—"

What happened to mini home? Oh, that's right. Only hers was a mini home; she always referred to Fred's as a trailer.

"Look at it now. It's gone worse than rat shit. Fred does absolutely nothing to it. I don't want to be responsible for that. And who knows how long he'll live. He's not well, but he could still live for years. It's gross in there. And, like I said before, he's acting weird."

"What do you expect? He's still grieving. He's elderly and men don't clean at the best of times." I spoke from experience. "So was he upset when you told him?"

"I haven't told him. Not that I really need to. I can turn it down after he's dead, but I thought I should come clean so he can pick someone else. My property lawyer is supposed to contact his lawyer. I don't imagine he knows yet. You know how slow lawyers are."

"How cruel." My words seeped out. But at least she had the decency to "come clean," as she put it.

"Cruel? Lawyers?" Then she clued in. "Oh, you mean me? But there's nothing left. What's in it for me? I'd have to clean the trailer, sell it. Gah! I can't imagine doing that."

"But you have everything. You got it early."

"I suppose you could look at it that way. Like an advance on a book deal. But if there's nothing left, and I know that, why bother? I have better things to do with my time."

"His trailer must be worth something."

"Yeah, right. You haven't seen the inside. Let his daughter deal with it. I'm sure he'll make her sole beneficiary and executor once he knows I'm off."

"Yes, likely." But I didn't know, of course. Who could know what cranked in an old person's mind? Who knew what churned in a younger person's mind?

Four months later when I pulled into Kelly's driveway, Fred was sitting on an old card table chair on the front porch. He motioned me over with one finger. I hesitated for a second and then sauntered across the yard. He wasn't well, that much was obvious.

"They're moving, aren't they?" He pointed to the glaring orange S-O-L-D plastered across the for sale sign dangling in front of their mini home.

"Yes, the closing is next week. I'm helping her pack."

"I haven't seen the girls around much," he mumbled.

"The weather's getting cooler. Kids like to stay indoors and play where it's warm." Even I didn't believe my words. The girls enjoyed frolicking outdoors, no matter the weather.

He didn't say anything. His tired eyes were red-rimmed. Sallow cheeks dragged his already doleful face downward. I felt sorry for the man and might have hugged him but for the smell. Cigarette smoke emanated from his dishevelled clothing, and his stained, nicotine fingers were hard to ignore. A grizzly stubble indicated he hadn't shaved in days. Despite the hour, around eleven o'clock, he'd been drinking. Or perhaps the smell lingered on his clothing from the previous day—or evening.

"Isabel loved those children. She'd always wanted children." His eyes glazed over. "So beautiful she was, like spring in the dead of winter. Until she got sick and couldn't smile any longer. After she passed, I let myself go to drink again. I shouldn't have, but the pain was unbearable. The pain in my heart as well as in my legs. My dear Isabel always made sure I took my pills. I forget now, now that she's gone, and I forget the pills and the pain takes over and the bottle, well, the bottle numbs all pain. All hurt." He looked at me. "You don't understand, do you? Ah, you're too young. That is good. I hope you never have to experience my kind of pain."

He coughed and wiped his sleeve across his mouth. "I had given up the booze when we married. I made that promise to her. And I never let her down. Not until she let me down when she got sick. Everyone lets me down. Everyone."

"She couldn't help getting sick," I said. "No one can stop cancer."

"I suppose not." He yanked at his gnarly fingers, thin and crooked like skinny, dried-up twigs that could be snapped like toothpicks. One bone sounded as if it had cracked. Had he broken it? No, he pulled at it again. More snaps. Too many brittle bones.

Smack!

He unexpectedly clapped his hands.

I jumped. My stomach somersaulted and my heart hurtled.

"Startled you, didn't I?"

I gasped for breath. "You did." Fool old man.

"Everyone startles me. How you think you know someone until they startle you."

Where was this conversation going?

"I thought I knew my daughter once. Kathy, with my wife Edith. But she startled me, too. They both did, and then I was alone. It was the booze, I know that now. Too much vodka in soda bottles. Do you know why people sometimes don't forgive? "

I pondered. "I don't know. Some don't, do they? They live in the past, I suppose. Keep the past too close and don't move forward. Some have their own agenda." I thought of Kelly, who pretended to care about others.

He read my mind. "Kelly's one of those agenda people, isn't she?" He didn't wait for an answer. "I used to be a good judge of character. I've lost my skills. Trusted too many who've taken advantage of me."

He droned on as if I weren't standing beside him. He rambled about his first wife, how she'd cleaned him out, furniture as well as bank account; how his daughter had deserted him; how he'd been unable to work after a car accident left him disabled. That explained his limp and the limited motion in his right arm that I hadn't noticed previously, which could give the impression of drunkenness.

His entire right side almost gone, he said. It would stiffen and he could barely move. He'd popped too many pain pills and had become hooked. Pills on top of alcohol. Not a good combination.

I thought he'd never stop talking. I was certain he had forgotten I was there half the time, but then he'd say something and I'd realize he knew darn well I was there.

He muttered something undecipherable and gazed down the unpaved road.

The sun, warm for a September morning, beat down.

"You should be wearing a hat," I told him. "The sun is hot." I pictured him in a Wild West movie, jumping onto a horse and clutching his Stetson while he hightailed down the dirt road into oblivion. In his younger days, of course, not now.

"Ah, don't matter. My days are numbered. Ya, the cancer has me now, too, but that's okay. Sooner it does its thing, the sooner I'll see my Isabel. She'll be waiting for me, at them pearly gates. She'll be wearing one of them white dresses, a short one, with lace around the bottom. She'll be able to show off her legs now. Everything's perfect in Heaven, you know, and she always said how ugly her legs were, but I didn't mind them blue veins and so-called spider trails. She was always my beautiful Isabel, and now I'll see how she looked before. Before I knew her. When she was younger. And she'll see me that way, too. We should have met up before we met others. Kathy might have been hers then, hers and mine, and Kathy's eyes would have been Isabel's eyes.

"Isabel was my golden angel." He rubbed his eyes and ran his hands over his sparse hair. "I couldn't give my angel the one thing she wanted. A baby. Her own little cherub. She was younger than me. By sixteen years."

I was surprised at the age difference because they had appeared to be around the same age. But then again, by the time I met Isabel, the cancer had already begun to ravage her even though she hadn't shared her diagnosis.

"She loved the girls. Treated them like her own. Knitted them sweaters. Gave them her things. Things she knew I had no use for. She'd never give away anything I needed."

I'd been quiet too long. "Yes, the girls sure did gravitate toward her."

He stared at me in the eyes, held my gaze until I thought I couldn't bear it any longer. "Would you ever startle me, Vicki?" I was taken aback he remembered my name.

"No, of course not. Not on purpose anyhow."

He continued to stare at me, delving deep into my soul. What was he discovering?

"No, you don't look like you would. Your eyes are different. Different from Kathy's and Edith's and Kelly's. The same as Isabel's." He paused. "Different from the girls, but they have young eyes. Innocent eyes. No one can predict what eyes they'll end up with, when or if the world will change them into other eyes. She—Kelly—wouldn't let them come around me after Isabel died. That hurt. But you know what hurt me more?"

He waited for me to speak. To give him permission to continue.

"No, what?"

"How startled I was when she didn't go to Isabel's funeral. Kathy didn't go either, but I suppose that was my doin'. I was startled. Hurt." He looked up at me again. "There was no one there. No one to help me mourn my dear Isabel. Don't people know funerals are for the living? I needed someone there, but no one came."

I bent over to take his hand. "'I'm so sorry. Someone should have been there with you."

His eyes glistened, but as quickly as they had glazed over, they darkened. I had never seen eyes change so dramatically. The whites darkened to grey, the blue to navy. Or had they been those colours all along and I hadn't noticed? Do we notice when people are hurting or are we so wrapped up in ourselves that we don't care about others? When had the world changed? Or, like his eyes, had it always been that way, that we make our own unique universes and don't see outside our pristine circles?

"I deleted her, you know."

"Deleted who?"

"Kelly. Kathy, too. Deleted them from my will." That faraway look returned and he glanced behind him, at his trailer. "No, it isn't much. And I've let it go to crap, but looks are deceiving, ain't they?"

"Sometimes, yes."

He pointed at Kelly and Mark's trailer. "A trailer is a trailer, isn't it? Some better than others. Just a metal shell, really, cold and harsh like metal is. Add the coverings, though, and it becomes warm. Add loved ones, and it becomes a home. No, my trailer ain't much." He sighed and fidgeted with his fingers. He smiled. A great big smile that lit up his face. His eyes glistened again. The whites of his eyes were whiter and cleaner, and the blue became bluer, an azure like the Caribbean Sea. He looked younger. "Yeah, I had to do it."

"I don't blame you," I said, "especially since they didn't bother attending your wife's funeral."

"They don't know the money I have. Well, not mine at first, but now, with Isabel gone, it's mine. She had no children from her marriage. I couldn't give her angels to love—oh, I told you that already, didn't I?" He looked down at his hands. "Oh, but we were too old by that time anyways. It was just a dream of ours that would never come true." He snickered.

"She left it all to me to do as I wish. 'See people's true colours, Fred,' she told me. 'See if they startle you.' She was a good judge of people, much better than me. She enjoyed Kelly's company, her talk, but she saw through her toward the end. I believe she did. And she so loved the girls. But no one came. I got rid of them both," he repeated. "Kelly and Kathy. My lawyer is executor now. He'll administer my estate, pay to clean up my trailer. Sell it." He spread his arms. "The land. It's worth something."

I knew from Kelly that the lots in this park were owned by the respective trailer owners and not leased as in other trailer parks. The lots were larger than most parks, too, but still restricted to trailers, single or double-wides—or mini homes, as in Kelly's case.

Fred jarred me to attention when he spoke.

"Isabel's money? Well, I've left it to the SPCA. Oh, I left the girls a little bit, for their education, just in case they grow up and have those special eyes. They have nice eyes, Isabel told me, but you can never know—I'll never know. But I'm not leaving it all to them, not like I had planned. I'd be helping Kelly too much if I did that. I already gave her that five thousand...a lapse in my judgement, giving that. But I'd like the girls to have an education. My lawyer will respect my wishes."

He was a smart man, that Fred, but a lonely man who needed a friend, as we all do.

He clutched his cane and hauled himself to his feet. "I must go inside. I've rambled too much. You have things to do. All young people have things to do."

"It's fine." I touched his arm. "You're a good man, Fred. The girls will remember you, I'm certain. And Isabel, too."

He smiled, revealing uneven yellowed teeth and one missing lower tooth. He ambled to the door, unsteady but sober. He slipped at one point, but I made no move to help. I sensed he wanted to do it alone.

He turned. "You have nice eyes."

"Thanks, Fred." I pointedly did not add *See you later*, as I'm prone to do because we'd never see each other again. With Kelly and Mark moving, I'd have no need to return to the trailer park.

You have nice eyes...different from Kathy's and Edith's and Kelly's.

I've always liked my eyes.

Mastress of Light and Dark

Mastress - female of Master

I pretended I was a terrible housekeeper. Only then could I forget I was incarcerated in a Mexican prison.

Looking out the tiny window, filmed from years of grime, was like trying to peer through a greyed veil that had been stored in an attic for a century. The round, thick metal bars on the outside of the glass were spaced far enough apart they didn't obstruct my view, not once I stuck my nose between them. I could pretend when I didn't notice those black vertical barriers.

The scene through that lacy window wasn't a sight to behold— nothing but a stone wall covered with dried vines and a dirt floor between me and the far wall. I was unable to see the sky. The view wasn't worth the effort of moving the sole chair and climbing atop it, but I had nothing else to do. Though moving the chair equated to exercise, climbing on the seat was a chore. At sixty-seven, my knees aren't as pliable as they once were.

But I had to see something other than four concrete walls, one marred with the steel door that shut me off from the world. If it weren't for that door that clunked against me three times a day, I could be home, surrounded by pictures of my family, seated in a comfy chair with a book on my lap and a glass of wine in my hand. Or even in bed, comforted by the down spread, my head resting on feather pillows. In the cell, I had one pillow, flat and stubborn as slate, and one sleazy sheet to warm me.

The naked light bulb above me, which I could turn on or off by unscrewing it from the socket, illuminated cockroaches scurrying across the dirt floor. (Unscrewing the bulb was a discovery I made after the first night when I realized lights weren't magically adjusted via a main switch as seen in movies.) In one corner, a pile of dirt grew while my eyes, entranced by the busy ants, remained glued to it. What the ants did, I didn't know, but they hustled as if chores had to be completed before dark. And the dark was in my hands. For when I sickened of staring at them—for what else was there to do?—that's when I unscrewed the bulb and shivered with trepidation, my heart pounding into my ears while I waited for a guard to jangle keys into the lock and rush in with a bayonet or some such weapon. But that never happened.

I became mastress of the light and dark.

The ants were there the next morning. Whether they woke when the bulb shone and began working as if they had never ceased or whether they laboured throughout the night remains a mystery. I wasn't privy, nor did I want to be, to the ants' world.

I knew night fell because of my watch. Due to my slim wrists, the stretchy bracelet sat midway between my wrist and my elbow, hidden behind my long-sleeved shirt. The officials missed it. I'm not sure how I would've survived without my watch, but although I constantly looked at it, I could've estimated the hours by the regular timing of the meals passed through the door.

Sleep never came the first night before I discovered I could control the light. Boldness came the second night when I unscrewed the bulb and slept off and on. I was never sure I'd make it to the third night. I became weaker, due to lack of sleep and sustenance. Despite having lived in Mexico for almost five years, I didn't particularly care for Mexican food. Beans make me fart and poop, and tomatoes are acidy. Tortillas add pounds.

Tortillas—always tortillas—and a conglomerate of mashed eggs, peppers, and onions constituted breakfast. Lunchtime brought a bowl of refried beans, two hunks of bread, and tortillas. A stringy piece of paper-thin, tasteless meat (which I prayed was beef), slices of dried-up tomato, a scoop of refried beans, a pile of rice, a spoon of hot salsa, and several tortillas made up dinner. No coffee, just grimy tin cups of water, and only three a day, one with each meal. If they'd given me a bottle of wine—even a cheap, sweet house wine—I'd have been a tad happier.

Dirt filtered in through cracks in the window. With every gust of wind, more dust collected on the six-inch-wide ledge. I'd run a finger through the layers, forming my initials or my first name as if to leave my imprint, lest I be forgotten. Often, teeny insects crept through the crumbling grout to reside on the ledge. One puff and I'd make them disappear.

Light bulbs shone constantly in the alley, mimicking twenty-four hours of daylight. Incessant light filtered through the dull window, but faintly, a glow like a lone star attempting to comfort me. And it did soothe me for, other than cockroaches, ants, and an occasional fly or unknown critter, there was nothing else.

***

"I can't see what's behind me, Neela," I said.

"Let me get out and see." Neela, my best friend and confidant, said.

A stone wall loomed at my left, a parked car on my right. A building and more parked cars were behind me. I didn't want to hit anything. I tried to be extra careful.

I backed up slowly, angling my head to see my friend. The May Mexico heat rushed in the windows. Neela was silent. I figured that was a good thing. I backed up a bit more.

"Neela, all okay?"

"Yes, back up, to your left. Lots of room."

I still couldn't see her.

I backed up a little. Gave the car more gas. Braked. Pushed the gas again.

A bump. A scream. The tires rolled over a hump, a rise in the uneven Mexican road.

"Neela?" I whispered.

Until I alighted from the car, I hadn't realized I had run over her. A woman—not Neela—still screamed.

***

They say your life flashes in front of you in slow motion as you take your last breath—your entire life floating by like a colourful parade, flaunting, haunting, daunting, clowns sporting garish grins—but it also parades when you have nothing to do but stare at achromatic walls. You wonder at your inadequacies, your failures—never your triumphs—moments that draw out your hidden tears. That's the way it was with me. My tears streamed. Not so much for me but for those I missed and years that flew by before I had a chance to stop and ponder them. And my regrets.

Neela.

I tried to push away unhappy thoughts—swatted at them like insignificant flies—but they remained a stain upon the colourless walls, there to torment me as if I wasn't tormented enough: holographs of my life, photographs I wished I could shred or burn, videos of incidents I'd sooner forget. All imaginary, of course, but as real as the fingernails I chewed to the quick until blood flowed that I lapped up like red wine.

My guards were three beefy men. I wasn't frail when they first locked me up, when those metal circles clasped around my wrists. I was theirs then; I was theirs. Frailty came later. It crept up on me, aged me, made me wonder who I was. What kind of woman kills her best friend?

Murderer, they chanted. *Murderer! You killed my mother. You killed my grandmother. You killed my wife, my sister.* Neela was all of those people. And I snuffed her out as one would extinguish a candle. Decimated the flame that provided light. And love. And life.

I hadn't meant it. It was an accident. An accident!

But I was still a murderer. I killed someone. No matter how you looked at it, I eradicated a life. Someone's last breath was taken because of me. Because I hadn't seen her. I had looked in the rear-view mirror. Even in the side mirror.

Except for when a lunatic barged through a red light and rammed into me, nearly killing me, I'd never been involved in an accident. My neck had hit the steering wheel. "A quarter of an inch farther down and you would have died," the doctor said. I was in my twenties then, when I was going to live forever, as young people assume. I could have died. Instantly. But I didn't.

But Neela did.

I could've become an alcoholic—had wine been provided. The bugs were getting to me, mocking me, grinning. I knew they were. *Stop! Stop!* But they persisted. Ants continued to work for their useless pay, carting leaves on their backs like motorized boats with unfurled sails. Flies buzzed around my face. Cockroaches zipped across the floor, like miniature horses clumping down cobblestoned streets. *Clomp! Clomp!*

I let them take over, the insaneness that rang around my ears. They came at me, charging as if soldiers readying for battle, careening down the mountainside. I was the villain, the enemy in the walker who waited patiently as if I had nothing else to do and nowhere to go. (Which I hadn't.) I existed solely to take the brunt of whatever those creatures threw at me. I was a murderer. A killer.

I didn't want to rot in jail. I wanted to go home. I was sorry for my friend—still am. More than sorry. I've cried and cried for her, but it was an accident. An accident I'll remember for the rest of my life, and not a day will pass I won't relive the scene. It'll be the first thought on my mind when I wake and the last sight I'll see before I fall asleep, but in that horrid Mexican cell, I fought for me. My life took precedence then. Grief for Neela would come later when I was safe at home. When I didn't have to worry about me.

The fourth day the steel door groaned, stealing me from my thoughts. I jumped from the bed. Could it be? My freedom? It was in between meals. What else could it be?

No, they were going to drag me away, stand me over an open pit, loop a rope around my neck. Or prop me against a stone wall and pull a burlap bag over my head, but not quickly enough that I wouldn't glimpse the nameless, leering faces and the aiming rifles. Gone! Dead! *Terminado!*

A noose or a bullet. It didn't matter. Death was the same.

A guard, one I didn't remember seeing previously, entered the cell. He spoke Spanish and motioned me out. Two other guards framed the door. Despite my years in Mexico, I didn't know much more than the perfunctory words *gracias* and *nada* and *buenos dias.* Even if I had, the heavyset, bronzed man's words were spewed too fast. Daylight hovered ahead. I yearned to race down the drab hall before he realized his mistake, shackled me, and tossed me back into that four-by-six pen where insects invaded my space (or perhaps I invaded theirs).

I felt the sweltering sun, visualized the waving palm trees and vibrant-coloured flowers scrambling over stone walls. Tasted the dirt skimming over the cobblestones, inhaled the balmy air and fragrant flower scents. Heard street dogs, choruses of birds, chickens' chatter, clicking of the *cicadas*. The rushing vehicles blasted their tunes and talk, jovial and awkward. I pictured everything as I never had previously, but the sights and smells and sounds were far in the distance.

The dark men in their well-pressed and clean but menacing uniforms, guns at their sides, spoke their gibberish. They barely looked as old as my grandsons, surely not as bright as my kin. If they made a mistake with my release, perhaps they wouldn't realize it until it was too late, long after I'd climbed that stone wall dotted with pinks and purples and yellows.

The taxi dropped me off at my rental in Ajijic, about forty kilometres from the tiny, obscure village Neela and I had visited. Yet, ironically, the village hadn't been too small to be without a jail. I was thankful the Mexican authorities had returned my purse and that my money was intact. I had signed numerous papers before they freed me, none of which I could read, all of which I signed in a haphazard manner. Later I could claim insanity, should I have signed something I shouldn't have, though non-knowledge of the Spanish language wouldn't count as a defence.

I had proclaimed my innocence every time those nameless, squat men opened the cell door. Obviously, they didn't understand me, but someone must have been on my side. After the statement I had given at my arrest, no one paid any further attention to me save for my three meals a day. That must have been law—*each prisoner must be fed three times a day*. I wasn't even allowed the requisite phone call. Wasn't that against the law?

After a drink to calm my nerves, I telephoned Pam. She and I, along with Neela, had been best buddies. Pam hadn't been feeling well the day Neela and I had gone on our day trip. Perhaps Pam was the culprit. Four eyes are better than two; circumstances could have been different had she been with us, but I harboured no ill will against Pam.

But why hadn't she come to visit me? Why hadn't anyone come to my aid?

"You okay?" she asked. "Where you were? What happened?"

What happened? "I was in jail. In Hell."

Pam didn't seem to have a clue. Where in the heck had she thought I'd been? Hadn't anyone missed me? Hadn't anyone cared?

"What!" she said.

"It was pure Hell," I said. "I never thought I'd be free. I'm not even sure why I am now."

"I'm so sorry. I had no idea."

Really?

"You okay?" she asked again.

"Yeah, I think so. I'm just glad to be home." I considered Mexico, my adopted country, home.

Silence.

"You there?" I asked. Mexican phone lines weren't the most reliable.

"Yes, still here."

"Did I miss the funeral?"

Silence.

"It's tomorrow."

"Tomorrow? We should go together," I said.

Silence.

"Grace, I don't know how to tell you this. The family. They're here. They're pretty upset. They said they want nothing to do with you. That you aren't welcome."

My stomach lurched. I almost threw up. "I don't understand…it was an accident."

"I know. But that's what they said. Neela's daughter and son. Both here. From Atlanta. Met them yesterday when I went to Neela's home."

"Oh." *You went to Neela's home?*

"Pretty mad. They…feel you killed her."

"Yeah, I did, I guess. But it was an accident. You know that."

"Yes, I do," Pam said. "It's a private service. A cremation. Then they're taking her back to the States. It's not a big deal, really."

The three of us had connected several years ago. We had come to Mexico for a more relaxed lifestyle and temperate climate. Neela had arrived first. I followed a couple of years later with my husband, Arnold. Pam, who had been divorced for seven years, arrived after Arnold and I. Neela's husband had died four years previous to my arrival, but Neela had remained in Mexico. After Arnold's death, I had stayed, too, despite the chagrin of my two children. I hadn't wanted to go back to Canada's cold winters. Ajijic's warm weather enticed me to stay. Even the draw of my grandchildren, young adults by that time, couldn't pull me back. I had made my home in Ajijic. Thankfully, Arnold and I had never bought a house but had merely rented long-term, which gave me flexibility after his death.

If only Neela and I hadn't driven to that village, somewhere north of Guadalajara—a name I couldn't even pronounce—to check out a pottery exhibition. I hadn't wanted to go. "Too far, Neela. I'm not comfortable driving in places I'm not familiar with," I had said. I owned a car; Neela hadn't. If only I hadn't gotten stuck in that alley, penned in between the wall and the other car. If only I had stuck to my instincts. If only I hadn't wavered. If only…

If only… Too many ifs.

"Gracie, I'm sorry." Pam sounded contrite. But was she? I felt abandoned, much as I had felt for several months after Arnold passed on. Alone.

"I don't understand," I said. "It was an accident. Don't you believe me?"

"Of course I do. Don't be foolish."

I heard tears behind Pam's words. Mine were coming.

But it was an accident. I didn't mean to…

"It's okay," I said. "I understand. I just wanted to pay my sympathies."

"I know you do." I heard the hesitation in her voice. "Let's get together for lunch on Thursday."

"Yeah, sure." I hung up, but I knew I wouldn't go to lunch or anywhere else in Mexico except for the airport. I wanted to go home, to my children and their children—my grandchildren, whom I had neglected for too long. Mexico, despite being my home for the past few years, would be my home no longer. I was glad I had listened to my son and had Arnold's ashes spread in Calgary. If I hadn't, I'd be stuck in Mexico forever. I couldn't have left Arnold behind.

I stared out the bedroom patio. Magenta petals of *bugambilia* splashed across the stone wall, the thorny vines creeping upward, higher and higher as if racing from me, running away as I wanted to. The three-tiered fountain, cascading its usual soothing tune, wasn't working its magic. The water spilling from the smallest top bowl down to the middle and then into the bottom largest bowl sloshed like buckets of tears.

I had always wanted a fountain.

I picked up the phone. Carol answered on the third ring. "Mom, how are you?"

"Fine," I said.

"What's wrong?" Perceptive Carol always knew.

"Mom," she said when I didn't reply. "You there?"

"Yes, sweetie, I'm here."

"You okay?"

My tears flowed, matching the bubbling fountain in the yard. My insides felt as if they would gurgle up through my esophagus and spew to the floor. "I just got out of jail," I blurted. I hadn't meant to tell her, but I had to tell someone who loved me and always would, no matter what travesties I might have committed. "I…killed someone. A friend."

"Mom! What?" She gasped. "Mom, what happened?"

"It was an accident. I didn't mean to." I brushed at my tears. I heard Carol in the background. Another gasp. Her tears. "Oh, Carol, I don't know what to do." I paused and took a deep breath. "I'm coming home. For good. Pick me up at the airport?"

"Mom, of course. I don't know what to say. You sure you're okay? When's your flight?"

"I'll book it tonight. Send you an email."

"Yes, good. Mom, sure you're okay?"

"Fine." I wiped my cheeks, which didn't dry. A steady stream of tears, like the fountain. "I gotta run. I'll e you later with my flight info."

I pulled myself together. My rent was paid until the following month. I'd leave cash for the utilities. My deposit of a month's rent would be lost. I'd be breaking my lease, but that was okay; I wouldn't be sued. Who could sue from Mexico? No one had my current address—the address I'd assume when I returned home to Alberta.

I possessed nothing in Mexico. My pension, which I accessed at ATMs, was deposited into my Canadian bank account. I owned a few knick-knacks, items Arnold and I had purchased when we first made our home in Mexico. Some I would take with me. I could handle two suitcases, even more if I wanted to pay extra to the airline. I could take what I wanted.

I sat at the desk and jostled the mouse. My computer came alive—a wondrous blue and white! I searched for the earliest flight. I'd be in the air before Neela's service began.

Published in anthology, *The Prison Compendium*,
by EMP Publishing, December 2016

Vengeance Is Mine

Dearly beloved, avenge not yourselves, but rather give place unto wrath: for it is written, Vengeance is mine; I will repay, saith the Lord. Romans 12:19 (King James Version)

I read the dictionary as some do the Bible. My battered College Edition of *The World Dictionary of the English Language* is always handy wherever I go, stuffed in my hot pink backpack. If I had attended college, this book might have been put to better use.

I enjoy discovering new words and their meanings, and I search for words to interject into my daily life. I used to be a voracious reader of all books—historical novels, romance, non-fiction, poetry, even the Bible. Later, I became hooked on the dictionary—maybe because it was less intrusive with simply words and definitions—a book one can read over and over, a book of new discoveries.

"Vengeance is mine," sayeth the Lord. I don't know how many eons ago the Lord said it, but soon I'll be saying it: *Vengeance is mine, says I— me—Polly.*

I'm not religious anymore. I don't remember anything I once knew about religion other than the quote about vengeance. The religion of my old life seems so far away now—someone else's memories, not mine. Maybe that's why I feel okay stealing words attributable to God. No sin in that, is there? Stealing words? Who can own words?

I don't believe in Him or in His son, J.C. I don't believe in anything at all, actually. Heaven and Hell and all that crap—what is the meaning of it? I haven't a clue, and I don't care to know. I'll never find out, apparently. Nemesis says once her goals are completed, I'll be banned from Heaven—and Hell. Yes, even from Hell because she says I'll deserve worse than Hell.

According to my trusty dictionary, vengeance is the *infliction of injury, harm, humiliation, or the like, on a person by another who has been harmed by him; violent revenge.* I've heard Biblical vengeance is promised by judgement in the next life, but the vengeance I seek is in this life, not the next.

She named herself Nemesis. Nemesis is a person in Greek mythology—*the goddess of divine retribution and vengeance.* A nemesis, the noun, *causes misery or death.*

Nemesis wants me to do these things. I'm still pondering whether it's misery or death I want to inflict.

My name is Polly. Or is it Nemesis?

I was christened Pollyanna, *an excessively or blindly optimistic person.* I was never an optimistic person, but I became blinded by life. My life as Polly began normally—normal birth, normal parents, normal home in a normal house. I attended school as did other normal children.

Normal—*conforming to the standard or the common type; usual; not abnormal.* In my early teens, my normalcy changed into abnormalcy. My standard of level dropped, became almost non-existent. I befriended the wrong crowd. Isn't that how bad things begin for normal kids? I did drugs and drank and engaged in sex. Gradually, I lost interest in school and dropped out before my sixteenth birthday.

My parents, both loving people—good people, now that I look back—were distressed. They did everything to prevent me from taking that twisted path, but I was headstrong and hard-nosed. I listened to nobody. I thought I knew it all back then. Much later, I realized how wonderful and normal my life used to be.

Enter Tough Love. My parents heard about tough love on a TV show. They decided it wouldn't hurt—and might even work—so they tough-loved me.

It didn't work.

They kicked me out, ass first, and I was on my own. In retrospect, I know they expected me to come crawling back to them, begging for forgiveness. I was proud, however, still obstinate, determined to make it on my own. Survival instincts kicked in, and soon I was off, living on my own with the help of the depraved crowd I considered my friends.

Many years later, I returned home, but I was too late. My mother had developed breast cancer and died. A year after she passed on, my father joined her when he suffered a fatal heart attack. Their deaths didn't affect me. I did mourn them, for a short time, but I wouldn't have stayed had they been alive. I was still too proud, still would not admit defeat.

***

My home is a shabby motel room in a shabby area of a shabby city.

Shabby—*impaired by wear, use, etc.; worn; showing signs of neglect; contemptible; meanly ungenerous or unfair, not up to par in quality.* The word "shabby" describes me, as does the word "nemesis." I'm not a quality person, and I'm definitely impaired by wear and use, in more ways than one. Nemesis, the person, is mean and contemptible, and we both show signs of neglect.

Shabby also sums up the description of my home for the past month, ever since I was released from prison. The prison was akin to a women's shelter, but it was a prison; I was shackled away in a cell. There were liberties: a TV room, a refrigerator full of snacks, a radio in each cell, free time to roam in the outside caged complex. It was quite peaceful, actually, much like a mental hospital. One didn't have to interact with other inmates if one didn't want to, and I chose not to. I wasn't giving up my soul to another human again. My lesson had been learned the hard way.

I open the battered door to my miserable home. This shabby motel has seen better days. Now it's home to prostitutes and drug dealers. I kick the door shut behind me and almost miss the folded piece of paper on the floor.

"10:00 p.m. tonight." The large scrawl is spread over the entire sheet. I fall to the bed in the dingy room and sigh as my fingers absently rub the threadbare comforter. I notice the streaked, yellow-green walls of my existence. How did I manage to arrive in this place? How would I escape?

***

The paper crackles beneath my hand when I wake. The glare of the naked light bulb startles me out of my light sleep. I don't need to re-read the note. Ten o'clock. It's not a question; it's an order. This time, however, it's okay. Tonight is the night I've waited for.

The bed, although saggy and lumpy, is soft beneath my tired body. I want to linger there forever, but I saunter into the bathroom, strip, and let the stinging cold shards of water caress my back. *Damn this crappy motel with its sporadic hot water.* My only caresses lately have been from the shower, and hot water would make them more pleasant. I wonder why I'm showering; I'll only get dirty again, but repetitious showers are the norm in my day.

The outside is pitch-black when I lock the door behind me. My expensive designer backpack is slung over my shoulder, and my red high heels click-clack while I trot down the unruffled street.

The dim streetlights highlight the star-studded sky. My favourite game is counting the stars, and I pretend each one harbours an invisible soul. I grant each shining twinkle a name and a heartbeat: Penelope, the Goddess of Perfection; Lola, the Goddess of Love; Rhonda, the Goddess of Right. All women, of course. Men are vile creatures. It has taken me twenty-plus years to discover that. How I wish I could soar up there tonight and become one of the goddesses instead of heading to my ten o'clock rendezvous. But which Goddess would I be if not Nemesis?

I arrive at another dingy motel and stand in front of another battered door. I check my watch. Ten o'clock. Right on time. I hear voices inside. Who else is there?

The door opens and he's in front of me. Butch. He spits on the concrete by my feet before moving to let me pass. The other voices are from the blaring TV. Butch turns down the volume while I nervously scan the room. Nothing has changed since the last time. Same old sagging bed, two cheap nightstands topped by several crushed beer cans, cigarette burns on the flowered comforter, butts on the floor. The sole lamp spreads its light over the leftover pizza on the desk.

Funny how all shabby motels look the same. Butch's place is almost identical to mine, but my surroundings are a notch higher in cleanliness.

I place my knapsack on the worn armchair by the large window concealed by droopy orange and green-stripped drapes. The thin comforter matches the drapes, with its gaudy orange flowers and striped border. A green wallpaper border trims the top of the wall, stained with years of cigarette smoke and age.

"Any smokes?"

Butch tosses me a cigarette from the top of the TV, and I reach for the lighter on the night table. I hope the nicotine will calm me down.

He disappears into the bathroom. I plop on the edge of the messy bed and wait. The toilet flushes, and he returns too soon.

"How ya doin', babe?" He's finally talking.

"Fine. Okay."

"Ya. Lookin' mighty fine, you are."

My stomach cringes, but I act nonchalant. Butch is not one of my favourite customers, but he's reliable and steady. And he pays. I've had my share of customers, and I've had worse than Butch.

I've also had better.

He comes closer, his lumbering body advancing faster than I would like. He's a large man—two hundred fifty pounds and over six feet tall. If he tidied himself up and adopted a new demeanour, he could be a cuddly teddy bear, but he doesn't care how he looks, and he sure doesn't care about bears. Butch lives for himself. Always has, always will.

His medium-blond hair hangs to his shoulders, greasy and stringy, and his bedraggled beard, which often harbours remnants of a meal, is darker than the hair on his head. The hair scattered over the rest of his body is even darker, almost black. Clumps sprout in obscene patches across his back and down to his waist, where they spider into a narrow line and disappear between the hidden recess of his butt crack. His chest is covered with even more hair, some older ones shining like slivers of silver. Thick furry arms and fuzzy squat legs add to the package I have nicknamed Blowfly Butch.

Blowfly is a word I discovered shortly after I met Butch—*large usually hairy metallic blue or green fly; lays eggs in carrion or dung or wounds.* Butch's favourite colour is blue, second is green. I'm the blowfly's carrion, the dung, the wound, a receptacle of sorts, here tonight merely for Butch's pleasure.

One meaning of fly, as everyone knows, is *a strip or fold of material along one edge of a garment opening for concealing buttons or other fasteners, used esp. on a man's trousers.* It's also *any numerous of two-winged insects*, not to mention *a fishhook dressed with hair*. Yes, Butch is definitely a blowfly, in more ways than one.

Lost in my thoughts about flies, I'm caught by surprise when Butch's meaty fist yanks my ponytail.

"Wench!" he exclaims as he gives another forceful tug.

"Ow! Butch, what the hell are you doing!" I screech, hating I acknowledge his infliction of pain.

"Just puttin' you in your place, babe." He gives another jerk.

"Stop it!"

He pulls even harder.

"Butch!"

He twists my head and plants his oily lips on mine. I smell garlic and decay. Butch's hygiene has always left something to be desired.

"Strip, babe," he orders before releasing his grip.

I see the thirst and hunger—a lecherousness—in his watery, bulging eyes, and a determined bloodlust. Butch is high. Strands of my long, blonde hair hang between his slimy fingers.

"Have you got what I asked for?" I ask.

"Yeah, it's here."

"Where?" I want to make sure before he has his way with me, not that I have any say in the matter.

"On the table, babe. In the bag."

I crane my head. I see a plastic bag. "Show me."

"Not now. We got other things to do."

When he clumsily straddles and smothers my body with his, I pretend to enjoy his frantic activity. I try to move when he moves, I reciprocate his kisses, I repeat his breathy shudders, but in his state of high, he probably doesn't notice my feeble manoeuvres. Thankfully, unlike some of my other customers, Butch is always fast, and then he's dead weight on my one hundred fifteen pounds.

He hoists himself up, his slobber drooling on my face from gaps of missing teeth, and twists my nipple between his thumb and forefinger as if to say, *Remember who's boss,* before he grunts and shoves me away. He slaps my butt when I roll over. I wince in silence while enduring the humiliation I've grown used to.

I inhale the musty odour in the flattened pillow. Crusty stains on the pillowcase chafe against my face. I lay exposed on the bed.

Butch pulls up his baggy jeans and buckles his belt. His slime oozes between my legs, and I wonder if I'm able to move.

"Come on, babe, things to do, places to go, people to see." He slaps my butt again, harder this time.

I grab my clothes from the chair and slither into the bathroom. I want a shower badly, but there isn't time. Butch is antsy; I'm antsy. I just want my package and to be on my way.

***

The street is darker now, even though stars are shining. I see my friends Penelope and Rhonda. "I wish I could be with you. Someday." I can't believe I'm talking to stars. I clutch my knapsack containing my night's reward. The streets are almost deserted and hollow, the way I like them.

Butch disgusts me, as do most men, but I have no choice. I need the drug like I need money. Last week, I pleaded with him to get me a drug in exchange for my services. I explained what I needed, and he assured me he could get it. I pray he got me the right stuff.

No doubt I'll see him again next week for our usual tryst if Hell doesn't catch me first.

Once home, I stash my haul in the closet and collapse on the bed before my shower. I'm exhausted. It's a long walk to Butch's.

Butch is kind of like me, in limbo, living in that shady motel. He used to have a house, apparently. I'm not sure what happened, not that I care. I'm not interested in him, don't want to know too much about him. I know more than I want as it is, what with his illicit drug deals.

Butch and I found each other two years ago, and except for when I was incarcerated, I've been servicing him one night a week since. Sometimes he'll demand an extra night and notify me by slipping a note under my door. This night is different, though. I used him for a change; I needed what he could give me.

Lately, Butch has been more abrasive, which scares me. He never used to pull my hair. We never used to have rough sex. He had never been gentle, but he was never mean, either. I dread our weekly appointments, but I need the money, so they will continue, at least for a while.

I let the shower fondle my back. It's the only time I feel loved, the only time I ever feel anything but disgust. The warm water—finally a temperature other than frigid cold—drizzles over my face and down my heavy breasts, erasing remnants of Blowfly Butch.

But it isn't Butch I'm thinking about. It's Henry.

I fell in love with Henry two years ago, about the same time I started with Butch. Henry fell in love with me, too. Then Henry fell out of love with me. But that was wrong. You don't lead someone on for two years and then change your mind. You don't fall out of love as Henry did. No, Henry is wrong, and I will show him exactly how wrong he is.

I don't know who speaks these words that invade my mind. Are they Nemesis's? Or are they mine?

***

An unexpected torrent poured down one night while I walked to the subway from an appointment. The rain was so bad, I had to take cover. I slipped into the Oasis Bar on Forty-Fourth Street and grabbed a stool at the bar. The smoke was heavy in the air, almost obscuring the half-empty room. I ordered a glass of Merlot, lit my cigarette, and sat, deep in my thoughts, until a man straddled the stool beside me. I didn't pay much attention. He ordered a gin and tonic before speaking to me.

"Rainy, isn't it?"

He was tall, fit, and dark-haired. His voice was pleasant. I didn't look like a hooker, and he didn't realize I was one. We chatted for a bit, and he bought another round of drinks.

"I'm in town on business," he said. "I'm staying next door at the Hilton. Want to come up for a nightcap? It looks like it's about closing time here."

I was tired, but he intrigued me.

"Oh, I'm Henry, by the way."

"I'm Polly. Nice to meet you, Henry." I debated for a few seconds before taking him up on his offer.

The door had barely closed behind us before we tore off our clothes and romped in the high, plump bed. Henry, a passionate lover, so unlike what I had been used to, smelled good. A nice smell always helps.

Henry was a politician from New Jersey. "I come to New York often," he told me.

Our affair progressed. We saw each other at least once a week, often spending the weekends together. Granted, most of the time was spent in the bedroom or in a nondescript bar or restaurant. In retrospect, that should have been my first clue. Isn't hindsight wonderful?

I was consumed with both sexual passion and desire for Henry. Even though he was a smaller man than Butch, he was warm, tender, and cuddly like a teddy bear. I was definitely in love. Henry told me he was, too.

Love: *sexual passion or desire, or its gratification; have sexual intercourse with; passionate affection for a person of the opposite sex; a love affair; warmth.*

I discovered early on Henry was married, but he told me he wasn't happy in his marriage; neither was his wife. "We're in the process of a divorce," he said. "I love you. I want to be with you. No one else."

A few weeks after we met, before I found out he was married, Henry set me up in an apartment close to Fifth Avenue. He paid all my bills. He never knew I was a prostitute. I made up stories about my life. I told him I hadn't been in New York for long and I'd been looking for a job and a place to live. "I don't want you to work," he said. "I want to take care of you."

I knew from the beginning he had ulterior motives and wanted me available at his beck and call, but I had no illusions; that came later.

I continued to see Butch one night a week even after Henry arrived on the scene. Maybe it was because Butch's payments were my own earnings and I needed a bit of independence. Maybe I needed the excitement of cheating on Henry.

I believed Henry's promises. I thought we'd marry once his divorce was finalized, but his excuse was always the same—he and his wife had matters to finalize that were taking longer than expected.

Two years later, Henry was still married; I still waited.

The last month of our relationship, he let it slip he had children. He said his wife had never wanted children. I realized then that all his words had been lies, but I kept his secrets as my secrets while I pondered what to do.

I felt like a fool. I should have known.

That was when an unnamed and foreign being grew inside my soul, some creature breathing fire into me. Nemesis took form, but I didn't know that until much later.

"Surprise!" Nemesis hollered at me. "You stupid dimwit, believing everything he tells you."

My heart was already broken, my dreams shattered. My life disintegrated. The beast inside me didn't need to berate me even further.

***

When my rage wouldn't stay hidden any longer, I confronted Henry.

"I'm sorry, honey," he mumbled. He said he truly did love me, but he couldn't leave his wife. There's always a "but." "I want to continue as we are," he said. "I'll keep taking care of you. I promise."

I wonder whether I should have accepted his offer. I was a hooker, after all. Just a scumbag prostitute. Isn't that what my kind does? Why did I think I was special?

Before I knew what happened, repressed demons tore loose, and I attacked Henry like a panther. My fingernails scraped across his clean-shaven, baby-soft face. My knee slammed into his crotch, and he emitted a howl like a banshee and escaped from my apartment. I tumbled to the floor while tears puddled on my lap.

That demon in me—the *evil spirit; devil; a person with great energy, drive*—was that Nemesis showing her face?

Henry stopped paying the bills after that night. Surprise, surprise! He also closed out my bank account, the one he had set up for me, the one I had thought was solely mine. I didn't know where to make bill payments even if I had the money to pay them. I was evicted soon after. Henry evicted me; it wasn't because of overdue bills.

A few days later, I stole a jar of makeup from Macy's. I was caught going out the revolving door.

I didn't need to shoplift. I still had a bit of money I had made from Butch. A whisper inside me, a tiny voice, made me do it.

I was in jail for six months, but it seemed like six years. Before I was released, Nemesis showed her real face.

***

Today is Monday. Today is the day. This is the day Polly gets revenge. Or is it vengeance?

I know Henry's schedule like the back of my hand. He still spends Monday nights in room 2902 at the Garden Express Hilton on Forty-Fourth Street, beside the Oasis, where we first met. How fitting is that?

I'm still sore from three nights ago when Butch had his way with me. Butch won't be treating me that way anymore, either. I've had enough of him. I'm leaving town when tonight is over, but I might take care of Butch before I go.

I shrug Butch from my mind. Today is Henry's day.

It's a long day of waiting. Everything I need is packed in my backpack, including my dictionary. At noon, I walk across to the deli for a salad and a glass of *vino*, where I sit and read the newspaper. A couple of guys eye me. Another day, I might have played the eye-game with them, but not today.

At four o'clock, I close the motel door behind me and walk to the subway. I unobtrusively enter the hotel and avert my eyes from the hidden cameras. *Thank you for that, Henry*. Henry slyly pointed the cameras out to me one night. Ever since then, whenever I joined him in his room, I looked the other way. I do that now.

I wait at the end of the hall on the twentieth floor. Henry usually arrives by six o'clock, which gives him time to shower and change before dinner. When I hear the dings of the elevator, I duck around the corner. The elevator deposited several groups of people before Henry arrives. I peek around to see him insert the key card into the slot and disappear into the room. I linger for a few more minutes before I approach his room.

I pose off to the side and turn my face while I bang on the door. It only takes him a few seconds to answer.

"Hello, Henry." I barge into the room. He is stunned, and I have no problem sneaking around him and closing the door. I fasten the chain across the jamb.

"What are you doing here?"

"Nothing much. What are you doing?" I glance around the room, noting the same four-poster bed.

"That's none of your business, Polly. Please leave. I have things to do."

"Yeah, I bet you do," I sneer. "Too bad for you. You have me tonight."

Before Henry knows what's happened, I've injected the vial of liquid into him. I pray Butch knows his drugs. Question marks loom in Henry's startled eyes. He stumbles over to the plush chair and falls heavily into it.

"Thanks, Butch. You're good for something," I mumble.

I told Butch I wanted a fast-acting liquid I could inject easily, something to put a person out for a good twenty minutes or so. Butch was concerned at first, unsure. Maybe he thought I had intentions of injecting him, but after more discussion, he said it would be no problem.

"What you doing?" Henry mumbles. Then he's gone.

Even though I'm a small woman, I manage to drag Henry to the bed. I undress him and fling his Armani shirt and other brand-name clothing across the room. Adrenaline kicks in, and I haul his naked body on the bed. I spread-eagle him and bind his wrists and ankles to the bedposts with the rope from my bag. I scan his lean, tanned body when I'm done.

I wipe an escaped tear from the corner of my eye. I have mixed feelings; part of me is not at all happy about this, but part of me relishes the upcoming celebration.

Celebration: *joyous diversion; the public performance of a sacrament or solemn ceremony with all the appropriate ritual.* Yes, this will be a joyous diversion, albeit a private, solemn ceremony. I need to right a wrong. And, of course, Nemesis eggs me on.

I thought of harming Henry's wife or his kids, but I wasn't sure where he lived and wasn't sure how I'd go about it. I didn't want to hurt his children; they were innocents in this fiasco. His wife, too, was innocent, although if it weren't for her, this plan would not be necessary.

Henry is out cold for approximately twenty minutes, right on schedule. He's groggy and confused when his eyes open. Then he's scared. I see the fear in his eyes.

"Polly...what...why?" Henry stammers, trying to formulate his questions.

Butch told me this drug might cause a bit of amnesia.

"Polly...where am I?"

I think he finally clues in.

"What are you doing? Polly, please."

"Henry, you hurt me. Badly. This is all your fault. You had no right."

He doesn't say much more. He's still dazed and weak. When he realizes he's tied up, he yanks his arms, tries to free his legs. His little wee-wee quivers. He looks down and shivers at his unexpected nakedness.

Silence.

He perks up like a light bulb switched on in the black of night. "Polly, I'm sorry. I was going to call you the other night. My wife and I are getting a divorce now. Things are really in the works. We can be together."

His words are slurred and spoken quickly, but I understand.

Does he think I'm a total fool?

"Too late, Henry. It's done. Over. You're done. You're over."

"What are you going to do?"

"Oh, you'll see, Henry. You'll see."

I'm a crazy woman as if something snapped in me, like a rubber band propelling across a room or a balloon unexpectedly bursting in one's face. I'm out of control, but it's a good feeling. Nemesis will enjoy this. Polly might, too.

Henry keeps trying to free himself. The mattress is so soft the bed doesn't budge, and he sinks lower and lower into the fluffiness of the bed covers. His eyes dart at me every few seconds while I stare back.

I'm mesmerized by his shrivelled privates. Man, I'm gonna have fun with these.

Henry sees me eyeing them, and I see more fear in his eyes.

"Polly," he whispers, "please."

I tickle his foot with my forefinger, which makes him squirm even more. But I want to do more than tickle, and I don't want to touch him with my fingers.

I go to the closet and select a coat hanger. All wooden, unfortunately. I sprint toward him and stop at the foot of the bed. I look at the point in the "V" of his spread legs. I move to the side and poke at his penis with the edge of the hanger.

He screams.

I run to the bathroom, grab a facecloth, and try to stuff it into his mouth. "Henry, if you don't open up, I'm gonna do something worse to you," I lie.

His trembling mouth opens.

I'm in my glory. I'm not sure what to do next. I know what I want to do, but I'm not sure Polly is that strong. Nemesis is. She's here, watching. Waiting.

I dig at him some more with the coat hanger. I jostle the little guy, poke at the two saggy sacs, jab at his nipples. Henry twists and turns. His eyes, frantic and watery, glare from his flushed face.

"Henry, you shouldn't have done this to me. What do you think I should do to you?"

Nemesis comes to life.

Henry moves his head, back and forth, back and forth. He clenches his fists, and blue veins pop on his hands.

Nemesis inserts the hanger underneath his butt but needs something new to amuse her. I go to the desk and spy a pen on the hotel notepad. Scrawled on the paper is "9:00 Urban Grill."

"Ah, Henry, a date?"

He flinches.

I return to the bed while Nemesis brandishes the pen in the air.

"Look at this, Henry. What do you think? Does this excite you?"

I have never seen a facial expression as I do on Henry. It's a mixture of fear and sorrow and hate all rolled into one, like a sandwich roll of butter, pimiento, and meat paste.

His once-little man, erect now, is a soldier standing at attention. I can't believe my eyes. He is turned on.

"Henry, you want this, don't you? What a horny guy!"

His head shakes. Gurgling noises emanate from behind the cloth, and snot rolls onto the facecloth. He cries. His fists open, and he splays his fingers. Little man remains erect. A drop of fluid glistens from the steeple. His hairy balls are tight.

I jab with the pen, but little man stands firm. I'm in awe.

"Henry, this is unreal!"

His eyes plead. I love dragging this out.

A knock on the door accidentally digs the pen into his balls.

Oh, no!

Another knock.

"Room service."

Will the waiter barge in if I don't answer?

"Can you leave it outside the door, please," I say in a muffled voice while peering out the peephole. The waiter acknowledges my words and walks away from the cart. I wait a few minutes before I wheel the order in.

"What have we here, Henry?"

I check the delicacies: two small deli sandwiches (not the rolled-up kind, however, which would have been quite ironic), an uncorked bottle of red wine, slivers of cheese and several crackers, and a small vine of green grapes, along with a wine glass, knife and fork, and a cloth napkin.

Henry is silent and still while I pour myself a glass of wine and take a bite of the sandwich.

"Hungry, Henry?"

I remember past times with Henry: fun times, exciting times. I remember how the two of us cavorted in bed—how we'd sip wine and accidentally-on-purpose spill red drops on our naked bodies and lap them up with delight.

I pour a bit of the liquid over Henry's not-so-private privates. I hate to waste good wine, however, as I'm not about to lap it up tonight.

He gazes at me. I'm not a mind reader, but he's remembering other times, as well.

"Too bad, huh?"

His body is dormant. Little man looks as if he's about to deflate, so I probe it with the knife, and it shoots right back up. He has sadistic tendencies, I suspect, a masochist turned on by knives and fear.

"It's only a butter knife, Henry."

He's transfixed by the ceiling while I continue to knife-poke him.

I pause. "What do you think, Henry? Are you a sadistic masochist?"

I show him my dictionary. "You never knew about this dictionary fetish of mine, did you?"

Fetish seems to be a word that fits right in with masochist and sadist. My dictionary reports one definition of fetish as *an object regarded as having magical power*, and I read the definition to him.

"Magical power, Henry. Do you believe that? My dictionary has magical powers."

Masochist. Am I using the right word? *The condition in which sexual gratification depends on suffering, physical pain, and humiliation, esp. inflicted on oneself.*

Henry isn't exactly doing this to himself, but I guess I can still use that word. I like the sound of it: masochist. It sounds like a mean word but in a sexy way.

And sadism—*sexual gratification gained through causing physical pain or humiliation*. Another sexy, mean word. I like them both.

Wow! At second glance, it appears from these definitions that it is me—Polly—who is the sadistic, masochistic creature, but I'm not receiving any gratification, at least not in a sexual way. This has nothing to do with sex.

I like to think Henry is sadistic. I like to think he is a masochist. "Yes, Henry. You are a sadistic masochist."

He ignores me.

I'm glad my dictionary is by my side; I'm glad I didn't leave it in my motel room.

I exchange the knife for a fork and bore it through the thick, dark hair that nestles little man. The prongs lose themselves in the wiry mass, but I delve through, roughly, bringing the fork up and out. Henry's body stiffens. Several hairs are tangled in the prongs. I run the fork through again, this time making sure the dull prongs dig into his tender skin once or twice.

"Isn't this fun, Henry?"

Did he know I had been in jail? "Henry, let me ask you a question. What do you think happened to me once you had me evicted? Do you know?"

Silence.

"I asked you a question, Henry."

More silence.

Henry's eyes beg me to stop.

"Well, okay, then. You're not going to answer me, you can suffer some more."

I take a couple more sips of wine. I savour the richness, the full body. Red wine. Merlot. My favourite. It's an expensive bottle, too. I pour a bit over the wadded washcloth in Henry's mouth so he can smell the fragrance and ache for what he is missing. His nostrils flap and flare.

"Henry, I have another vial. Should I inject you again? Or do you want to stay awake?" I asked Butch for two vials in case I needed a double dosage.

I receive a sudden flash and decide I should keep the other vial for Butch. Oh what fun to do this to Butch! Plus, I want Henry awake and alert. I want him to enjoy this as much as I. "Okay, no answer. I guess that means you want to be awake. Good!"

I gulp more of the sweet nectar and swirl it around in my mouth before swallowing.

Nemesis takes over, and I'm powerless to stop her. She does things to Henry that are beyond my comprehension, things I'm sure I could never do.

Afterward, I see the blood-red sheets, once pristine and white, and the bloodied fork and knife resting by Henry's hip.

I pour the last of the wine over what remains of his man jewels, the burgundy melding with the scarlet.

It is over.

I shudder when I look down at him. What has Nemesis done? I'm not sure I wanted to go that far. Or did I?

Show-off, sadistic Henry always carried a large amount of cash in his pocket. I help myself to the bills in his wallet and stuff them in my bag, along with the empty vial and my beloved dictionary. I towel off everything I've touched—the wine bottle, the wine glass, the knife, the fork—and hope I haven't forgotten anything.

Thanks to that voice, my fingerprints are on file, and I don't want to be back in jail. After all, I didn't do anything, at least not this time—it was Nemesis.

I survey the room one more time, take a last peek at Henry, and shrug into my backpack. I wrap the towel around my hand before I open the door.

Vengeance is mine I realize when I fling the towel into the room just before the heavy door swings shut.

Yes, vengeance is truly mine.

The Lone Leaf

I remember when Mom spouted her goal to the three of us. "I'm going to live to be one hundred," she said, which didn't sound like a goal to me, but a proclamation. Had it been a goal, she would have written it in a diary, perhaps flipping ahead to page 100: I want to live to be one hundred.

But Mom didn't have a diary.

None of us believed her because one hundred sounded like an unattainable number and a massive amount of years, but as well-brought-up children, we agreed on the outside and snickered silently inside. "Yes, Mom, you'll live that long. And way beyond that." In retrospect, Mom was still young then, in her early forties, even though she appeared ancient to us teenagers, and what teen thinks that far ahead?

Later, on her deathbed, while watching a lone tear slide down her withered cheek, we remained positive. No matter how elderly and frail she was, not one of us wanted her to leave us. We pretended positive, knowing positivity had been tossed away like the hospital breakfast she'd picked at.

Mom had always been the pillar of the family, the one who held us together. Perfect, in retrospect, though at the time what did we know about perfection? She was innocent; naïve, too, I had thought. Oh, so naïve, a trait I had wrongly attributed to her, which I didn't discover until much later.

As teens, we selfishly proceeded with our daily affairs. In our eyes, our parents were ancient; they'd not age any further. Neither would we. Teens and young people were immortal—in our own minds.

Dad was not quite so perfect, not with his dalliances and flings. Then again, had everyone been aware of them, they wouldn't have been classified as meaningless episodes but secret liaisons. I'd always been grateful Mom never knew; the knowledge would have killed her in her prime, obliterating her wish—her goal—to reach one hundred.

Dad died at sixty-two. A massive heart attack. *Probably from your frequent floozies,* I had wanted to scream. But I never did; we respected our elders. Plus, I had to pretend I was as clueless as my younger two

152

siblings, Becca and Ben. Dad had sworn me to secrecy. "Betsy, it'll kill your mother," he had said. He begged. Pleaded. Whined. Bribed.

The bribe worked. "Okay," I had said, "I'll never tell. But if Becca or Ben find out on their own, I can't be responsible." "Fair enough," he had said. We even shook on it. What father and daughter shake hands? What daughter should ever be placed in such a despicable predicament?

A riot would have ensued had the other three found out. Okay, not a full-blown street riot with tear gas and batons, but the news would have torn our family to shreds. Mom, especially, and I would never hurt her. None of us would. I'm sure Dad didn't want to, either, but he had uncontrollable impulses. Booze and cigarettes. And women.

It was autumn when Mom landed in the hospital for the last time. Her shortness of breath scared me. "We need to go," I had said. She fought with me, and I sensed the "goal" she had harboured for years. I figured she thought she would reach her hundredth year if she remained at home rather than being admitted to the hospital. And if I succeeded in taking her to outpatients, they would surely admit her.

I'll never forget leading her outdoors. It was autumn, as I said, the time of year when leaves turn brown and plummet, disintegrating into the ground like dirt. She scanned the yard and pointed to the many fallen leaves. "The kiss of death," she said, waving her arms.

When we reached the driveway, one lone leaf scuttled in front of us, as if to taunt us when it stopped at Mom's feet. Okay, it wasn't so much the leaf that stopped, but the wind. The leaf was flawlessly shaped, a healthy green instead of sickly brown, and even without picking it up, I could tell it was rubbery instead of crinkly—one of those perfect leaves that sensitive people insert between pages of a thick book to preserve forever.

"It's an omen," Mom shrieked, disregarding her previous comment which had sounded more like fear. "It's a good sign. There's always a good one in every bunch."

Huh? What did Mom know about leaves? What did I know about leaves? Was there a special meaning in a lone leaf? "What do you mean"? I asked, humouring her.

"I'm going to reach my goal." At the exact moment she stopped to glare at me, the prize scurried away with a sudden gust. "Even if you're thwarting my plans by forcing me to the hospital."

Thwarting? Forcing?

"Mom, I'm looking out for your interests, remember? You need to be in the hospital so they can prolong your life. That's what doctors and nurses do." My words sounded lame, even to my ears, and no doubt even more so to hers. "And soon enough, you'll be back home. All better." More untruths to bolster a sagging spirit, but she had no one to trust but me. After Dad died, I had moved back to our family home and had been taking care of her ever since.

She watched the leaf disappear into the neighbour's yard until I opened the car door and helped her in. She thrust out her hand at one point as if to stop me, and I half expected her to race after the leaf. I knew she wanted to.

Memories careened at me like an avalanche. Mom, so trusting and dependent, as most elderly are, and I hated my father at that moment. More so than I usually did. Sure, he'd been the bread and butter of our family, bringing home the bacon as the cliché goes, but Mom had been the glue that kept us together when times were tough, like when Becca lost her son and when Ben became suicidal after his job loss, and me, too, when my husband, Jeremy, left me for a younger woman before I'd even had a chance to become pregnant. After Jeremey deserted me, I had pictured duct-taping him and Dad in a pine box and burying it six feet under. Jeremy had crushed me like a worthless, weathered autumn leaf under his feet.

Crazy—we all were. Mom must have used Crazy Glue to bind us together. Regular white paper glue wouldn't have worked, not for our dysfunctional family. Mom had been right, I suppose, to want to catch that unfettered leaf. One last hope. A miracle. A memory to hide in a book.

***

We stood around Mom's deathbed. Becca, Ben, and me. Waiting for her to die; not wanting her to die.

She was sicker than the previous day when I brought her to the hospital. She was right: she would have lived longer at home.

All was quiet. Too quiet. Was this it? Was this how dying starts? In the silence? What if we were jovial? Would that keep death away?

A nurse skipped into the room, as brash as her bold-fabric scrubs, interrupting my mentation, asking if everything was okay.

I recognized her instantly and inwardly screamed. I rubbed my arms, feeling goosebumps beneath my sleeves.

She didn't recognize me, of course, but surely Mom's last name beeped a chime with her.

Though she had bounded into the room like a three-year-old, she had to be in her sixties. Thirty or so years younger than Mom and Dad. Can that be?

I hadn't known how old the woman was when I caught her and Dad in bed together. She had bounded from the bed then like she bounded into the hospital room. Her hair, still bottle-blonde, flowed around her face, but surely her breasts wouldn't be as perky. My eyes lingered on her chest as they did years ago, like a lesbian might. Being a divorcee and single most of my life caused nosey people to gossip.

"My, my, what have we here," she asked in that old-fashioned, fussy, placating tone, a question not requiring an answer. She scanned the room, either to lambaste or embrace us. She did neither, but hurried to Mom's bedside, brushing us aside like burnt toast crumbs, and checked the IV.

My gaze reverted to Mom, still alert despite her breathing issues.

Her eyes flashed. She raised her hand, the one free of the needle. What was she doing?

"I'm gonna win," she mumbled. "I'm gonna make my goal. To heck with all of you."

She had four days left.

***

I was alone with Mom when she passed to the other side, as she called it. The other side? What waited on the other side? A fairy tale life?

I call it what it is: death. The end. Finito!

Becca and Ben, disgusted with frequent, close calls at night, didn't heed that last call. But that was okay. I was closest to Mom, the one who cherished her the most, and I was happy to be alone with her at the end.

"I knew all along," she said to me.

I stroked her withered hand. "Knew what, Mom?"

"I Knew. Your father."

"Dad?"

Was she hallucinating? I was aware the end neared, but she was fairly alert and communicative as if she had received a reprieve. Did the dying receive a second wind to rid themselves of burdens before departing for the pearly gates? Life was supposed to flash before the dying within seconds before death, but who lived to support the tale?

"What do you mean?" I asked.

"That nurse. Didn't she look like her? Could have been her twin."

"Look like who?" I grasped her hand a little too tightly.

"Remember? You went into the house. You saw them, together. In bed. I did, too."

I dropped her hand like I would a too-fast burning match. "You saw?"

"I came in after you. I snuck out just as quietly."

"What? Mom, what are you saying?" How could I not have known Mom was there?

"It's okay, Betsy. Oh, I'm sorry. I should have told you years ago. I shouldn't have let you suffer with that your whole life."

"You knew?"

It had been the weekend before my prom. Ben was overnight at a friend's. Becca, Mom, and I had gone shopping. Mom wanted a contrasting material to make a scarf to go with my prom dress. I had forgotten the slip of fabric at home, so Mom drove home, a good thirty-five minute drive. Mom was like that. Kind and forgiving, and she never chastised me for the wasted time and gas. Naïve, too—or so I thought.

Happy-go-lucky, I had bounded into the house. When I heard a noise in my parents' bedroom, I opened the door. A woman had leaped out of bed.

"It wasn't that nurse from the other day? When Becca and Ben were here?"

"What? Of course not. No."

"It sure looked like her."

"Oh, sweetie, that was many years ago."

"But that woman—girl—was young, Mom. This nurse is the right age. And she looks just like her. I recognized her right away." The hair, I almost added, not wanting her to think it was her breasts.

Mom managed a laugh, but there was a slight cough mixed in. "Oh, sweetie, no, that wasn't her. I thought so at first, too. And when I saw your face, I knew you thought the same. That's why I needed to tell you. To ask forgiveness."

"Oh, Mom, no, I've never blamed you. I still don't."

"I'm sorry it happened, that you had to see."

"But how could you have been there? I didn't see you."

"I was there. I saw. All these years...I've ached that you saw."

I caressed her bruised arm, feeling the pulsating vein. "It's okay, Mom. I've never blamed you. I felt bad for you. I was mad at Dad. Hated him."

"Mmm, I did, too. Hated him. But I loved him still."

What to say? Why does someone maintain their love for someone like that? Another cliché: love conquers all.

Too many clichés in the world.

Too much suffering and death.

I was amazed at the strength Mom had possessed to speak those last words, but her face relaxed. For the first time since she'd been in the hospital, she looked at peace. Another phrase I hated: at peace. What's that mean, anyhow?

The end was close. I felt it. She did, too. I prayed the "other side" would be wonderful for Mom. Would she meet up with Dad? Heaven forbid, would he be there with his look-alike nurse? I shrugged away that last vile thought. That was Mom's business. And Dad's.

Hours passed while I sat by her bedside. She slipped in and out of unconsciousness.

Her eyelids fluttered open. "I beat them all," she muttered, her voice faint and weak.

No third winds for her.

I stroked her cheek while death sucked her last breath.

Mom achieved her goal: one hundred years.

Plus four days.

I left the hospital in tears. A breeze, mild like balmy Caribbean breezes, washed over me. Too warm for September.

I headed to my car. I had managed to find a parking spot on the street. On Sundays it wasn't necessary to feed the meters.

I heard a slight rustle and saw a flicker of dark. By my feet.

A leaf! A lone leaf?

There wasn't a tree in sight, not in the downtown core. Concrete had long ago removed all living thing except for breathing souls.

I crouched to pick it up. Rubbery. Green, with spikes of burgundy veins threading from the sturdy stem to the outer edges, reminding me of Mom's patchy, mottled flesh, and my fingers feeling her faint flutter of life.

"It's an omen." I heard Mom's soft voice.

I smiled and hurried to my car. When I arrived home, I'd insert the leaf between two pages of a thick book for a few days until it became perfectly perfect.

How nice it would look in a frame. I'd hang it on the wall, beside a picture of Mom.

Memories to cherish: Mom and the lone leaf. And I'd write about it in my diary. On page 100.

Between the Good and the Bad

y stomach churns so loudly and uncontrollably that I'm afraid I'm going to be discovered. I press down hard on my belly, hoping to mute the sound, but it ignores my plea, another instance of my body having its own mind, with no regard for its master. Yes, my body has betrayed me previously as it will likely turn on me again in the future.

Some things are uncontrollable.

The night draws to a close. Dawn will soon appear and display its fresh face for those who want to see.

This October evening, not yet Halloween, is when his life will end. I see him out of the corner of my eye…

Michael doesn't notice me creeping behind him. He turns left and when he's almost adjacent to the alley between Northwest and Highcrest, I seize my chance. I grab his hands and shove his wrists into the cuffs. He's a big man, six feet tall and two hundred thirty pounds, but he's defenseless in his inebriated state. The element of surprise helps. I force him into the dark alley.

He screams. My black hooded cloak is long, flowing, and mysterious—not to mention scary—and I keep my face shielded. I throw him to the ground. Shards of glass lay about, which could be hazardous, but glass and other debris are the least of his worries. The surface is abrasive on his backside, even through his clothing, and I know it makes his ass chafe. He moans. It's a moan of fear, but unconscious sexual connotation seeps through. He's more frightened, especially when I throw myself upon him.

Michael, by his own admission, is over-sexed. I'm not sure what over-sexed means in his convoluted mind. Does his wife not put out as much as he likes and could never meet his expectations no matter what she did? Or does he desire sexual gratification and ego-stroking from any woman who will look his way? I believe it's the latter, but I'm sure he applies the first instance to rationalize his wanton ways and cheat.

He sees a flash of my face when the moon saunters above, and he knows I'm a woman although there's no indication from his expression that he's recognized me. Despite being pinned, he squirms. Freeing himself is hopeless. He realizes he's screwed. In more ways than one.

His fear evaporates a bit, yet he's still scared, especially when I drop my hood to reveal my gorgeous face. I know I'm gorgeous because everyone tells me. Over time, you believe what you hear. Recognition flashes across his face. He sees lust in my eyes but also something more, something indescribable, and for the first time in our sexual escapades, he's petrified. Wheels spin through his head; he's wishing he had never taken this cheating path, at least not with me. Yet, in a perverse way, he's aroused. His eyes lock into mine.

He glares, almost begging, as if he has no strength with which to resist, as if he knows he's doomed. There's also something else in his eyes, an element of intrigue. He doesn't want me to stop, anxious to experience what I have in mind, but I'm not certain he's aware it'll culminate in his death. Michael is like that, enjoying a taste of surprise, and he's always savoured what I've dished out. Fantasies, real or imagined, turn him on.

I'm in so deep now I can't prevent my actions even if I want to.

I gaze at him. His lower lip quivers. I envision his brain roiling like a hamster peddling on its never-ending journey.

I'm shocked he doesn't speak. He simply stares and shivers. Perhaps he knows.

After one last look at him, my face falls upon his. My mouth seeks his neck, and I latch to his flesh. The blood streaming through me exhilarates me. The nectar of his fluids goes down like swallowing warm, creamy yoghurt. I suckle on him like a breastfeeding baby.

The unexpected thud when his head plops to the concrete after I release him jars me. I glance at him: his open eyes plead with me.

"Sorry, Michael." But am I sorry I sucked the life out of him? Wouldn't I rather have fucked him one last time? A tiny twinge of regret wafts through me.

I close his eyelids. Perhaps I want to block the sight so I don't have to stare into his godforsaken soul. Or perhaps I want to close his pain.

I had not been nice to Michael, but he deserved it. That was my rationale.

I lick my blood-coated lips. If it were lipstick, it would be a dark shade—crimson. His blood tastes especially good. I don't dwell on the why. I savour the taste. Fresh is best.

With his eyes closed, Michael resembles the man I once knew. Our times were spent in bed, where his eyes, when I looked, were almost always closed.

Good old Michael. What lies did he tell his wife? Where was he supposed to be when he wasn't home?

I went to Michael's house one evening when he told me he had to work late. He had never given me his address or last name, but I had skimmed through his wallet when he was asleep after an encounter.

When I arrived at his house, it was eight o'clock. I hid behind a tree on the avenue of white-picket-fenced homes with gardener-tended lawns. Once darkness descended, I'd see more clearly into his home.

About ten minutes later, Michael appeared, which was odd since he said he'd be at the office. He was a cheater. One can't trust cheaters, but he promised to remain faithful, saying I was his one and only. I believed him.

He drove toward Wiltshire. I lost him when a taxi veered behind him. I would have preferred being in that taxi instead of on foot, but my legs sped along as fast as the cars until both disappeared.

I turned left on Wiltshire, hoping that's where they had gone. Bingo! Michael turned at King, where he parked. He backtracked on foot to Lincoln, stopping at a brownstone. He glanced around and went to the front door. Before he rang the doorbell, the door flew open. A slinky redhead emerged, wrapped her arms around him, and yanked him in. The door shut.

I knew what would ensue. He'd remove her robe and attack her breasts. After he devoured those, he'd throw her to the floor and ravage her. His thick fingers would prod and knead and enter every orifice before his engorged cock filled her cunt. He'd hump and thump, his heart beating as though he'd suffer a heart attack. He'd groan and moan, and when he orgasmed, he'd screech loud enough to wake the dead. His body had a mind of its own. With mistresses, he gave himself permission to let inhibitions roam free, something he couldn't do with his wife. At least that's what he told me.

Just as Michael's body had its own mind, so did mine. Thinking about him ravishing another woman set my juices flowing. My panties became wet, and my fingers longed to massage my clit. I calmed down before I skulked to the window. I peeked through a broken blind, which afforded me full view of her living room.

Michael was on top. His hands rubbed her thighs. She was a slim woman except for her fake boobs. Her flaming hair fanned across the floor like a red-headed snow angel.

He moved off and slurped a nipple, suckling longer than necessary. The woman's open mouth and her tongue licking her lips goaded me. I wondered why Michael hadn't taken that opportunity—an open, inviting orifice—yet he ignored it, concentrating on her breasts. After he finished with the left one, he latched on the right. I willed my body to remain still.

When he moved down to her lower half, I left.

The day after Michael's escapade with the red-headed tramp, I spied on his wife. I was curious about her. According to Michael, though she wasn't a dog, she wasn't a beauty. I was taken aback by his crude comments. What husband put his wife in the same category as a dog?

As I did the previous night, I leaned against the tree. It was two o'clock in the afternoon, and Michael would be at work. His wife's green BMW was parked in the driveway. After twenty minutes, I realized how ridiculous it was loitering in daylight. I decided to ring her doorbell and pretend I had the wrong house. Before I had a chance, though, a car appeared and pulled to the curb a few houses past Michael's. The driver crossed the street, and when he reached Michael's house, the door opened. Dorothy. He glanced around, scampered up the walk, and disappeared into the house.

I got a good look at Dorothy. I'm not sure what I expected, but neither a silly, overgrown-child/woman Dorothy from the *Wizard of Oz* nor the gorgeous blonde peering out the door.

I glance at Michael's lolling head. This is the last time I'll see him before they cart his decrepit body to the morgue. I brush my fingers across his blanched cheek. He's peaceful as though the devil seized his sordid soul to allow him to rest in peace. The devil is wrong; Michael shouldn't reside peacefully for the rest of eternity.

I loved Michael more than any other man. Once a man lies, that's it. Finito, kaput, done. That's when my rage erupts. That's when I exact revenge.

No one messes with Vanessa.

The next day dawns sunny. I thank the gods (for I believe there's more than one) for miracles such as the warmth of the sun and the glow of the moon and the twinkle of the stars, small yet important things, for where would we be without the sun, moon, and stars?

I run to the store to purchase *The Gibson Star*, our local newspaper, and sit in the nearby park. Michael's death blasts from the front page as if he's Jesus Christ risen from the dead:

> *Gibson native, Michael J. Larson, 39, was found dead*
> *early this morning by a local passerby just off Mason*
> *Road. Until the investigation is complete, the police*
> *won't release further information.*

Yeah, right. The police aren't releasing any so-called information because they don't have any information. They don't know what to make of a blood-drained body. I snicker. The press will have a field day if this gets out.

I wonder how Dorothy took the news. How did they tell her? And when?

Michael and his wife have one daughter, Leah. I remember the first time he mentioned her. "See if you can figure out the significance of her name," he said. I never could, not that I tried that hard.

He bragged about Leah's ballet prowess. She had taken lessons since she was two years old. According to him, she was perfection in motion—a prospective ballerina ready to perform in a production of Swan Lake. His daughter meant the world to him. He'd climb mountains for her, but I didn't get the impression he'd do the same for his wife. Shouldn't wives mean more to husbands than children and vice versa? Sure, fathers and mothers should cherish their children, but spouses should cherish respective spouses more than children.

Spouses come first; the couple is the glue in a marriage. That's the way my parents were, with a bond so great only death could break it apart.

***

I began stalking Dorothy a few weeks after Michael's funeral. I don't know why. Perhaps I needed to find out what made her tick. Was she as frigid and cold in bed as Michael had depicted? She appears to be a sexual individual, but looks can be deceiving. I don't understand why Michael had been on the prowl, not with a wife like her.

Although I consider myself attractive, I'm not as gorgeous as Dorothy. Men usually like long hair, but Dorothy's hair is fashioned in a bob. She's one of those women who look better in short hair. I could never pull it off nor would I want to try. Michael used to face me, gather my long black hair behind my neck, and run his fingers through the strands. "So silky," he'd say. "Don't you ever cut it."

I love my hair as much as Michael did. I love the way it cascades down my back like a dark waterfall lit on fire by the rising sun.

***

The day of the funeral dawns dark and gloomy. The night before, I made up my mind to pay my respects to dearly departed Michael.

I sit in a middle pew at First Baptist Church of Gibson Hills, and while we wait for the family to arrive, I discretely observe everyone as if I can discover tidbits about Michael that I don't know, something to help me understand why he acted the way he did. I suppose that's a ridiculous idea since it's a man thing—a man not being able to keep his fly zipped, much like a woman not keeping her legs closed. Lust is all it boils down to. Why am I still stunned by his actions? Men are fanatics for sex, the more the merrier and with as much variety as they can manage.

The church is packed, and a crowd congregates outdoors. It's not a huge church, but neither is it one of those small country churches you drive past while on a Sunday drive. There is a sudden silence when the family congregates at the back of the church.

A man escorts Dorothy up the aisle. She's crying crocodile tears. Surely she's not that upset. Or is she? Her other hand clutches Leah's. Leah's little girl face is white, marred by blotches of pink. I feel sorry for Michael's daughter. She's at that young, impressionable age. Too young to lose a father.

The customary funeral poppycock transpires—the minister preaching his pious sermon, the congregation kneeling to mundane prayers, everyone singing sorrowful hymns. Michael's best friend recites the eulogy, and we listen to never-ending saccharine words about the dearly departed. It's funny how death brings out the very best in an individual, and suddenly, he or she is everyone's best friend and the most wonderful person ever.

With the service finally over, everyone retreats outside to the cemetery. A heavy green tarp, mimicking grass, camouflages the empty plot. The plastic covering is a bit ridiculous as if we mourners are a dumb bunch who doesn't know a gaping hole lies beneath.

Outdoors, even in the day's dullness, tears are more obvious. The weather cooperates fittingly, the light mist blending in with tears. It's a great day for a funeral and burial.

The pallbearers lug the burnished coffin toward the burial plot, and two funeral home employees remove the fake grass. I step toward the hole's edge where I have a clear view of Michael's final resting place. I see the bottom, but it's still deep, still abysmal. I envision Michael posing there for all eternity. Sure, maybe his soul will depart, depending upon one's religious beliefs, but he'll be there forever. That thought warms my insides as his blood did. I can still taste his sweet and nourishing fluids.

Without realizing it, I've dug at a finger and pulled away the skin adjacent to a nail. I suck my finger, tasting metal, thinking how appropriate that my bloodletting occurs precisely when Michael is lowered. I watch him slowly enter the hole, much like he's entered mine numerous times before. Most apropos.

The coffin thuds when it hits bottom, an unsuccessful attempt to slip it down carefully. Even in death, Michael has a mind of his own. The sudden noise startles me as it does everyone, and I back away.

Dorothy, her face white in the doom of the day, stares down the pit as does Leah, as if in disbelief he's down there instead of holding their hands. Dorothy pulls a tissue from her pocket and wipes her face for the millionth time. Ghastly dark smudges rim her eyes, and the black has stained her tears and runs down her cheeks. Who applies makeup on the day of a funeral, especially a widow? Doesn't she know that mascara, waterproof or not, will smudge and smear? Maybe it's all for show. Is she role-playing?

Leah, outfitted in a frilly black dress garnished with tiny white polka dots, short white socks, and patent leather shoes, is dry-eyed but bloodshot. Perhaps she cried her tears through the night. She seems in shock and doesn't move unless her mother takes her hand.

A slight breeze materializes, and my mid-length black dress sways about my bare legs. Without the sun, my wide-rimmed black hat and huge sunglasses are unnecessary, but it's easier to keep them on than hold them. I feel powerful in black, but I may have dressed too much like a mourner despite a mauve scarf draped around my shoulders.

***

Two days after the funeral, I stand outside Michael's house, watching Dorothy and Leah get into the car. They drive down the street, and I follow, alternately running and flying, skimming so fast I'm unseen. Dorothy pulls into the parking lot of Leah's school and leads her into the building. When Dorothy returns, I trail her down Oak Street. She makes a right turn on Pine Avenue and a left on Spruce, turning into the parking lot of Gibson Gym. She parks and enters the building, carrying her classy fuchsia gym bag.

I debate the merits of purchasing a membership or waiting for her to leave. I decide to go inside.

"Do you offer trial memberships?" I ask the girl at the front desk.

"Yes, we do. Four sessions to try out our facilities. Then it's $199.99 for six months." She waits for my response.

"Can I have a tour first?"

"Certainly. Let me find Rocky." She picks up the phone and carries on a conversation. With Rocky, I assume.

A few minutes later, a hulking black man appears. He's vaguely familiar, and for an instant, I wonder if I've dated him. When he ogles me, specifically how my black jeans and turtleneck hug my body, I realize we haven't met. He would have remembered me if we had. I smile, wink, and lick my lips. His eyes glaze. He's aroused. It doesn't take long for men to become horny in my presence.

"So you want a tour?"

"Yes, please."

"Come this way." He hesitates. He'd prefer I lead so he can lust over my backside. Instead, my eyes wash over him. His gym attire—the navy skin-tight stretch pants and body-clinging white t-shirt—reveals every nook and cranny of his body. Almost. A couple of body parts are left to my imagination, and I conjure images of him naked while he grinds into me.

He turns to ask, "You haven't been here before?"

"No. I haven't."

While he points out the Olympic-size swimming pool, the shower and locker room, and demonstrates the equipment, I'm on the lookout for Dorothy. She suddenly appears, steps on the treadmill, and turns it on. Her endless slender legs run as fast as they can. How long can she keep up the pace?

"I forgot to show you something." Rocky touches me on the shoulder, and I follow him back to the women's lockers.

The room is deserted. He turns around and pulls me to his chest, almost smothering me.

"I saw the way you looked at me." He grasps my chin and leans down to kiss me. His thick tongue invades my mouth. I tongue him back, my small tongue no match for his.

"Ah, baby, I knew you'd like this," he gasps and stares at me. "You're so lovely."

"Yeah, well I'm here for a tour, remember?"

"That's it, babe. That's the tour. How about later? Want to get together?"

"What do you have in mind?"

"Meet me at Riverside Pub. Eight o'clock. We can take things from there."

His eyes bore into mine, and I stare back, uncertain what to do. Finding a fuck isn't in my game plan.

"Busy tonight," I say.

"Aw, babe." He grabs me again and kneads one breast. I collapse against him. I've been chaste since Michael, and I'm ready for some loving. I fondle his crotch and feel the looming manhood that perks up at my touch. I yank down his pants, and his cock points at me, a gun aiming to shoot its bullet.

"Come here." He drags me into a stall. It's a changing stall, no toilet, with a wooden bench built into the far side. He sits, pulls down my pants, and impales me. There's pain at first, but once our rhythms are in sync, I'm comfortable. His hands slip under my blouse, and he tweaks my already erect nipples. He is much larger than Michael and fills me completely.

Soon, Rocky's done. So am I. And then we hear someone in the room. How long has she been there? Has she heard us?

"Ssh," I whisper.

Rocky's eyes narrow. He shouldn't be in the women's locker room, but I suppose he can come up with an excuse if need be. I pull up my pants. He stays on the bench.

"I'll go out," I mouth. "You stay here."

I open the door to see Dorothy. She doesn't know I know her, and there's no rush of recognition from the funeral. She says, "Hi," like anyone would to acknowledge someone who enters a room. Since she's seen my face, I'll have to be careful in the future. I don't want to arouse her suspicions.

After she disappears into one a stall, I flag Rocky to leave.

I wait for him outside the locker room. "I'll be back," I say before leaving. I'm not certain I'll return, but I want to keep my options open. And I still have four free visits.

***

I'm not your run-of-the-mill vampire or even a witch. I've known since I was small that I was different, and my parents didn't know what to make of me. They were frightened—frightened for me and for them. But they were my parents; I'd never hurt them, and they gradually realized that. Other than my "gift," my childhood was normal, for my parents ensured that and instilled in me the values I have today.

"Don't kill without a good reason," they told me numerous times.

My parents called me their little Vitch, which was their definition of a cross between a vampire and a witch. Although they realized I wasn't a full-fledged vampire or a full-blown witch, they didn't know exactly what I was.

I thrive in the dark, but I don't fly on a straw broom nor am I doomed when I face crosses and holy water. My eyes and teeth are normal, but I possess a fierce bite that allows me to easily break skin and suck up one's life. I have the ability to speed by humans so fast they can't see me. I can lurk in the shadows unseen, but I'm not invisible. I don't exist solely on blood. I eat food although blood is required to energize my mind and body.

Blood is a treat, much like dessert is for others, but I don't eat sweets. My parents learned early on that sugar took me to a high they didn't want repeated. At the age of three, after eating my birthday cake, I attacked Fluffy, our four-month-old cat. I sank my teeth into her neck and gorged. My parents watched, with revulsion and disgust tinged with a bit of awe, but were powerless to stop me, for once I began, I latched on until life exited that poor animal.

My parents had never been ones for desserts, and that was the first time they'd let me dig into a cake. After a similar episode a few months later with another pet, they added two and two and came up with sugar.

I don't kill without reason, at least not anymore, not once my sugar problem was discovered. Sometimes killing for blood is a necessity, such as my need for caffeine, similar to a human's need that drives them to drink cup after cup of morning coffee. I've learned to use my skills to help the world, and I'm selective with my prey.

My witch gene enables me to cast magical spells. I've conjured formulas to carry out my deeds, and I'm somewhat of a poet when I recite chants.

You've heard of those unexpected, unwarranted deaths where an individual dies in a sole-vehicle accident? Although people keep their thoughts to themselves, everyone assumes those individuals are suicide victims, for how could a driver veer off a deserted road into a ditch at three o'clock on a beautiful summer's day? Some of those deaths are instances when I've assisted; there are plenty more. Sure, some of those motor vehicle deaths are accidents, but the majority are due to my spells. Of course, no one will ever know the difference between the two.

There are more mysterious deaths than I can take credit for. Are there are other individuals like me in this town who perform the same acts? If so, I haven't met them. It would be difficult, not to mention dangerous, to approach a suspected individual and ask.

There are those who are too mentally diseased, too down in the dumps to live. Suicidal they might be, but killing themselves is something they would never accomplish successfully on their own—or even attempt—so I help out. I brew special liquids and cast the spell of death or, at least, ensure suicide attempts are successful.

I've also helped others die earlier than they would naturally. One such individual was Germaine, a woman in her sixties, who feared aging. She'd had numerous facelifts, so many that her face resembled Michael Jackson shortly before his untimely death. I put her out of her misery; she requested it, in a roundabout way. Another face job would have killed her if I hadn't, and an operation was scheduled.

Another was Amy, a beautiful twelve-year-old so full of cancer she didn't stand a chance. Another year might have been afforded to her, but it would have been a painful and horrific one—for her and her family. Something had to be done to relieve them from misery.

Phillip experienced a different type of death, the hands-on treatment. He had cheated on his wife, but that was the only similarity between him and Michael. Phillip, a sex offender, had served a six-year prison term before being released on a technicality. Six years for molesting eight little boys? And he would have hurt more children. A sentence of endless years wouldn't have been enough for him; he needed to burn in hell for eternity. No spells for him.

So, one late night, I confronted Phillip, much like I had Michael, and I performed slow, painful acts on him like he had on those poor defenseless boys. He suffered horrifically and begged for death before I was halfway through.

There are numerous other Genevieves and Amys I have helped, all with similar circumstances and pre-determined fates, and there will be many more. And there are the Phillips—males and females—who don't deserve to live.

Although I can last several weeks without gorging on blood, there's no shortage of innocents and victims, not in this depraved world, so I don't have to worry about where my next feed will come from. And when I have an uncontrollable urge, I am selective and pick an elderly individual.

***

From the window seat in my tenth-floor penthouse, I stare at the street below. People resemble tiny toy characters coming and going, and I wonder which of them has been naughty or nice, much like Santa ponders children at Christmas. Will one of them be my next conquest? Which one needs my help? It hasn't been long since Michael, but I feel the urge.

I take another sip of Merlot, thankful sugars in wine don't affect me. I prefer red wine, the more full-bodied and richer the better. The liquid reminds me of blood, especially when I look in the mirror and see teeth stained red.

The wine soothes my soul and calms my mind, and I pour another glass. I continue to peer at the walkers. I think about Rocky and the quick fuck we had. I'm not usually one for quickies, but Michael had been on my mind, and I regretted not having used him for one last selfish purpose.

I suppose I'm like a spider; I snare men in, use them, and toss them away like trash. But that's the female in me. It's the witch in me that performs other acts, the ones relieving people's pain or punishing them for bad deeds.

I had my first sexual experience at thirteen after my first period when I blossomed and flowered into a woman and became more aware of my capabilities and limitations. My parents saw the change in me, but no one could have changed me; they were aware of that. I was born that way. A quirk of nature, an unlikely blending of genes or cells that hadn't formed correctly. Perhaps my parents would have prevented their one and only pregnancy had they known, for they didn't have more children after me.

My parents were killed in a car accident when I was fourteen. That's when I began avenging. Roger Thomas Thorne, the driver of the car that had careened into my parents' vehicle, perished in a horrific vehicular accident less than twelve hours after my parents' deaths. His car slammed into the brick wall of Carter Construction Limited, where it caught fire within several minutes. While the flames snuffed out his life, I stood and watched. He recognized me sneering at him and realized his fate.

After my parents' death, I shuffled from one foster home to another. I kept to myself and never shared my secrets. In too short a time, I had matured and snuck out at night to kill. More than anything, it was my way to cope without my parents.

For a short time back then, I picked victims at random, not caring who or when. Now, however, I help those who deserve to die—those who have no hope of a successful suicide, those whose remaining lives will only lead to despair and untold pain, those savages who deserve death.

I pour the last of the wine and guzzle it down.

I'm feeling pretty good. Wicked, actually. Wicked and happy. And I feel the urge.

***

From my vantage point, I see Leah. She sits alone, her face down, and a woman, presumably a teacher, approaches her. The teacher takes a tissue from her pocket, wipes Leah's face, and says a few words to her. Leah nods. The adult's gentleness doesn't have any effect because after she leaves, the child's tears begin again. She swipes at them before brushing her long blonde hair from her face though wisps remain plastered on her pale face. The once-rosy cheeks are gone, and she looks older than her seven years.

Flashbacks from when I was seven, before I understood my powers, wash over me. Notwithstanding the love for my parents and how I wish they were alive, I'd give anything to be Leah—despite the loss of her father since my father would be dead no matter what I had or hadn't done. This so-called gift is more a curse than a blessing. How I long to be normal.

Leah wipes her face again before scanning the yard as if looking for her father.

The longer I watch, the more I realize I can eliminate her pain. I have the capabilities of reuniting her with her father, but I don't want to help Michael. But his daughter? She had no part in this fiasco, and causing her this enormous grief hadn't been in my plan. She'd be happier with her father.

Dorothy? She'd miss her daughter, but I have to think of the child's misery. Several weeks have passed since Michael's funeral, and Leah's been upset for too long.

After the teacher wanders off, I slink from the tree and lean against the metal fence.

"Leah," I whisper. She's only a few feet from me.

She doesn't hear me.

"Leah."

She looks up. Her watery eyes stare at me.

"Come here." I motion for her to come.

Her teacher's talking to another adult.

Leah glances around the yard and saunters toward the chain-link fence. "What do you want?"

"Come with me. I have a message from your father."

"My father? He died. He's gone to Heaven."

"Meet me in the front of the school, and I'll give you his message."

I turn and veer toward the other side of the building where I pray she'll meet me.

***

Today, I don't know whether I did right or wrong. All I desire, really, besides ridding the world of monsters who don't deserve the air they breathe, is to help others deal with their pain.

Yesterday, I wanted to help Leah. Everyone knows a daughter needs her father. Heaven knows, I needed mine—and still do. My dad was taken from me much too soon, too, but I don't regret taking Michael's life despite hurting Leah. Michael deserved it, treating me that way. If he had remained faithful to me—or to his wife—he'd still be alive. But he had to lie and stir emotions in me I couldn't repress. Despite my strict guidelines as to whom I kill, if you incur my wrath, you pay the price.

Leah would be happier in Heaven with her father. Amazingly, I do believe in Heaven and Hell, and despite Michael's faults, he'll reside in Heaven. All he did was cheat on his wife and mistresses, not exactly a crime, not when the mistresses knew he had a wife. Dorothy didn't seem upset at his death, so I figure she knew of his dalliances and didn't care.

Besides, she cheated, too. Remember Rocky from the gym? Hoping for a repeat, I returned to the gym a few days after our first encounter. When I entered the ladies' locker room, I heard rustling in one of the stalls. I didn't think much about it at first, but my curiosity sparked at the unmistakable sounds of sex. After slipping into one of the other stalls to change into stretchies, I lingered by the sink, not knowing what possessed me to stay other than intuition.

Within minutes, Dorothy appeared from the stall. "Hi," she said, careful to shut the stall door behind her.

There was no recognition since she didn't really look at me. Her flushed face was a tell-tale sign of too much exertion.

She washed her hands and splashed water over her face before leaving the room.

With her absence, the room breathed an eerie quiet that warns someone is near. I remained quieter than that silence until the stall door opened.

Rocky and I faced each other. And recognition dawned. He was the man from the vehicle who had parked down the street from me, the man Dorothy had welcomed into her home while Michael was at work.

I should have listened to that niggling suspicion before the tour that day, but I had been transfixed by his body. Of course, had I recognized him, nothing would have changed. I still would have fucked him. He and I had no understanding, not with one dalliance, but rightly or wrongly, it still pissed me off.

I grabbed my bag and my clothes and left. I'd never return, and I had no desire to see Rocky again either.

Dorothy and her feelings be damned. I was within the boundaries of my guidelines to suck the life out of Leah that day.

***

When I reached the front of the school, Leah stood by the door. She saw me and advanced.

"I'm not supposed to be out here. Teacher will get mad if she finds out." She scanned the yard, apparently looking for someone who might tattle, but there was no one else around.

"Let's go over there by the trees so no one will see us." I grabbed her little hand, and we escaped to the trees bordering the driveway. "Over here."

When we were safely hidden behind trees and shrubbery, I garnered my first close-up look at her. She was gorgeous, every bit as lovely as Michael had said. She'd mature into a beautiful woman if she lived that long. Her large, blue eyes stared into mine.

"What do you want?" she asked. She was still scared, especially away from the security of the school.

"I have a message from your father."

"But Daddy's dead. I told you that. The angels took him."

"I know, sweetie." *Sweetie?* When had I ever used that word? "But sometimes the dead can talk, you know."

"Really?" Her eyes grew even wider. "How come he hasn't talked to me, then?"

"I don't know, but he talked to me."

"What did he say?"

"That he loved you very much."

She glowed with the words, but her eyes glistened. I hoped she wouldn't break down.

"Did you know my daddy?"

"I did."

"How did you know him? Are you friends with Mommy?"

"No, I just knew your father. We met once, a while ago."

"Where?"

Little minds want to know everything.

I opened my mouth but changed the words I had intended to say. "He helped me with my car one day when it broke down."

"Oh," she said, obviously still confused.

171

"He mentioned he had a daughter then. Later, after he died, he came to me. Told me to come talk to you."

I noticed the sheen of her pale pink skin. So smooth. Not a mar. Her neck was exposed above her flimsy jacket. I hesitated, wondering when to latch and suck that innocent blood.

"I miss him so much," she said as a tear formed.

"I know. I miss my daddy, too."

"But you're old."

I laughed. "I know, but I still had a daddy, and he was killed when I was little like you. And I still miss him."

"Really?"

"You'll miss him for a long time probably."

"I want him back."

"I know, sweetie. But he loves you. You always have to remember that. And he's always around you, even if you don't know it."

"How do you know that?" she asked.

"I just know."

Leah stared at me for a second and then perked up. "Do you know my middle name?"

"No. I don't."

"It's Kim."

"Kim? What a pretty name. Leah Kim." Sounded kinda dumb, really, not that anyone asked for my opinion.

"Yeah, I'm named after Daddy. I'm glad I have his name. Now that he's gone."

"How so?" I asked, confused.

"It's a puzzle. Can't you figure it out?"

I thought for a bit, pretending to wrack my brain. "Nope."

"Daddy told me only special people would know the secret. Or smart ones who could figure it out."

"Oh," I said. Obviously, I wasn't a special person, nor was I smart. "So tell me."

"Leah Kim." It's Michael spelled backwards.

I pictured the letters in Michael's name. Then reversed them. Something seemed off, but without pen and paper in hand, I couldn't figure it out. "I still don't get it."

She giggled. "Cos Kim is spelled with a 'C' not a 'K'. Get it now?"

I mouthed the letters. "Okay. Yeah, I get it." *Stupid*, I thought. "Kinda neat."

"I miss him so much." Leah's eyes brimmed with tears again.

I kneeled and wrapped my arms around her. Her neck, juicy and inviting, stared me in the face. I leaned down, my mouth aiming toward her. Succulent. My tongue reached out and lightly grazed her neck.

I jerked back and stood. I couldn't do it. Despite missing her father, Leah had the right to live the rest of her life as naturally as possible. There was no good reason to end her life, and I had my self-implied code of ethics. I could pick a dozen people on the street who deserved to die. I didn't need to take a young, defenseless girl. Death was a part of life. She had to learn to deal with her loss as everyone had to. She'd survive. Kids are resilient.

I gulped at what I had almost done. I patted her hair and removed strands caught in her mouth. "Honey, didn't your mother ever tell you not to talk to strangers?"

"Yes, all the time."

"Then why are you here? You don't know me. You shouldn't have listened to me and come here. I could be dangerous."

"But you look nice."

"All people look nice until they do something wrong." I caressed her hand. "Promise me something?"

"What?"

"Listen to your mommy from now on. Don't talk to strangers. Don't listen to strangers. Don't follow them anywhere, okay?"

"Okay."

"And always remember that your daddy loves you. Very much. He'll never forget you even though he's in Heaven. You don't forget him either, okay?"

"I won't."

"You better get back to class now. Do you think you can sneak in so you won't get in trouble? Maybe say you were in the bathroom?"

Leah glanced at the school. "I'll try. I don't want to get yelled at."

"Okay, you run back now. I'll watch and make sure you get in the door safely. And remember, no more talking to strangers, okay?"

Her eyes examined my face a second before she ran to the entrance. She stopped at the door and turned around to search for me in the trees.

I stepped out and waved. She waved back and disappeared.

Straw People

Hey, kiddos, wanna hear a story?"

Aunty G huffed and puffed into my bedroom where my brother, Steven, and I sat on the floor playing Monopoly. Even had her floppy, fluffy, fake rabbit-fur slippers been soundless on the carpet, she announced her presence with her laboured breathing.

Steven and I dropped our game pieces. "Yes! Yes!"

She leaned toward us and whispered, "You ain't real siblings. Ain't real at all." She stuck a bony finger into my cheek. "And you, little missy, ain't legit."

I strained to hear and ignored spittle spraying my face. "Legit?"

She looked at me first and then at Steven. "Your mother ain't your mother. She ain't who you think she is. Ain't so high and mighty just 'cause she goes to church every Sunday. She's a sinner. Her past will haunt you, mark my words."

Aunty G wheezed and coughed before rambling further, but I heard nothing else. Steven and I weren't brother and sister? I was illegitimate? And Mom? What was Aunty G saying about my mother? I'd always been closer to Dad than Mom. Was that a sign? Was Mom forced to love us or put on a show to keep our father's love?

I raced downstairs and into the parlour where my parents sat quietly. With my hands on my hips, I shouted, "Who are my parents? My real parents?"

Mom dropped her book.

Dad made a funny noise in his throat and scratched his chin as he always did before a serious discussion. "What brought this on?"

I glared at my father. "Aunty G told me and Steven that Mom isn't our real mother. That we're not real brother and sister."

Dad glanced at Mom, whose face had turned scarlet. For several too-long minutes, he remained silent, and then he sighed. "I guess you're old enough to know." He hesitated, rubbing his eyes as if he'd just awakened, and sighed again. "Steven's mother died when he was born. Your mother," Dad patted Mom's leg, "adopted him after we married. But I'm your father and your mother is your mother."

"Mom is my mother but not Steven's?"

"Exactly."

"So, Aunty G was right? We're not real brother and sister?"

"Of course you are."

"But Aunty G said I was illegitimate."

Mom looked at Dad before saying, "I'm your mother, Susan." I detected a tear in her eye.

"Yes, she's your mother and I'm your father. That's all you need to know."

My heart thundered in my chest. Mom wasn't Steven's mother, but she was mine?

"I don't want to discuss this again. And ignore Aunty G. She doesn't know what she says," Dad said.

"But you're my real dad? And Steven's real dad?"

"I am." Dad stood and brushed the tear from my cheek. "Steven is too young to know about his biological mother, so let's keep this our secret, okay?"

"When will you tell Steven?"

Dad pondered for a few seconds. "When he's your age. Thirteen's a good age to know, right?"

I wasn't sure. Perhaps Steven would be happier thinking Mom was his real mother. "But Aunty G says I'm not real. Why would she say that?"

"Drat that drunken woman! She lives in the past, an old woman of regrets. Of course you're real. What a stupid question. Pinch yourself."

When I hesitated, Dad pinched my upper arm.

"Ow, that hurts." I glared at him.

Dad laughed. "See? You're real. You're spirited, healthy, and happy. That's all that matters."

I sauntered back to my room, where Steven sat alone on the floor. One of Aunty G's too-big pink slippers lay beside him as if she had evaporated or ran fast away before the boogieman could get her. Or the monster that caught those who lie?

Perhaps I was another big-mouth Aunty G, for I blabbed to Steven what Dad had said. Steven acted unconcerned. Maybe he was too young to comprehend my words. Or maybe he just didn't care. Despite that, we stood before the full-length mirror, trying to find resemblances—a minute detail to tie us together. I examined my face and pointed to a freckle. "There's that. And you have one, too."

"A freckle? Everyone has freckles."

"But what else is there? Your skin is darker than mine. Your eyes are darker, too."

"Our hair," Steven blurted. "We both have straight hair."

"Ya, but yours is brown. Mine is blonde."

"Yours is yellow. Mine is light brown. Pretty close. And your hair is like Mom's."

"I'm not sure she's my mother. I think they're lying. Something doesn't add up." Aunty G's word "illegitimate" burned in my mind. Why would she say that if it wasn't true?

I peered closer in the mirror. "Do we even look like Dad?"

"We're too young to look like him. He's old. When we're older, I'll look just like him. We're men, you know." Ten-year-old Steven stood taller as if that made him a man.

***

Aunty G, Dad's father's sister, was really Gertrude Grace Bennett. She never married nor had children of her own, so when Dad's mother died young, Gertrude became his surrogate mother.

Her words "not real" resonated with me for many years, and when I was younger, I had mulled over the meaning. If not real, were Steven and I fictional? We grew up together. Weren't we real since we breathed, suffered, and laughed?

When Aunty G was in her eighties, Dad convinced her to move from her apartment to Stonebrooke Home, where she'd have companionship and less stress. He felt so beholden to her that he brought her to our home on weekends and holidays. Since liquor wasn't permitted at Stonebrooke, he allowed her a stash at our house, and as soon as she'd consumed dinner, she'd drag out the amber-filled bottle. Although he agreed with Mom that liquor was a magnet pulling Aunty G to our home, he shrugged off her drinking habits.

Aunty G hated Stonebrooke and complained about lumps: lumps in her food, lumps in her bed. Oversized clothing camouflaging an obviously sizeable body made me view her as a life-sized lump.

When I was fifteen, she left Stonebrooke and came to live with us. The first day, she went off on a drunken tangent at the dinner table. "I tell ya, incest ain't right. And children born out of wedlock ain't right." Aunty G eyed Mom who glowered at Dad.

"Watch your language, Aunt Gertrude. Children are present." Dad sounded mad.

My head swivelled from Aunty G to my parents and back to her.

Steven had often jumped into my bed at night, and we would snuggle under the covers. If we had a flashlight, we read or played tent. Other times, we talked, comforted by the nearness of each other. When the hall floor creaked under our parents' footsteps, we watched the light shine through the partially open door. If one of them neared my room, the last one down the hall, a shadow entered first, which prompted Steven to slip down the far side of the bed and slide underneath—a frequent scenario that had taken place several times with neither Dad nor Mom the wiser. Once I discovered the meaning of incest, I no longer wanted him in my bed, but I missed our closeness, especially after Aunty G's rant.

How had Aunty G known Steven and I cuddled in my bed? Did Mom and Dad know, too? Did they think we had done "it?" That had happened years previously. How could blabber-guts Aunty G have kept a secret that long?

Mom glared at Dad again before leaving the room. Dad raced upstairs after her. Aunty G leaned back in the wooden chair, snickered, and poured another drink. Steven remained preoccupied with his food.

I snuck after my parents and listened outside their bedroom door. The door was ajar, and Mom sat on the bed with Dad's arm around her, his fingers kneading her upper arm.

Tears streamed down Mom's face. "God forgive me, but she needs to keep her mouth shut. All that talk of me not being their mother. It's upsetting the kids. And today was the last straw. Susan's acting like I don't love her, and you allow your aunt to get away with everything, like a spoiled child."

Dad dropped his arm and sighed. "She's almost ninety. She's not right in the head. The kids don't know what she's talking about."

Mom huffed. "You don't know what the kids know or don't know. You could take away the booze. Her lips might not be so loose then. A woman her age shouldn't be drinking anyhow. At least she's semi-sane when sober."

"She's set in her ways. She'd die if I restricted her drinking."

Mom didn't give up. "I'm afraid the kids will become alcoholics. And I'm positive she gets up in the middle of the night for swigs. And her words are horrid. Just horrid."

Dad kissed her on the cheek. "Ignore her. She likes to push your buttons. The kids know she drinks too much and talks nonsense. Besides, what do kids know?"

I called Mom "Ruby" a few times, especially when I got mad over a punishment, more to rebel than anything. Despite Steven's adoption and Mom and Dad's denials, I felt like the odd one. Were there more secrets? Was Steven not his dead mother's son? Scenarios crept through my mind.

Mom wouldn't elaborate on Aunty G's words, and Dad became annoyed if asked. Until Aunty G opened her blubbery mouth, Steven and I had thought Mom—Ruby—was our biological mother. Thanks to Aunty G, had Dad concocted a tale? Or had he told the truth?

One day, Dad came into my room. He gazed out the window for a few minutes until he spoke in a harsh tone. "Every time you question me or Mom, you disrespect your mother. Your real mother, the mother who is here now, alive in the flesh. I won't speak of this matter again. Understand? And don't ever call her Ruby again."

I stared at the spinning carpet, wanting to disappear beneath it where I used to hide boogers in the dark of night after picking my nose until it was clean and empty.

***

I entered Great Aunt Gertrude's room. Her eyes, wide open, stared at the ceiling. A few seconds passed before I clued in. I screamed, and Ruby—Mom—bounded into the room. One look and she knew.

She gathered me into her arms. "It's okay, sweetie. Don't cry."

I couldn't help it. I had never seen a dead person before, but mostly I cried for answers that had died with her. Aunty G had been bedridden for much of that year. A woman from town who had tended to her needs probably knew more than I.

After the funeral, while mourners congregated in the stifling hall, devouring teeny sandwiches and sweets and drinking ice-cold lemonade to beat the heat, Steven and I huddled in a corner. "What now?" I asked. "Who will tell us our answers?"

Steven whispered, "Maybe there's no answers. Did you ever think of that? Maybe Dad told the truth. Aunty G was a nutcase, you know."

I didn't answer.

Life progressed. Mom became our "real" mother again, and Steven and I were once again "real" siblings.

Mom and Dad seemed happier than ever. Was the demise of Aunty G and the burial of secrets the reason?

***

Seventeen-year-old Steven bounded into the kitchen. "Hurry." Tears streaked down his red face. "Help! They're after me."

I dropped the dishtowel. "Who's after you?"

"Mr. Hornberger. He's coming. With his shotgun." Steven flailed his arms and hopped about the room. "I have to hide. Where can I hide?"

Mom and Dad had gone into town, which left me in charge, and I deemed the situation serious. Ordinary hiding places like under the bed or in the closet wouldn't suffice.

I grabbed a straw. "Outside. Come on." I bolted through the back door, Steven at my feet. I stopped at the barn and pointed to the rain barrel. "Jump in."

Steven's face turned white. "What? It's full of water. I'll drown."

I held out the straw, and his face relaxed. I helped him in. Cold water splashed over me. He dunked below the surface, the straw pointing to dark clouds.

The situation escalated quickly. An enraged Mr. Hornberger and his oldest son, hefty Colin, emerged from the side of the house. I walked toward them, distancing myself from the barrel.

Mr. Hornberger's head swivelled back and forth. "Where is he? I know he's here."

"Who?"

"Your damned brother, that's who."

"Steven?"

"You have more than one?"

"No."

"Then it's Steven. Quit being the fool that you are."

Colin twirled a monstrous axe, like a weightless pencil, at his side. Mr. Hornberger brandished a rifle. "Let me at him. I swear to God I'm gonna kill him."

"He's not here."

"He's here. I smell your fear. And rightly so."

My stomach lurched, and I stepped back. I screeched, but the nearest neighbours, the rest of the Hornberger clan, wouldn't be of assistance even if they had heard me. When Colin raised the axe, I motioned behind me. "In the woods."

They advanced toward me. And then the water gurgled. All eyes fixated on bubbles emerging from the overflowing barrel.

Colin heaved the axe, aiming it at the middle of the barrel. Instead, the blade hit the rim with a great crunch, splitting the ancient wood down the side like a sharp knife slicing a tomato. Out tumbled Steven.

Dazed for several seconds, as were the Hornbergers, he regained his senses and tore into the woods, the Hornbergers charging after him.

Hunter and prey disappeared between the trees. I hoped my brother had the sense to shimmy up a tree. He excelled at gymnastics, but the hunters, bigger and stronger, would prevail; they always did.

While I wondered what to do, Mom and Dad returned. I had barely explained the situation when the Hornbergers reappeared, dragging Steven like a deer carcass.

I screamed.

Dad lunged at them. "Let him go."

They dropped Steven's arms. Covered in dirt, Steven remained on his back, his chest heaving.

"He done knocked up my Isabelle." Mr. Hornberger's spittle flew.

"Calm down," Dad said to the Hornbergers before yanking Steven to his feet.

Dad's forehead wrinkled, and his eyes blazed. "Is that right, son?"

Steven stared at the ground. Tears plopped to his feet. "I don't know."

Mr. Hornberger rammed the end of the rifle into the soil. "That's what my Issy says. She never lies."

Phooey, I thought.

The Bennetts and Hornbergers had never been the best of friends, but we'd been neighbourly. They thought us too hoity-toity, probably 'cause Dad had been to college; we thought them too hillbilly. Two such diverse cultures would never meet in the middle.

And now this.

And why hadn't Steven confided in me?

"Son?" Dad repeated.

"I don't know, Dad." Steven blubbered liked a beached whale. "We may have done it once—or tried to."

Dad flushed. "I don't need details."

The Hornbergers loomed before us as if waiting to pounce.

"Come into the house," Dad said. "Let's talk."

Mr. Hornberger's eyes flared, and he jabbed the rifle into the dirt again. "We don't need no talking. And if'n we do, it can be done right here."

Defeated, Dad shrugged. "My son will do what's right, won't you, son?"

Steven, without raising his head, mumbled. "Yes, Dad."

Mr. Hornberger raised his rifle. "No, not what you're thinking. No Hornberger will ever marry a Bennett. Us Hornbergers take care of our own."

And with those words, Mr. Hornberger and Colin stomped off.

***

Isabelle Hornberger was shipped to Vermont to live with relatives until the baby's birth. The plan, from what I had figured, was for her to give up the baby for adoption and return to Millville, Nova Scotia, as if nothing had happened.

Out of sight, out of mind, and we erased her from our lives. Since she never returned to town, the task was easy.

The subject wasn't discussed again, and the Hornbergers and the Bennetts never again spoke. We avoided each other if we happened upon them in town, and at town meetings or events, we sat on opposite sides of the room.

***

After Mom and Dad passed away, Steven and I were alone. Life happened and passed us by. Neither of us married. The small community of Millville must have thought us incestuous, for we remained together in the family home. Perhaps they thought us as loony as Aunty G.

Steven was unconcerned. "It's the old kids' saying: sticks and stones and all that. We know the truth."

Did we? Our snuggling in bed flashed before me. We weren't teenagers then, and our parents hadn't yet discussed the birds and bees. We hadn't known those experiences were anything but two loving, innocent siblings.

Dad had been the first Bennett to attend college. Steven and I were supposed to have had better educations than he, but Steven wanted to be an auto mechanic and completed a two-year course at Millville

Community College. I had no interest in college and secured a secretarial job at Kramer's Warehouse, a kilometre from our house.

Steven achieved his dream of opening his own auto shop, which he did on our property. Before his death, Dad had advanced him funds for the building. The business started small, but soon Steven was overwhelmed with work. Dad would have been proud had he lived to see Steven's success.

One day, a visitor appeared at the front door. A young woman in her early twenties peered down at me from stilettos. "Is Steven Bennett home?"

She emitted an air of seriousness. Politeness didn't permit me to ask what she wanted, but I sensed she wasn't in need of an auto mechanic. I pointed to the dirt road alongside our driveway, noticing the fancy sports car parked in front of the house. "He's out back."

"Thanks."

When the shimmering red car disappeared down the lane, I lingered out of sight on the back porch. She stopped in front of the auto shop, pulled down the rear-view mirror, and adjusted her hair before exiting.

I sneaked across the yard and peeked through the open side window, where I had a good view of the two of them.

"I'm Cynthia, your granddaughter," the woman said.

I almost fainted. Steven frowned. He had no clue. *It's Isabelle's granddaughter*, I wanted to yell. *Your granddaughter!*

"Isabelle Hornberger was my grandmother."

Steven dropped the wrench. He stared at her for several seconds. "I see."

She broke the silence. "Don't worry. I don't want anything from you. I live in Vermont. Just here for a few days, checking out my roots."

Steven remained silent.

"Genealogy is the new fad, didn't you know?"

"No, I didn't."

"Everyone wants to know where they came from. Even celebrities."

How true, I thought, still not having resolved my parentage. Nice that she could. And nice that celebrities could. She, of course, referred to the popular television show *Who Do You Think You Are?* I had thought the show a bit of a farce and didn't believe for a second the show portrayed the truth. Then again, with celebrities' fortunes, they could hire anyone and everyone to research their pasts. What about us lowly folk left floundering? Life wasn't at all fair.

"I suppose," he said.

Would Cynthia's unexpected appearance prod Steven's interest in his biological mother? Everyone we loved was gone, and though it had been years since my curiosity had piqued, my desire for answers had never waned.

Cynthia examined his face. "I don't think we look anything alike, do we?"

"I'm not great at that sort of stuff, but no, I don't see a resemblance."

"Mind if I take a picture?" She withdrew a camera from her purse. "Mom might like to see what you look like."

Poor Steven, who hated to have his picture taken, didn't have a clue how to get out of the predicament. "Okay." His mouth formed a funny, fake grin; she clicked.

"I must go."

Steven's face crinkled. "That's it?"

"Yes, just wanted to see you."

"Okay. Ah… if you need your car worked on before you go, let me know."

She laughed. "My car's fine. It's brand new." She pointed at the open door.

"Porsche. Nice."

"Yes, isn't it gorgeous? Must go. Dinner with long-lost family tonight."

Steven brushed grey hair from his forehead, leaving a strip of grease across his weathered skin. "Perhaps I'll see you again."

"I doubt it. This is my first and last trip here. Not really my cuppa tea, know what I mean?"

Steven nodded. Did he know what she meant? Little Miss Hoity-toity was more hoity-toity than we'd ever been.

When she turned, I ducked. I slithered to the side of the building and watched her speed down the lane, dirt flying everywhere.

I giggled. The car's shine would be gone when she reached her destination.

***

Had the reunion between father and granddaughter been more amicable, Cynthia might have lingered around, enabling me to glean pointers on how to proceed in my parentage quest. Because of her sudden appearance—and disappearance—the nagging uncertainty that had plagued and perplexed me since Dad had closed the subject struck me like a barrage of bullets from Mr. Hornberger's rifle.

Who do you think you are?

The truth hit me—or, rather, the questions. I was older than my brother, and my parents married after his birth, so how could my supposed Mom—Ruby—be my mother? My head spun with flashbacks and falsehoods.

Steven's granddaughter had found her past. Shouldn't I? But I hadn't a clue how or where to begin.

Steven was still uninterested. He had believed Dad's explanation. "My biological mother lived and died having me. That's all I need to know. Dad and Mom will always be my parents."

"But I need to know about *me*," I said, selfishly emphasizing the "me."

"Dad told you the truth. What more do you want?"

I regretted allowing people to pass on without demanding answers, but our parents had taught us to respect elders—to be seen and not heard, most times not even seen, stored away like winter coats stuffed in the closet at springtime.

The most logical place to start was with my birth certificate, which I hadn't seen for a coon's age since I hadn't had any use for it. I didn't travel so had no need for a passport, and I'd never needed it for a marriage licence. I hadn't yet turned sixty-five. Would I need it for Canada pension? Had Mom and Dad kept our birth certificates from Steven and me for a reason? If the documents had been needed for school, neither of us had handled them.

Dad, a stickler for paperwork, stashed anything of importance into a metal box in the linen closet. After placing Dad's and Mom's death certificates in the box, I had placed it on the shelving unit in the parlour.

I delved into the box. The information on my birth certificate appeared correct, but why did Steven's certificate show his parents' names when mine didn't? Vernon Thomas Bennett was listed as Steven's father, and Dad's first wife, Augusta Jane Simmons, the woman rarely spoken of, was shown as Steven's mother.

Why were my parents' names omitted?

Nothing jumped at me from other papers in the box. How I wished answers could magically appear. Was Dad, even in death, controlling information?

My place of birth was Halifax. Would I have to travel two hours from Millville to search records? I rarely travelled to the city.

***

I presented the birth certificates to the clerk. "How come my parents aren't listed?"

The young woman examined them. "This one is the long form, the other the short. The short form doesn't list parents."

"Really? That's the only reason?"

"The short form is cheaper."

Stunned, I asked, "Could you look up my parents?"

"We can't give out that information." The clerk withdrew papers from a drawer. "You'll have to request the long form."

"I can't find out now?"

"We don't provide that information in person. You have to complete the forms and mail them back with the funds."

***

Weeks passed before the anticipated document arrived. Heartbeats hurling to my throat increased the closer I neared the house from the mailbox. My very being depended upon answers in the envelope clutched in my hand—answers no one had seen fit to share. Perhaps either to delay or to savour, I sauntered as if the paper in my hand were a mere flyer and then, when the screen door slammed behind me, I debated where to sit before slitting the envelope. Perhaps I'd slit my wrists, too, when I was done.

I sat and opened the envelope. Blood rushed to my head. I read it a second time. I felt faint. I read it a third time.

Dad's words pounded at my ears. *"Ignore Aunty G... ignore her, ignore her, ignore her,"* and *"I told you your mother was your mother."*

The document slipped to the floor.

***

I loathe Stonebrooke, and now I understand why Dad took Aunty G from here. My room is horrid. Food is horrid. Staff is horrid.

And the lumps never end—lumps in the mashed potatoes, lumps in the mattress, lumps in my body.

Dad, his voice strong and sure, haunts me. *"I told you Mom was your mother. Why wouldn't you believe me?"*

And I want to scream: *Why couldn't you have given me the truth.* No, he didn't lie, not technically. But he lied by omission, and aren't secrets just as bad as lies?

So what if Mom birthed me before Dad and she married? But why didn't Dad and Mom marry when she was pregnant with me? Why did he marry Augusta Jane Simmons? Did he cheat with Mom on Augusta? Did he even know Augusta when Mom became pregnant?

Obviously, Mom was his second choice or he would have married Mom first. Or could Mom have not told Dad about the pregnancy? Maybe she didn't want to force him into marriage. Was Augusta's death the catalyst for Mom and Dad to reunite, and if so, what prompted their reunion? Did Dad love one wife more than the other?

I sigh and wipe away tears. Despite having facts, I wish I had all the answers.

"Ignore Aunty G...ignore her..."

Author's Note:
This story is fiction although there are two instances creatively written from facts. While researching my MacKenzies around 2000/2001, I conversed face to face with several elderly individuals in Kenzieville, Pictou County, Nova Scotia. From these conversations, I heard about a

young man who several years previously had been searching for his MacKenzies. With no one remembering the man's name, I was unable to locate him, but in 2015, he—Vincent—found me online. His story was similar to that of fictional Isabelle's in that his great-grandmother Elizabeth had been sent to the United States to deliver her out-of-wedlock baby. Vincent (my fourth cousin once removed) relayed the barrel story, which actually happened to his great-grandfather Ernest MacKenzie, the father of Elizabeth's baby. Ernest and his sister, Isobel, my second cousins twice removed, never married and remained together in the family home for many years. Coincidentally, Isobel had an out-of-wedlock child, too, and moved out west after she became pregnant, where she delivered her baby who was raised by her married sister.

Published by the Evergreen Writers Group in anthology,
Off Highway, October 2017.

Perfect People

Hilda and Peter decided to plan a vacation, just the two of them if they could pawn their children off on grandparents. They had travelled often the first few years of the marriage, before his job and kids absorbed their lives.

"Should we have had children when we did?" Hilda, her mind on a cruise, asked her husband. "Perhaps we should have waited until we were older."

"We waited as long as we could have," he admonished her. "How much longer do you think we could have waited? It's not healthy for women to have children in their forties. No, our timing was perfect. Everything's perfect."

Hilda was silent.

"Aren't you happy?" He answered his own question. "Of course you are."

Don't I have an opinion? But why had she questioned him in the first place? He was always right. He knew the answers to everything. He was the perfect husband with the perfect children and the perfect job. Perfection. Peter Perfection Phillips.

Was he happy with her? Did he think she was the perfect wife? Did she fit into his mould of perfectionism?

"You're right. Of course I'm happy." She sighed. "We're all happy, right? Happy husband, happy wife, happy children."

He laughed. "You know what they say: 'A happy wife is a happy life.' And I aim to please."

What could he do to make her happier? She was so bored with the supposedly perfect life, she could scream. Can you unbore someone? Can you make someone happy? Happiness came from within and not something one could control. It was like the perfect personality: you either had it or you didn't, though perhaps that wasn't the best analogy. She didn't have the perfect—or any—personality, but she faked it.

How long could someone dupe life? Did one bottle emotions until the inevitable burst of the overblown balloon? She could fake her personality to some extent, and if she donned a happy mask and sported her quirky smile and spouted meaningless trite words, others might be persuaded she was worthy of speaking to.

But she couldn't hide from herself.

As if aware of how inadequate she felt, Peter was gentle that evening, not his usual fast, "get-it-over-quick" loving. He was kinder and more considerate of her feelings, a side of him she didn't often see, but when she did, she luxuriated under his touch. He could make her feel so good when he wanted. Trouble was, he didn't often want to.

Peter wasn't, in fact, the perfectionist he claimed to be, but she'd never tell anyone. Who would she tell? And why? No one would listen even if she found willing ears. Or ear. One ear was all it took; just one.

And, in fact, she wasn't the perfect wife Peter thought she was. Though cordial, the women at church didn't like her, not really, and she couldn't be a perfect wife if she wasn't liked by churchgoers. They pretended to like her: *Nice to see you, Hilda. How are you today, Hilda? Pretty dress, Hilda.* None of them were perfect either. If they were, they'd be real friends to her, not just a figure to greet.

And hers and Peter's bodies? They weren't perfect—not at their ages, not once they stripped naked. Sure, Peter strutted around the bedroom, head high, shoulders back, and chest expanded as if showing off the perfect bode. Hilda, more modest, would never do that in Peter's presence; he might see a flaw. She saw enough of them and was sure he'd seen all she had to show, but he'd never said anything derogatory, never mentioned the purple spider veins on her legs or the raised mole on her breast or the deep scar on her back.

Other than their vacation, which was too far in the future to be excited about, she had an upcoming event for which she'd have to sport a happy face: the James Street United Church tea, held the last Saturday of every month from one to four. They were stifling, stuffy afternoons when everyone would be polite and she'd be polite back, and if no one invited her to a table, she would sit at a corner table alone and pretend she didn't care. She'd smile prettily to passersby, and everyone would think she was happy and content in her alone world just as they were happy and content in their unique cliques. She'd been a latecomer to the neighbourhood; she'd never fit in no matter what she did.

She dreaded those afternoons but always forced herself to attend because, as the perfect little wife, it was expected of her. Of course, she could have pretended to have gone. Peter wouldn't have known, and the women wouldn't have cared or even noticed her absence. She could have gone to the mall to window shop or sat at the park to watch pigeons. She could have done any myriad of activities. And when—if— Peter ever questioned her, she could have lied: *The tea was wonderful, dear. I enjoy talking to the other women. Such fun!*

But she wouldn't lie—at least not to Peter. She was the perfect wife married to the perfect husband. And perfect wives didn't lie.

Except for the monthly church social, Hilda didn't socialize much other than within Peter's circle of co-workers and their wives. A boring bunch, the lot of them, just like her and the socials. But everyone donned masks and flashed teeth and flaunted fancy clothing, and all pretended to have an outrageously wonderful time.

For some unfathomable reason, Hilda looked forward to this month's church tea. Perhaps it was the gossip. Oh, how they loved to gossip. From her usual table for one, she had overheard conversations: who was going where, who had just returned, who was fucking whom. The names didn't mean much to her, and conversations flowed through her like a horrid bout of diarrhoea.

Or maybe it was the sweets—a church bribe that ensured she and the other women attended. So many varieties of sweetness to savour with every chewy morsel, and piping hot coffee to which she added heaping spoons of sugar and lengthy pours of heavy cream. Peter didn't allow cream in the house. Too fattening.

Hilda wasn't much of a cook, baked goods especially. She never purchased even three-quarters of the ingredients needed for confections: raisins, currants, figs, finely grated coconut, walnuts and pecans and hazelnuts, dried candied fruit. All the good stuff her family wasn't allowed to eat. "Must keep up appearances," Peter would say, meaning their figures.

When grocery shopping, she might purchase cookies, pies, or cakes, and despite his comments, he'd act unconcerned when she served them, and the four of them enjoyed the desserts. But those occasions were rare. Her husband was right as always; best to avoid temptation, especially anything that added pounds to already bulging waistlines of women approaching middle age.

Men didn't suffer the weight problems most women did. Men could eat and eat without worry; of course, some women ate without abandon, not caring what they stuffed into their mouths or the resultant consequences. Hilda couldn't do that; she wouldn't be perfect then—save for that monthly Saturday afternoon when she joined the ranks of those who didn't care.

***

"Hilda!" Jane rushed to her side. "You came. You told me last month you wouldn't be here."

"I did?" Had she said that? How could someone remember what someone had said a month previously unless it was of dire importance? Hilda not attending a church tea was hardly news. "I'm here," she added.

Jane had taken a recent liking to Hilda. Hilda appreciated that someone wanted to be her friend and sit with her. This would make two teas in a row Hilda hadn't sat alone. Perhaps they could be friends at other events besides the teas. Maybe go shopping or "hang out" as teenagers phrased it.

"I'm glad you're here." Jane yanked Hilda's arm. "Let's grab this table near the kitchen before someone else takes it. We'll get served faster. Won't that be lovely? And we can sneak into the kitchen if we're so inclined—you know, to help ourselves to extra food if they don't serve fast enough. It's a table for four and if someone wants to join us, they can. Otherwise, it'll just be you and me." Jane, breathless after her spiel, turned red and gasped for breath.

Hilda neglected to remind the other woman that it had been the two of them the previous month. And what were the chances another woman would join them?

After she and Jane sat at the table for four, Sandra Clipper appeared almost instantly to collect their six dollar donation. Alice MacIntosh took their drink orders, filled Hilda's mug with coffee, and placed a small metal pot of hot water and a packaged teabag by Jane. Cream and sugar had already been placed on the table.

Hilda helped herself to the creamy liquid that she so craved. Dee Williams arrived with a plate of dainty sandwiches—all crusts removed, of course—that she placed in the centre of the table. Jane dug in, but Hilda preferred to fill up on sweets. Sandwiches could be made at home, even tuna fish, egg salad, and cheese. Despite the fancy appearances of the pinwheel sandwiches and the delicately filled rolls, all tasted the same once chewed.

Jane stuffed her mouth with one of each kind. "You just have to try this," she said after every bite, each new variety increasing in deliciousness.

Hilda nibbled on a salmon swirl, taking the teeniest bites possible. It wouldn't do to be too full for dinner; Peter wouldn't be happy. Besides, the sweet treats were still to come.

Jane eyed her. "You're not eating much. You're making me look like a pig."

No, you're making yourself look like a pig. Hilda stared at Jane for a second and then leaned across the table. "Want to hear a secret?"

Jane's eyes lit up. "Yes, please."

Hilda had always longed to ask, *"Want to hear a secret?"*, and then reveal an innermost deep, dark secret. "I'm waiting for the sweets," she whispered.

Jane almost choked on her food. "That's your secret? I was expecting a juicy tidbit, something as delicious as these sandwiches. Or the sweets you're waiting for."

Hilda smiled. "Sorry to disappoint. I don't have any worthwhile secrets, unfortunately."

Jane examined Hilda's face as if not quite believing her. "Really? Nothing earthshattering, gob-smacking delicious?" She demolished the last bit of a tuna fish and Swiss cheese pinwheel.

"Nope, nothing."

"Well, drat. I might as well eat another then." Jane selected a small roll with a sliver of roast beef dangling on the almost empty plate.

Hilda kept one eye glued on the kitchen door, waiting for the first hint of sweets. The basement hall had filled up. "Good thing we sat when we did. We might not have gotten a table."

Jane scanned the room. "Yes, before all these old biddies scoff the food. The best of the best. It's all good, but some are better than others, as in life. There's always the best of the best."

"I suppose," Hilda replied. *Like Peter Perfect.* She leaned toward Jane again. "Want to hear a real secret?"

Jane's eyes lit up for a second before darkening. "But you said you had none."

"I do have one. I was afraid to tell you before."

"Do tell."

"My husband, Peter. He's perfect."

"Your husband is perfect? That's your secret?"

"Yes, but the thing is, he's not really perfect. He just thinks he is. He puts on airs to make everyone think that. I'm sorry that it's not a secret, not really, but it's something I've wanted to share. Don't you ever feel the need to get something off your chest?"

Jane opened her mouth to reply, but the moment was lost when the sweets arrived.

Diane Doland set down the plate and snickered. "I'll leave these here. Looks like you're both hungry."

"Thanks," Hilda said. Her hand hovered over the sweets, her eyes lighting up as Jane's had. She selected the fattest brownie, brimming with chocolate chunks and nuts, with creamy chocolate icing drizzled over the top. "Yum."

"The biggest one, eh?"

Hilda nodded. "Delicious." She ran her tongue over her teeth to relish every last morsel.

Jane hunched over the table. "So tell me."

"Tell you?"

"What you started to tell me about your husband."

Hilda selected another sweet, a butterscotch one, and held it at her mouth. "I already told you. He thinks he's perfect, but he's not. Peter Perfect Phillips. My nickname for him." She blushed. "Please promise me you won't breathe a word of this. Don't tell my secret." She bit into the sugary sweetness.

"It's hardly a secret."

"Oh, but there's more. Promise you won't tell?"

Jane ran her forefinger across the length of her mouth. "My lips are zipped."

"He's having an affair with Mary Frances Simmons."

"Who is?" Jane gasped and covered her mouth. "Oh, not your husband?"

Not Peter Perfect. Hilda hesitated. "No, Diane's husband."

"Diane's husband? With Mary Frances?"

"Yes," Hilda whispered. "And you promised, right?"

Jane ignored her question. "Well, I never. Mary Frances."

"I hear she's having an affair with another man, too."

Jane's hand flew to her mouth again. "Oh my. Who?"

"I don't know. Might be more than one. Several."

Jane became more and more horrified, yet Hilda could tell she craved more. The other woman inched to the edge of her seat, clinging to Hilda's every word.

Hilda scanned the room and whispered, "Could be your husband, for all I know." She paused for effect and added, "Frank, is that his name?"

Jane's flushed face relaxed. She sighed and leaned back in her chair. "No, thank God. Simon. Simon is my husband. Frank? Could be Trudy's husband. Frank and Trudy Greyson."

"Oh my. Simon? Simon is your husband?" Hilda's eyes widened, and she clasped her hands, staring at the other woman.

"What's that look for?" Jane's face turned white. "Noooooo. Tell me it's not Simon."

Hilda giggled. "I don't know, really. Rumours and such. But who can believe rumours, eh?" She patted Jane's hand and smiled, revealing her perfect white, even teeth. "I'm sure you're safe, dear. But—"

"But?"

Hilda looked away. She couldn't bear to see Jane's ashen face. Or could she? She eyed the stricken woman across from her, the only woman in church who had ever asked to sit with her, the only woman who had ever shared more than two words with her. Hilda chuckled. "I'm sorry, Jane. I'm sure it's not your husband. Don't worry about it. Simon's a common name, isn't it?"

Jane's wild, dark eyes darted about the room as if searching for her husband or his supposed lover.

Hilda had never been formally introduced to Simon. She'd seen him in church, and he seemed a decent enough guy, but looks were deceiving, and she had no clue whether or not he cheated. Or why she enjoyed upsetting her only friend.

She examined the plate of sweets. She'd only eaten three, and her friend hadn't sampled one. "I'll take a few of these home with me. You don't mind, do you."

Without waiting for an answer to a question that wasn't a question but a statement, Hilda spread her paper napkin on the table and slid the contents of the plate onto it: another brownie delight; a coconut bar; a cream-filled croissant; a date bar; two pieces of fudge—one chocolate, one vanilla; and a mammoth molasses cookie. Carefully, she folded the corners of the napkin over her haul and stood.

Jane, her eyes glistening, hadn't budged.

Was that a tear rolling down her cheek?

Hilda suppressed a smile and stifled a snicker. "I'll see you next month, Jane."

She placed the booty into her purse. She would share the treats with her family, one for each of them, leaving four for her. Yes, that was fair.

And perfect.

About the Author

Catherine A. MacKenzie escapes from her self-perceived mundane world by writing fiction and poetry. Although she dabbles in all genres, she invariably veers toward the dark. Her mother once asked, "Can't you write anything happy?"

Cathy's stories, essays, and poems have been published in many print and online publications. She has also published several short story collections, books of poetry, and children's picture books. *Wolves Don't Knock* is Cathy's first novel, published June 2018.

She is a member of several local and online writing groups, including the Evergreen Writers Group, The Spot Writers, and Seven Fates Writers.

Cathy also edits, formats, and publishes other authors' books under her imprint, MacKenzie Publishing.

She lives with her husband in Fall River, Nova Scotia. They often winter in Ajijic, Mexico, where her works have appeared in local publications.

Her amazing, gorgeous grandchildren provide much joy and inspiration.

Cathy's collections of short stories (available on Amazon) include:

Between These Pages
Paper Patches
Broken Cornstalks
The *Creepy Crazy Christmas* series of books
Hidden Places (Young Adult)

Her debut novel:
Wolves Don't Knock

Connect with the Author

Email: **writingwicket@gmail.com**

Blog/website: **http://writingwicket.wordpress.com**

Facebook**: https://www.facebook.com/cathy.mackenzie.790**

Facebook "Writing Wicket" author page:
https://www.facebook.com/writingwicket/

"Granny MacKenzie's Children's Books" Facebook page:
https://www.facebook.com/grannymackenzie/

Smashwords (e-books):
https://www.smashwords.com/profile/view/camack

Amazon.com Author Page:
http://www.amazon.com/Catherine-A.-MacKenzie/e/B006HSUD9W

Twitter: **@GrannyMacKenzie**

LinkedIn:
https://ca.linkedin.com/pub/catherine-mackenzie/24/15/a5b

MeWe:
https://mewe.com/i/cathy.mackenzie

***
Thank you for purchasing.

Reviews, good or bad, are important to authors. If you have a moment,
please leave one.
***

WOLVES DON'T KNOCK

(a novel)

A blend of thriller, suspense, mystery, romance, and family dynamics.

Twenty-two-year-old Miranda escapes from her abductor and the wolves that have tormented her soul for six long years. She returns to her childhood home where her mother, Sharon, caring for Miranda's son, Kevin, has feared for her daughter's fate. Uncertainty and distrust taint the first year after Miranda's return. Miranda and Sharon hide secrets they dare not reveal while constantly wondering when the kidnapper will reappear. Can mother and daughter bury their demons and repair their strained relationship? Can Miranda bond with the child she never knew and find the love she so desperately wants? Will Kevin's father play a role? Will Sharon find the answers she needs to recover from her own troubled past?

Though dealing with sensitive issues, there are no graphic sexual scenes.

REVIEWS:

I love the parallel mother/daughter relationship. The knock-knock jokes are a stroke of genius. The author has wonderful symbolism and uses it well throughout. All the "wolf" connections and descriptions are soooo perfect this should be in a lit course to teach symbolism! —PL

A five-star novel. So many elements of suspense are weaved through Wolves Don't Knock that you feel you can't read and turn the pages fast enough. The many threads left me exhausted by the end...a very good thing. The introspections, often beautifully written, are some of the best passages. Joyce Carol Oates uses intensive character introspections in a lot of her work. She can get away with it because she has the skills to make those introspections fascinating. So does this author.—RA

A spell-binding novel that delves into the mysteries of a traumatized young woman's psyche as she fights to regain a sense of worth. Thumbs up and five stars to this talented author. —KB

What a story! What a read! It reminded me a bit of The Room and a couple of other similar stories. It is engaging though it has difficult themes and elements. —ML

AVAILABLE ON AMAZON AND FROM THE AUTHOR.

www.ingramcontent.com/pod-product-compliance
Lightning Source LLC
Chambersburg PA
CBHW070016260626
47159CB00005B/1831